"No!" Veronica and Simon shouted in unison

Deacon yelled in triumph as he held up the Midas Stone like a primal hunter after a kill. Veronica swore Deacon's eyes looked like they were glowing. She and Simon took a step back.

"I'll be damned," Simon whispered, pointing his flashlight at Deacon. Veronica corrected her earlier assessment. Deacon didn't seem to glow. He *was* glowing. His hands, to be specific. They had an aura about them like a halo from an eclipse. His right hand was clenched around the Stone. In his left, he held a solid gold flashlight.

"Thank you, Veronica," Deacon said, his smile almost splitting his face. "I would never have found this if it wasn't for you."

What had she done? She knew he couldn't be allowed to keep it. She'd started this, and now she'd finish it. "Put it down, Deacon," she said, aiming the gun at him.

"You want this, don't you?" Deacon held up the Stone. "Your entire career depends on it," he said cruelly. Without warning, he dropped to the ground and placed his hands on the floor of the Temple. "You can have it!"

Around Deacon, the floor turned to gold in a circular wave that rippled toward them. *My God, he meant to kill them by turning them into gold....*

Dear Reader,

What's hot this spring? Silhouette Bombshell! We're putting action, danger, romance and that exhilarating feeling of winning against the odds right at your fingertips.

Feeling wild? *USA TODAY* bestselling author Lindsay McKenna's *Wild Woman* takes you to Hong Kong for the latest story in the SISTERS OF THE ARK miniseries. Pilot Jessica "Wild Woman" Merrill is on a mission to infiltrate the lair of a criminal mastermind—but she's been thrown a curveball in the form of an unexpected partner....

The clock is ticking as an NSA code breaker races to stop a bomb in *Countdown* by Ruth Wind, the latest in the high-octane ATHENA FORCE continuity series. This determined Athena woman will risk her career and even kidnap an FBI bomb squad member to save the day!

Indiana Jones and Lara Croft have nothing on modern legend Veronica Bright, the star of author Sharron McClellan's *The Midas Trap*. Veronica has a chance to find the mythical Midas Stone—but to succeed, she's got to risk working for a man who tried to ruin her years ago....

Meet CPA Whitney "Pink" Pearl, heroine of *Show Her the Money* by Stephanie Feagan. Blowing the whistle on a corporate funny-money scam lands her in the red, but Pink won't let death threats, abduction attempts or steamy kisses from untrustworthy lawyers get in the way of justice!

Please send your comments to me c/o Silhouette Books, 233 Broadway, Suite 1001, New York, NY 10279.

Sincerely,

Natashya Wilson

Natashya Wilson
Associate Senior Editor, Silhouette Bombshell

Please address questions and book requests to:
Silhouette Reader Service
U.S.: 3010 Walden Ave., P.O. Box 1325, Buffalo, NY 14269
Canadian: P.O. Box 609, Fort Erie, Ont. L2A 5X3

SHARRON McCLELLAN

THE MIDAS TRAP

Silhouette®

BOMBSHELL™

Published by Silhouette Books

America's Publisher of Contemporary Romance

SILHOUETTE BOOKS

ISBN 0-373-51353-4

THE MIDAS TRAP

Copyright © 2005 by Sharron McClellan

All rights reserved. Except for use in any review, the reproduction or utilization of this work in whole or in part in any form by any electronic, mechanical or other means, now known or hereafter invented, including xerography, photocopying and recording, or in any information storage or retrieval system, is forbidden without the written permission of the editorial office, Silhouette Books, 233 Broadway, New York, NY 10279 U.S.A.

All characters in this book have no existence outside the imagination of the author and have no relation whatsoever to anyone bearing the same name or names. They are not even distantly inspired by any individual known or unknown to the author, and all incidents are pure invention.

This edition published by arrangement with Harlequin Books S.A.

® and TM are trademarks of Harlequin Books S.A., used under license. Trademarks indicated with ® are registered in the United States Patent and Trademark Office, the Canadian Trade Marks Office and in other countries.

www.SilhouetteBombshell.com

Printed in U.S.A.

SHARRON McCLELLAN

began writing short stories in high school but became side-tracked from her calling when she moved to Alaska to study archaeology. For years she traveled across the United States as a field archaeologist specializing in burials and human physiology. Between archaeological contracts, she decided to take up the pen again. She completed her first manuscript two years later, and it was, she says, "A disaster. I knew as much about the craft of writing as Indiana Jones would know about applying makeup." It was then that she discovered Romance Writers of America and began serious study of her trade. Three years later, in 2002, she sold her first novel, a fantasy romance. Sharron now blends her archaeological experience with her love of fiction as a writer for the Silhouette Bombshell line. To learn more, visit her at www.sharronmcclellan.com. She loves to hear from her readers.

To Robert Hobart—
For all the advice on weaponry and creative suggestions
on how to commit various illegal acts, for being the
voice in my head telling me to "suck it up"
when I whine, but mostly, for reminding me about
what's important.

To Julie Barrett and Richard Curtis
for believing in me at the same time…
and as they say, timing is everything.

Prologue

She had put off death long enough.

Standing in the tiny boat, Thalassa watched Menophaneses, a general for Mithradates VI, race his ship toward her across the Aegean Sea. In the bright, clean light of the full moon, all was as visible as if it were day.

She curved her fingers around the leather-wrapped hilt of her knife and drew it toward her breast. She could not let him take her.

Her hands shook with fear. The heat and shame of tears burned her cheeks. She gazed up at the moon and prayed to Artemis for courage.

A star fell from the heavens, and her breath caught in her throat as she followed its path to the horizon. A sign? She glanced across the sea. Another ship. Roman. Its bank of oars sounded like thunder across the waves. She lowered the short blade. *Thank you, my Goddess.*

Menophaneses changed course and raced to close in on the Roman ship.

There would be a battle now. If the Romans won, she was saved. If not, there was the blade in her hand.

Menophaneses matched the Roman ship and slowed. The Romans drew alongside the large enemy craft.

Thalassa watched as Romans boarded the ship from Pontus, Mithrades VI's empire that sprawled along the southeast coast of the Black Sea. Voices carried across the waters. But there was no shouting. No battle cries. No screams of mercy.

The reality of the events washed over her, and Thalassa's heart skipped a beat.

The Romans were not here to save her, as was their duty. Quite the opposite, they were joined with Menophaneses.

Her stomach roiled at the betrayal.

The blade burned in her palm, and once again, she raised it to her breast.

She hesitated, but the memories of her sisters raped and beaten—their very lives taken—steadied her hand.

She would not give these men the wealth and power they craved. They would not see the gold.

Her resolve set, she waited for the ship to grow closer. Let these *men* see her defiance. Let them watch her death.

Let them taste failure.

For she was the last of her temple. The one sent to hide the Stone. The chosen one of Artemis.

The ship slowed to a halt. Thalassa waited until it drew alongside her small craft. Menophaneses peered over the wooden railing at her, his lips curled in a smirk. Thinking he'd won.

Thalassa lifted her chin and spat in defiance.

Then she turned her eyes upward. She had waited long enough.

Thalassa smiled at the moon even as she plunged the knife into her heart.

And she knew the Midas Stone was safe from the hands of men. Forever.

Chapter 1

Present day New York City

"Quiet night, Dave."

"For a change. Let's hope it stays that way."

Guards. Veronica Bright, crouched among the bushes and hidden by the deep shadows of the moonless night, held still and waited for the two men to walk past her. The taller one stopped and with a flick of his lighter, lit a cigarette. He inhaled, the bright ember illuminating his face.

The acrid smell of burnt tobacco wafted toward Veronica, tickling her nose. She wrinkled it, trying to squelch the need to sneeze. It didn't help. Panic reared its unwelcome head. In a moment, she would sneeze and they would find her.

Move! Silently, she willed the pair to continue their rounds.

"You know Mr. Grey doesn't permit smoking." The shorter guard crossed his arms.

"Yeah, inside. Which is why I am smoking outside." He inhaled again, then moved off with the other guard following.

Careful not to rustle the foliage, Veronica reached up, rubbed her nose, then pinched it closed. The men turned the corner toward the lower garden and out of her line of sight.

She couldn't hold back anymore and sneezed into her shirtsleeve, muffling the sound as best as she could.

She hesitated, waiting for the guards to come running back and yank her from her hiding place.

Only blissful silence reached her ears. With a quiet sigh, she laid her palm against her sternum.

Her heart pounded in her chest.

She took a deep breath and willed it to slow.

This wasn't the first time she'd been compelled to enter a place that was considered off-limits, but those had been tombs sealed by men and time and guarded with the occasional booby trap—not Glock-toting bodyguards.

The dead were much safer.

That didn't matter. Michael had stolen from her, and she wasn't going to let him get away with taking what didn't belong to him. Not again.

Her jaw tightened as the last of the fear flowed away, leaving a burning anger and the need for revenge in its wake. *Time to go.*

Dressed in black jeans and a long-sleeved black cotton shirt, and carrying her backpack, Veronica skirted the side of the hedge just a few feet from the outer rim of the lit yard. She glanced back at the path the men had walked down, but it remained empty.

Quickly, she made her way to the left side of the mansion until she was underneath one of the main balconies.

Pulling a rope and grapple from the main pocket of her backpack, she swung the climbing gear up and over the second-floor marble railing.

The grapple broke the night's silence, clinking, then scraping across the tiles before catching against the railing's edge. Again, Veronica hesitated, but no shouts of discovery sounded.

Muscles straining, she climbed hand-over-hand up the rappelling rope. Gripping the top of the cool marble railing, she slipped over the edge and onto the balcony, not giving herself time to contemplate her actions.

Crawling on her elbows, she snaked over to the French doors that led into Michael's private study.

She rose to her knees, and taking the glass cutter from the pouch at her waist, she suctioned it to the windowpane and drew a circle next to the door handle.

Veronica pulled the glass disk free, set it down on the tiles and took a deep breath. Now came the hard part. She took the small electronic code-breaker from the pouch.

She glared at her assistant's newest invention. Veronica hated depending on electronic devices, preferring the physical weight of the shotgun resting between her shoulder blades and a direct confrontation to subterfuge.

Reaching through the small, round hole, she turned the handle and opened the doors.

No alarm sounded, but she knew the lack of noise meant nothing. The alarm was on a thirty-second delay to give Michael time to turn it off, and in thirty-one seconds, all hell was going to break loose.

Leaving the balcony doors ajar, she ran to the room's main entrance.

Four seconds.

The keypad was to the left of the door—just as she remembered.

She put the small flashlight between her teeth and pulled the cover off the plastic alarm box. *Red wire. Red wire.*

She found it and used her pocketknife to strip away the plastic surrounding the copper threads.

Ten seconds.

Clamping the code-breaker's alligator clip on the wire's bare spot, she hit Enter and prayed the tiny machine would do its work. If it didn't find the alarm code within the next twenty seconds, she'd have to depend on her wits.

She glanced at the red number screen of the code-breaker. It found three numbers. Three more to go.

Twenty seconds.

The numbers flashed as it searched for the rest.

Four numbers. *Twenty-three seconds.*

It flashed faster now.

Five numbers. *Twenty-seven seconds.*

Her heart beat faster. "Come on. Come on."

The code-breaker beeped, its work done.

Twenty-nine seconds.

Veronica let go the breath she'd been holding.

Unhooking the device, she shoved it back into her pack.

She headed over to Michael's desk. She'd seen him open his walk-in safe while sitting in the oversize leather chair and knew there was a button in the desk itself. Using her knife, she pried open the middle drawer. She ran her gloved hands over the inside of the desk and touched a small bump on the back right corner. She pressed it, and a door-size section of wall slid open.

She smiled, relieved.

Time to get her prize and go.

Flashlight in hand, she rummaged through the walk-in safe, tempted to take all the artifacts. An Incan mask. A Greco-Roman sword. Even pottery.

She picked up a glazed vase and ran her hands over its simple, elegant lines.

Tempting, but she didn't steal from others. She wasn't like Michael. She only took back what was hers.

A small, cloth-covered object at the back of the safe caught her eyes. She flipped open the material. A clay jar, incised with line art and painted with red ochre, shone dully in the light. The protohistoric Turkish burial urn.

She picked it up, and her skin prickled as the familiar excitement coursed through her. Recovering the artifact from a safe wasn't the same as excavating it from an overgrown burial mound in the Turkish countryside, but no matter, it still felt like Christmas, Thanksgiving and the Fourth of July all rolled into one to touch something that no one had seen for more than two thousand years. She ran a fingertip along a painted lightning bolt. "Beautiful." And if she were right, it was the burial urn of a holy woman. Perhaps one of the first.

She shrugged the pack off her back, unzipped it and pulled out the padded cloth. She wrapped the urn, then stuffed it inside.

"Put it down, Veronica."

Michael.

He continued, his deep voice resonating in the dark. "I'd hate to shoot you. After all, I know how perfect your body is."

She bit her lip at the comment, drawing blood.

Worse than the intimate remark was the *click* of a gun being cocked.

"Damn." She didn't need the lights on to know there was a gun pointed at her head, and she started to tremble. She blinked hard, forcing back panic.

Rebecca had said Michael was gone for the evening. Playing rich benefactor at some charity event with his girlfriend du jour. If she got out of here without being killed or thrown into jail, her assistant was going to have to do some explaining.

But now was not the time to give in to fear. Taking a deep,

calming breath, Veronica set her backpack on the floor of the massive vault.

"Thank you. Now, turn around, hands in the air."

Shadowed in dark, Veronica faced her captor. He stood in the doorway, a familiar image.

Once, they were friends and even lovers. Both raised in archaeological families, they'd spent summers together while their parents worked at whatever site they happened to be excavating.

As a child, she'd had a crush on him. Loved him with all the love a thirteen-year-old girl could muster for a sixteen-year-old boy.

Later, when she'd graduated with her doctorate, they'd become lovers, and she'd thought her life complete. Their parents were thrilled with their relationship.

Hell, she was beside herself with joy at the thought of spending her life with Michael Grey.

She'd shared his bed. Shared her body. Shared her soul.

And he'd betrayed her.

It had been worse than simply using her, then leaving her like a plaything. Instead, he'd done the unthinkable—stolen an artifact and abandoned her in a Brazilian jail cell to meet the consequences of *his* actions.

She shuddered at the memory.

She had helped Michael break into a private estate after he told her the owner had stolen a Mayan fertility statue from Michael's employer. Michael had been so passionate, so righteous, in his need to "save" the stolen property that she hadn't hesitated to help him.

Standing in the darkened mansion, Michael had taken the statue, kissed her in the dark and gone out a side window while she'd run to the back door to make her escape.

That was when the police jumped her. Not knowing who

they were, she'd fought and ended up being beaten for her effort. It wasn't until her opponents cuffed her and she saw their cars marked with the word *policía* that she realized what had happened.

Michael had lied. They weren't *saving* the statue. They were stealing it.

Shoved into the police car, she was taken straight to jail—do not pass go, do not collect two hundred dollars. There wasn't a hearing. No judge. No jury. The statue was gone and she was caught.

Once at the jail, the interrogation began. It wasn't like the movies. There wasn't good cop, bad cop.

There was just bad cops.

They'd slapped her. Punched her. Ripped her shirt off and humiliated her. They wanted the name of her accomplice, but even then, she wouldn't give it. Instead, she held on to the hope that she was wrong. That Michael would return the statue. Save her. Do something.

But he didn't come, and she finally realized he never would. He'd taken her innocence, crushed it under his heel and left her to the wolves.

And for what? Money.

Humiliation washed over her as she remembered her naiveté in delivering Michael the statue and actually protecting him. Stealing the urn and catching her was simply adding insult to her already bruised ego. She glared at Michael, amazed that she once loved the man standing before her. Now she felt nothing but contempt for him and an anger so hot it scorched her from inside out. No panic. No fear. Just rage.

She managed a grim smile. "If I'd known you were here, I'd have knocked."

Michael gave a snort of disbelief. "And if I'd known you were coming, I'd have poured the wine." He motioned with his gun. "Now, step away from the safe and take a seat while I decide what to do with you."

Veronica stepped out of the vault and back into the half-lit room. "It's not as if I was stealing something that belonged to you."

Michael chuckled and walked closer, stopping at a small table next to the couch. With the hall lights behind him, she could make out his features—his chiseled chin and thick, dark blond hair. He wore silk boxers and nothing else.

With his lean, muscled body and all-American good looks, he could be a model.

Too bad he had no conscience. In her eyes, that made him less than human and as attractive as a cockroach.

She waited for him to pick up the phone or shout for his guards.

He did neither. Instead, his face softened, and for a moment, he resembled the man she once thought she knew. "Why did you come here, Veronica? Why couldn't you leave it alone?"

There was a familiar tenderness in his voice that caught her off guard. She knew they were no longer talking about the urn, and it tugged at the buried place in her heart that had once been his. "Why did you take it?" she asked, her whisper carrying through the dark.

"I had no choice."

"There is always a choice."

"A client…" He hesitated, and now the darkness almost pulsed with unspoken words. "I wanted to see you. Talk to you. Explain."

He had never been shy about revealing his feelings for her, but why did he even have them? They were at odds now. Enemies. "Michael, why can't you just let it go? Let me go?"

His eyes glittered. "You are my first love, Veronica. The

only woman who ever touched me. Understood me. Even when we were kids…" His shoulders slumped as if carrying a great weight. "No matter what I did, you were there. No accusations. Just understanding. Remember that time we stole the camel?"

Her lips curved upwards in spite of her precarious situation. She had been sixteen and both her and Michael's parents were in Turkey on the same dig. Bored, she and Michael had stolen the camel and gone riding under the moonlight. They hadn't thought anyone would notice but when they came back, the camel's owner *had* noticed and was anything but pleased.

They'd pulled water duty—carrying water from the oasis to the diggers—for the next week.

But it had been worth it. He'd kissed her under the moonlight, and for Michael, she'd have done anything. "I remember, but we were kids. It was a camel. This is different. This is real life. This is illegal."

"We're meant to be together, Veronica. We belong to each other. We pledged it, remember? How can you just forget that?"

Belonged to each other? That's what this was about? She chewed her lower lip. He'd always been obsessive about his things and what they represented to him. Once, she'd borrowed his archaeological toolkit without asking and he'd been furious for days.

It was just a toolkit, but it hadn't mattered to him. *It was his,* he'd raged. She'd had no right and if she'd respected him, she'd have known that.

It seemed she was reduced to being his metaphorical toolkit. "I remember, but I don't belong to anyone, Michael. Least of all, you."

His eyes narrowed. "You're supposed to understand. I thought maybe, if you saw me again, if you just listened, that you would see the truth."

"I do understand," she countered. "I understand that you've deceived me twice. Stolen from me. Used me. I understand that when it came down to helping me or meeting your client so you could sell an artifact on the black market, the client won."

"It wasn't like that."

She didn't miss the tension and restrained anger in his voice, and she wondered if he had always been like that. How had she missed it?

"There was nothing I could do to help you until the next morning, so I went ahead and met my contacts. It seemed like a reasonable plan." The tension in his voice ratcheted upward. "They wouldn't let me leave. They practically held me hostage, for Christ's sake."

None of it mattered. In his own sad, twisted way, he loved her, but love wasn't a word and it was more than an emotion.

It was an action.

And his actions had spoken volumes. "I understand all that," she replied, remembering how he'd begged her to stay with him. That he never meant to leave her behind. That he did it all for her. To buy her *things*. To create a life for them.

What he didn't understand was that she'd been happy.

Until Brazil and the awful truth.

No—he might tell himself that he did it for her, for them, but he did it for himself.

"If you hadn't lied to me in Brazil, put me in that situation, I would never have been thrown in jail."

She raked a hand over her hair, thrusting a wayward piece behind her ear. "And you broke the biggest rule. You're an archaeologist, and you stole an artifact for personal gain. You sold it to the highest bidder. That goes against everything our parents taught us."

"Is that so different from what you do?" he replied. "Private collector or museum. We're both stealing from the past.

Mine just pays better." He waved his free hand to indicate the opulent room that surrounded them. "A lot better."

She hesitated. On some level, he was right. In fact, on more than one occasion, a native from wherever she happened to be excavating said the same thing. Last year, she'd been excavating a site on the outskirts of Ankara, Turkey, trying to beat the highway construction team that would be going through the middle of the site in less than a month.

She'd hoped the locals would assist her team, but instead, they accused her people of stealing their Turkish heritage. Far from helping, they'd gone as far as sabotaging the site—filling in the excavation pits to slow her down.

Reexcavation cost time and only half of the site was recovered before the bulldozers arrived and destroyed what was left. Artifacts were picked out of the backfill, but precious information was destroyed when they were moved and their location in relation to each other was lost.

The loss made her want to cry. And it was concern for preservation and heritage details that made her different from Michael—not simply concern about where the artifacts ended up.

She raised her chin, glaring at Michael. "I am nothing like you." She spat the words, angered at the comparison. "I do this for knowledge. So we can learn from history. Teach the knowledge to others. Not for profit."

He stiffened, and she knew she was losing him, but she didn't stop. Didn't care. She'd wanted to say this before but had faltered. Now, in the dead of the night with her heartache behind her, there was no hesitation. Not any longer. "Not for a mansion. Not for a fancy car. Certainly not so I can betray those whom I love."

He strode toward her, his expression dark, his hand tightening around the gun pointed toward the floor, and for a moment, she thought he might shoot her. "It wasn't my fault," he said through gritted teeth.

Whether he meant Brazil, the burial urn or even their failed relationship, his excuses were just that—excuses. She steadied her nerves. "I. Don't. Care."

They stood there, facing each other. Staring. Silent.

Finally, Michael took a step backward and raised the handgun level with her face.

The moment of honesty was over, and they were back to the status quo of hating each other.

It was a tangible relief.

"I take it that you're not going to let me take back my urn?"

"Not likely."

Veronica worried her lower lip but had to try again, even as she knew it wouldn't work. "It's a valuable part of history. It belongs to the people, not stuck in some private collection."

"If it's so important, why didn't you put it in the museum's vault right away? Why keep it in your apartment where anyone could take it?"

The worst part about having an ex-lover as an enemy was that they knew all the soft, vulnerable places in which to strike. Her cheeks burned in embarrassment at the dig. She'd been careless. She'd recovered the artifact last week, and after gaining clearance from the Turkish government, she'd flown with it back to the United States, planning to take it to the museum in the morning.

She should have called the museum Director of Archaeology and Ancient Cultures of the Smithsonian and asked him to secure it, but she hadn't, and someone on her crew had obviously contacted Michael and told him of her find.

Her jaw tightened as another course of anger rushed through her. She shook it off. She'd find the loose-lipped grunt later. Now she needed to escape, somehow, with the urn.

She sighed. "Mike—"

"Michael," he corrected.

"*Mike*. Where's the satisfaction in stealing ashes? Give them back and I promise not to call the police."

"If you were going to call the police, you'd have already done it." Michael grinned in satisfaction. "You're so predictable, Veronica. Want to save your parents the pain of your inep-titude? Of knowing their daughter mishandled a sacred artifact?"

He thought he knew her so well. And he did. Once.

That was no longer the case.

"Parental approval? That's what you think makes me tick? Our parents are friends. Good friends. If they knew about you. About how you paid for this *monstrosity* of a mansion, it would break apart a thirty-year alliance. *My* parents would hate you and *your* parents would be compelled to defend you. How can you jeopardize them for the sake of a burial urn?"

"As you said, my dear, money. And the power and luxury that come with it." He picked up the phone. "You didn't want to call the police, but I will. I believe that breaking and entering a home, with a gun, is a felony."

Rage burned through Veronica's veins. He wouldn't win. Not again. "Go ahead. Call them. I'll tell them about the urn." She leaned toward him. "My excavation of it is well documented, so when this is all sorted out, you'll be in jail for theft."

Unless they believed him about her breaking and entering and he had the sense to hide the urn.

"I know what you're trying to do." He hesitated, the phone receiver in his hand and the number undialed.

Veronica held her ground, keeping her focus on Michael's face and not at the gun that was still pointed at her. "What?"

"Give you the urn. Let you go. Get a little payback for me dumping you."

"Dumping me? Is that what you call it? Is that how you live with the knowledge of what you did?" The memory of his betrayal rolled through Veronica in a red wave.

He shrugged, and she shook the anger off. Now was not the time to lose her temper. He was baiting her, and going over the Brazil incident was like flogging a dead pony. She was tired and the pony was past caring. Besides, she wasn't here to debate right and wrong with a person who refused to see the difference.

She took one last stab at reason, no matter how pointless. "Let me leave with the urn and we'll call it even. No one has to know about this."

Michael gestured at her shotgun, his dark blue eyes unforgiving and unrelenting in their determination to have his way. "Hand over Lily."

Damn. He knew her *much* too well.

"Now."

Slowly, Veronica drew the Remington 870 police issue shotgun from her back holster. He would pay for this.

Michael leveled his gun. "Careful."

She held her weapon out, butt first.

Sorry, Lily.

She dropped her.

The moment of distraction was all Veronica needed. Using all her strength, she stomped on Michael's instep as hard as she could. He yelled and automatically reached towards his foot, the gun still in hand.

Veronica grabbed for the weapon and they wrestled for control, Veronica fueled by anger and fear and Michael fueled by pain. "Let go or I'll shoot," Michael growled in her ear.

"Bite me," Veronica retorted, trying to bend his hand backward. He didn't give an inch, and she knew that while she might match him strength-to-strength for a few more seconds, he was stronger than she was, and in a battle of brawn, she'd ultimately be the loser.

Quickly, she tried to stomp on his already sore foot and he instinctively pulled away.

Dropping to the ground, Veronica grabbed Lily and swung her upwards, knocking the pistol from Michael's hand with Lily's barrel. His weapon skittered across the floor. Pointing the shotgun at Michael as he lunged to recover his weapon, she forced the shells into the double barrel even as she leapt to her feet.

The familiar *krch-krch* sound of the pump action caught Michael's attention. He stopped, resting his weight on his good foot.

A surge of adrenaline rushed through Veronica. It was moments like these—the look of shock in Michael's eyes—that made all the pain she'd tolerated worth it.

Michael's eyes narrowed and he took a tentative step toward his gun. "You wouldn't do it."

She ignored the taunt, realizing he wouldn't fire on her even if he were armed. Not when pushed. He was a coward. The kind of man who paid others to do his dirty work, then left them to hang. He didn't have what it took.

She did.

She leveled her shotgun. "God help me, I would."

The truth behind the statement surprised her. She loathed that single, brutal piece of her soul, but there was no denying it. Their families and their past be damned, she could put up with Michael and his lies no longer.

Michael hesitated and dropped his gun.

Veronica kicked it away. She pointed to a wing chair. "Sit."

Michael crossed the room. "Don't do this, Veronica. You don't want to get on my bad side."

"You should be more concerned with getting on mine." Veronica tightened her grip on Lily. "Now sit!" She shouted the command.

He sat.

Footsteps echoed in the hallway outside the room. Damn. Another dose of adrenaline shot through Veronica. Keeping Lily trained on Michael, she sprinted to the door, slammed it and turned the deadbolt.

Seconds later on the opposite side, someone pounded on the wood with a solid thud.

With Lily still trained on Michael, Veronica grabbed her pack with the urn, threw it over one shoulder and edged back toward the balcony. Beyond the expensive French door, the night was silent.

Someone pounded on the door to the study.

So much for silence, Veronica thought.

"You know I'll steal it back."

She couldn't see him, but she heard the sureness in his voice and it unnerved her. She squared her shoulders to hide the uneasiness, then looked back and gave a nonchalant wave as if his words meant nothing to her. "I'll let the curator know you said that."

He smiled from under hooded eyes. "You do that."

Her eyes narrowed and she steadied Lily. "If you steal it, anyway, I'll remember what you did to me and take measures to make sure you never bother any one ever again. I'm tired of you, Michael. The games. The lies. If you come near me or mine again, I swear you'll end up with something more serious than a bruised foot."

The pounding on the door grew louder. Another minute and Michael's guards would break through. Her heart beat harder. Veronica stepped onto the balcony and hurried to the edge. Sheathing Lily in her holster, she stepped over the railing.

Looking back into the room, she watched as Michael rose

from the chair and sprinted toward her with murder in his eyes. Veronica grabbed the rope, sliding down and dropping the last few feet to the damp grass.

Shouts from above reached her ears. In seconds, she was running to the bushes, then through them. The dense branches scraped the bare skin on her cheek and tugged at her clothes.

In another few seconds, she was on her bike. The Kawasaki Vulcan Classic roared to life between her thighs, and she sped into the night.

Her feet dragging, Veronica entered the small outer office of Discovery Incorporated, her archaeological firm that contracted to excavate sites, and set her leather backpack on the floor. It had been a long night with no rest. She'd arrived at her apartment exhausted from the adrenaline crash but unable to sleep for fear of Michael making good on his word to try to steal the urn back. She'd managed a shower and a change of clothes, but even those were done with both Lily and the urn resting on the floor beside the tub.

She'd ridden into the city as soon as the world woke up and delivered the urn to the Museum of Ancient History, reiterating its value to the curator. She'd watched as he locked it in the vault until further studies could be done on it.

Now she needed sleep. About eight hours of it. But first, paperwork, pay some bills that were late, and then she could go home and collapse into bed.

She sniffed, and the full-bodied scent of a Sumatra-bean coffee tickled her nose. "Thank God."

Taking off her jacket, she unstrapped her custom holster, slid it off her shoulders and placed it, and her shotgun, on the floor next to the backpack. Generally, she didn't carry Lily to the office, but after last night's fiasco, she wasn't taking any chances with Michael.

Rebecca came around the corner and stopped midstep, her periwinkle-colored, semi-sheer dress swirling round her ankles, giving her an ethereal quality. "Hi, boss. What happened to you? You look like something the cat dragged in."

"A bright good morning to you, too." Wearing her favorite Levi's jeans, sneakers and a clean cotton shirt, Veronica eased herself into the wing chair across from Rebecca's desk with a sigh. "Michael was home."

Rebecca's wide blue eyes narrowed, and she went from ethereal assistant to obsessed computer whiz in the time it took her to sit behind her desk and turn to her computer. Veronica fought the urge to roll her eyes. Rebecca's ability to find information—no matter how well protected—bordered on the supernatural.

"There's no way," Rebecca muttered, as lights from the computer screen flickered across her face, framed by blond corkscrew curls. She didn't look like your typical top-level hacker, but she was.

"He was out for the evening. I checked."

Veronica shook her head. "Tell that to Lily. She had to have a *chat* with him last night."

Rebecca's head jerked up, and she eyed the shotgun. Her face paled. "You didn't...uh...she didn't have a serious conversation did she?"

"I didn't kill him, if that's what you're asking." But she remembered her willingness and shuddered again.

The color returned to Rebecca's cheeks, and she returned her attention back to the computer screen in front of her. A few seconds later, she frowned. "I should have been more vigilant."

"About what?"

"According to the limo records, he left the party early. They dropped him off at his mansion just before midnight." She leaned back in her chair, lips tight. "I'm so sorry. I was careless. I should've checked. Kept checking." She curled a strand of hair around her finger. "I could've gotten you killed."

Veronica waved off the apology, all traces of annoyance gone with Rebecca's obvious chagrin. "It's okay. He knew I'd come for the urn. Counted on it. You can't know everything. Especially when it comes to certain devious minds."

"Still, I should have caught it."

"Next time, you will."

"Well." Rebecca managed a weak smile. "I know something that might change your mood."

"Did I win the lottery?" Veronica asked jokingly.

"No, but it's something almost as good." Reaching into her desk, Rebecca pulled out a thick manila envelope and tossed it to Veronica.

Opening the flap, Veronica spied the familiar green of cash. All vestiges of weariness slipped away. "Son of a…"

She paged through the bills, counting. "There's two thousand here." It had been weeks since she held more than a few hundred in her hand at any given time. Ever since her return from Brazil six months ago, she'd been off her game.

It appeared she was back on.

Licking the edge of the envelope, she sealed it and tossed it back to her assistant. "Did you rob a bank?"

"No, but there is a paying client waiting for you in your office."

Veronica sprang to her feet. "Why didn't you say so?" she sighed in exasperation. "Next time, call me on my cell so I can change." She ran a flattened palm down her shirt, trying to smooth out the wrinkles.

Her assistant rolled her eyes. "I tried. Is it turned off? Again?"

Veronica didn't have to find the palm-size phone to know

the answer was yes. She hated her cell phone. She ran a hand over her dark hair, smoothing her long ponytail as best she could. "How's this?"

Rebecca reached into her purse and tossed her a compact. "You might want to try to minimize the damage."

Veronica flipped open the mirror. She looked like hell. Dark circles from lack of sleep made her hazel-green eyes appear a muddy brown. Her olive skin was sallow. Gingerly, she touched the large scratch that decorated her right cheek. She must have done it when she ran through the bushes to escape. "It's going to take more than powder to hide this."

She could run down the hall to the ladies' room and put on makeup, but she doubted that it would make much difference. Only a good night of uninterrupted sleep could accomplish that.

Besides, clients didn't pay her to look pretty. They paid her to recover artifacts and provide a detailed report on where they came from, the condition of the site and anything that might help give a history to objects that had no voice of their own.

"Good enough." She snapped the mirror closed. "Who's the new client?"

"His name is Simon."

"Simon what?"

"Simon Mitchell."

It didn't sound familiar. "What does he want?"

Rebecca waved the money-filled envelope. "I asked. He didn't say. Who am I to question someone who offers us a wad of cash? Besides, he's a hottie, and I never argue with a hottie."

Veronica reminded herself that she'd hired Rebecca to run the office—that and for the recent college graduate's ability to hack into any computer system on the planet.

Granted, she didn't plan to infiltrate another's computer

system, but after her experience with Michael and Brazil, she felt better knowing she had the ability to ferret out a liar before she took on a job.

If she wanted someone who wasn't subject to the whims of her libido, she could look in the mirror. "Good point." Veronica smoothed her shirt one last time and picked up Lily. Taking out the shells, she checked the barrel, then handed her to Rebecca. "Can you take care of Lily for me? She needs a cleaning."

"Of course." Rebecca sighed, reached across the desk and took Lily. "You do realize that, for most admins, cleaning weaponry is not in the job description?"

Veronica flicked an imaginary piece of lint off her pants. "Most don't know how."

Rebecca rolled her eyes. "When I said I wanted to learn the business, this wasn't what I meant. I thought you'd teach me how to excavate."

Veronica flashed her a smug grin. "I will. Just consider the cleaning reparation for last night." Turning on her heel, she walked down the short hallway to her office before Rebecca could reply. Her admin loved making comebacks almost as much as she loved hacking.

Smiling her best *thank you for the money, please don't ask me to kill for it* smile, Veronica opened the door.

The client stood at the window, staring out at the New York skyline. He wore a black leather jacket over a plain black T-shirt and faded jeans. His dark brown hair was tied back in a ponytail.

She shut the door behind her, and he turned.

Her eyes narrowed and one simple fact overwhelmed her.

His first name might be Simon, but the last name was *not* Mitchell.

Chapter 2

"*Simon Owens.* What are *you* doing here?" Veronica asked through tightened lips.

She'd first met Simon in graduate school. They'd had a few classes together and while she found herself drawn to his dark good looks and sharp mind, she hadn't bothered to pursue the attraction, preferring to keep her focus on school.

Then came the Anthropology Department's graduation party. It was the last time she'd spoken to Simon, but there hadn't been much talking going on.

He'd just completed his Ph.D. and she'd finished her master's. Both a little drunk, they'd ended up kissing in a dark corner while the party raged around them.

He'd left the next morning for Russia before she had a chance to say goodbye. He'd never called or written. She'd been disappointed—but that was the life of an archaeologist. Always heading off for the next exciting dig.

The night spent kissing him faded into the back of her mind to exist as a fond memory and nothing more.

Two years later, she saw him take a seat in the back row at the Northwest Archaeological Symposium just as she was about to give her presentation. Archaeological field experience had given him a leaner, hardened body, and she'd planned to talk to him afterward. Perhaps even pick up where they'd left off if he was still single.

It wasn't to be. She presented her paper, claiming some myths were not simple tales to promote social order and morality, but were histories based on real-world accounts.

She gave her data and backed it up with the established doctrine that verbal histories were as good as written in many cultures. In this case, the myths were the verbal histories.

Asking for acceptance of her theory was risky, and even when she'd first considered the notion, she'd almost dismissed it out of hand.

But something in her gut told her to believe. Something deep inside told her that she was right and that if her ideas were accepted and supported by both doctrine and funding, she would change the archaeological world and secure her place in history.

So, she'd made the leap of faith and, foolish girl that she'd been back then, she'd thought the leap possible for her colleagues.

Instead of the kudos for innovation she'd anticipated, she received humiliation in the form of laughter and disbelief. A few people actually heckled her as she tried to talk.

Simon wasn't the worst, but he joined in the ridicule. The mouth that once kissed her in a dark corner now accused her of inept archaeology.

Veronica touched her lips, the memory of Simon's touch tangible, as was the humiliation she'd felt at his disbelief.

"I need—"

"Forget I asked," she cut him off before he could finish. "I don't care what you want." It took all her willpower not to cover the few steps between them and punch him in the jaw. Just when she thought her luck had turned, she had the misfortune to meet up with the two most exasperating men she knew within the span of twenty-four hours. "Get out."

"Not until we talk," he replied, his voice determined.

Arms crossed over her chest, she debated the possibility of shoving him out the window. Would it be classified as murder or self-defense? "There is nothing you can say that I want to hear."

"It's important." He clenched and unclenched his hands at his sides, drawing her attention.

She knew those hands. The night of the party, they'd gripped her waist before unhooking her bra and tracing a path to her breasts. Then she'd wanted more of his caress.

Now she wanted to break his fingers.

Her heart pounded in her ears. "The only words of importance you can say are 'I'm sorry for helping ruin your career, Veronica.'"

He gave a single, quick shake of his head. "You can blame it on me if you want, but you did it yourself by presenting a theory with less-than-stellar evidence," Simon countered.

Her cheeks blazed at the truth of the crack. Her colleagues, Joseph Connelly and Christopher Morganstein, had tried to warn her. All three were part of the research, but she was the lead researcher, or as Chris called her, *the pusher.*

Their evidence was scant but noteworthy, as often was the case in archaeology. They had two tablets, written by a scribe to Pope St. Victor I. One described the golden apples of Atlanta, giving details to their size and weight. The second talked about the music of Orpheus's lyre and its effect on animals and humans when played.

Backing up the information on the tablets was a letter written by a librarian from the 1700s. It was addressed to his fiancé, and it told her that the vaults of the Vatican held "great wonders," some mentioned in Greek mythology.

It was interesting and had potential, but it wasn't enough. They told her to wait. Be patient. Get more supporting evidence. Something concrete.

But impatience was her downfall, and she'd refused to listen. Instead, she'd *pushed* them until they agreed to let her present.

And fail.

"Give me five minutes and then I'll leave if you still want me to." He stilled his hands and crossed them over his chest. Simon had clearly dug in, and short of her physically tossing him from the office, he wasn't leaving until he had his say.

Veronica took a deep breath. Held it. Released it. Visualized the tension leaving her body.

It didn't help. Her muscles ached. All she wanted to do was go home and forget men—and that didn't seem to be an alternative, as the ones that annoyed her most kept intruding at the most inopportune times. She clasped her hands together to keep from punching him. "Why would you even want to talk to someone who, you claim, panders to Hollywood?"

His eyes narrowed, but in anger or embarrassment, she wasn't sure. Still, Veronica smiled to herself, pleased that she'd struck a nerve.

"If I remember correctly," she continued, "you said I played to the simple-minded people who also believed in aliens and that my working for the University of Columbia, even as a teaching assistant, was questionable." She shifted her weight onto one leg and looked down her nose to gauge his discomfort. "It seems you got your wish. Now I work for myself. And here you are. Offering me money."

The tension in the room ratcheted up a notch. Still, he said nothing, but she didn't miss the way his lips pressed thinly or his jaw tightened.

Veronica shot him a wicked, unrepentant grin. Now that she'd drawn metaphorical blood, she'd see what he had to say.

After all, Simon coming to her for help was not a scenario she'd ever envisioned. The reason behind his motives was bound to be interesting. She could give him a little time.

Little being the operative word.

"Five minutes and make it good." Shoving past him, Veronica fell into her worn leather chair. Taking off her watch, she set it on the desk facing her. With forced casualness, she leaned back, hands steepled in front of her lips. "Tell me why you're here, asking help from a woman you once despised."

Simon settled his large frame into her too-small wooden client chair, but his back remained ramrod straight and his shoulders as set as stone. "Don't let your head get too big." His tone chastised her, but she ignored it.

He continued. "It wasn't as if I didn't speak to anyone else. Dimitri Kalakos. Jonathan Caddo. Liza Samios. But they didn't have the information I needed."

Veronica leaned forward, interested in spite of herself. She knew those people. They were all experts in Greek archaeology. "And now you're here...." She didn't need to finish the sentence. Her unspoken sentiment hung in the air as loud as if she'd screamed it. *Asking a favor from the woman you both kissed and crushed.* He was stuck between the Scylla and Charybdis and they both knew it.

"So it seems." He shifted in the chair and it creaked under his weight. "I considered going to your ex-colleagues, but Connelly is, well, Connelly, and I heard Morganstein died last year."

Veronica blinked at the unexpected reminder of Chris's death. Just when she thought the loss was bearable, a twinge of pain surprised her.

She missed Chris. Him and Joseph both. After the archaeological community all but crucified them, she'd tried to convince Joseph and Chris to help her search for irrefutable evidence to prove their theory. They'd refused.

Hurt by what she saw as their betrayal, she'd finished her Ph.D. as quickly as possible, but instead of working for the college as was her original plan, she created Discover Incorporated. Once her small firm was up and running, she found a plethora of companies willing to employ her and her team of freelancers. If a pipeline or any other large structure was going through a burial mound or ancient village, she was contracted to excavate the site and save the artifacts.

And she found work beyond the borders of the United States. Being raised in the countries that surrounded the Mediterranean gave her an edge over other U.S. archaeologists, and she found herself employed by private firms in both Europe and the Middle East.

But she never forgot Joseph and Chris. With work and time, she'd forgiven them, but by the time she was ready to say the words, it was too late.

Chris was dead.

She no longer knew what to say to Joseph. With Chris's death, the chasm between them might as well have spanned the ocean.

Simon continued. "I was sorry to hear about it. Chris was a good archaeologist."

She gave a sharp nod and pushed the sudden, awkward tears back, not wanting to share her grief with someone she barely knew.

Simon's dark eyes glittered with sudden intensity. "Are you familiar with the legend of King Midas?"

Warning bells went off in her head, but Veronica ignored them. Let him talk. Let the story unfold. Then she could react. "Of course. Dionysus granted him a wish, and the moron wished that everything he touched turned to gold. He almost starved to death before Dionysus took the gift back."

Simon hesitated. "What would you say if I told you Midas wasn't a myth?"

"I'd say, 'so?' He lived around 740 B.C."

Simon shook his head. "No, not the man. The gift."

She stiffened. The warning in her head rang louder now, like the whooping sirens that accompanied a prison break. "You mean the ability to transmute anything to gold?"

"Yes." Simon leaned forward, resting his forearms on his knees, his focus as narrow and tight as a laser. "It's true, Veronica. It's all true. You were right."

What felt like every possible emotion roared through her like a freight train. Anger. Distrust. Hope. Excitement. Fear. Everything and anything. So many thoughts and feelings that she couldn't do anything but manage an incredulous whisper, "What is this? Some kind of joke?"

"No joke." Simon's expression remained impassive as he rose and locked the door.

His movement broke the spell, reminding her that this man, this archaeologist, this enemy, was one of the ones who condemned her and her colleagues for such thoughts. Her hands clenched into fists. Her short nails dug into her palms. "What do you think you're doing?" Her nerves were raw, her brain fried from lack of sleep, and the question came out harder than she intended. She didn't care.

Simon turned around and glared at her, his dark eyes intense. Gone was the polite man who needed her help—if he had ever been real. In his place resided someone much harder. "There's something I need you to see."

She shook her head.

He dismissed it with a glance, staring down at her from where he stood and making her feel like an ant under a magnifying glass. "It wasn't easy for me to come here. I knew you'd be angry." He retrieved his backpack from the floor and set the worn, leather bag on the table between them like a peace offering. "What do you want? An apology? Contrition?" The words spoke apology but his strong hands fisted tightly.

Veronica stood before she could think to stop herself, hands planted on the desktop. "I want my reputation back!"

He leaned over to meet her. Face-to-face. Almost touching. His breath was warm on her skin. "Then listen," he said, his voice low and steady.

She didn't know what to think or feel as the myriad of emotions continued to rush over her, drowning her in their intensity. Taking a deep breath, she slapped the top of the desk with her hands hard enough to sting. It was enough. She reined in the chaos that was crowding her thoughts. "Get to the point, Simon. Now, tell me why I shouldn't toss you out."

Unzipping the pack, he took out an accordion folder. "Read this, and afterward, if you're still unsure, you can take a few whacks at me."

Was he yanking her chain or was this real?

Simon continued talking. "What I need from you are facts. You referenced a number of myths and objects in your paper. Orpheus's lyre. Pandora's box. Even Thor's hammer from Norse mythology."

"I referenced them. I didn't have them," she replied.

She took the folder and pulled out the contents. They weren't notes. The size, width and height of a hardback novel, the pages were bound into what she could only describe as half of a codex. She turned the manuscript over. The back was missing and, she guessed, a number of the pages along with it.

Carefully, she rubbed a page between thumb and forefinger. Calf vellum. Durable and lasting but still thin and yellow. She sniffed. It smelled familiar—like the earth and old skins. From the top to the bottom of each page were paragraphs written in ancient Greek. This wasn't a recent creation. From early Greece or Rome would be her first guess. Perhaps the fourth century—give or take a few hundred years.

Her hands skimmed the blank page that passed for a cover. The writing style, texture and even the scent triggered a sense of déjà vu.

She knew this codex. Or at least the missing piece.

And she wondered just how much Simon knew. "A diary or journal of some sort?" she asked as she skimmed the words and picked out a few phrases that she recognized.

Simon raised his right eyebrow in an exaggerated vee. "You read Greek?"

"Of course," she scoffed. Although she knew it wasn't a skill most archaeologists bothered with. "However, I am out of the habit. If you had done your research, you would know that my mother is Greek and an archaeologist who believed in making sure her daughters knew their heritage. How do you think I ended up with a name like Veronica?"

Simon gave a nod. "Touché. Means 'honest image' or 'true image,' doesn't it?"

Perhaps he was as smart as she remembered. That, or he'd done *some* research before he approached her. Either impressed her. A little. "Very good."

His mouth turned up in what she thought was his first real smile since he came to her. "Anyway, according to this codex, the transmutation from organic and inorganic materials was done with an artifact called the Midas Stone."

"The name coming from the legend?"

"That would be a good assumption," he replied. Reaching

over, he turned the pages and pointed to a sketch of a rock. "This Stone is hidden at the birthplace of Artemis."

"Delos." The small, uninhabited island off the Greek coast. "Then why are you here? Just go get this Midas Stone."

"If it were that simple, I would. But the Stone is hidden, and while the island is barely a square mile in size, that's still to big for a random search. Part of the text describes the Stone. What it did. How people both used and misused its powers. It also refers to it in conjunction with the Eye of Artemis and explains that this Eye is the key to retrieving the Stone. Specifically, it says that the Eye is the key to all that is gold."

The Eye of Artemis? Her skin tingled. She knew the Eye. Or learned of it, at least, when she was last in Rome doing research. "So?"

"I'm here because you referenced the Eye of Artemis in your paper, and that's the only other place I've found it mentioned. I hoped you had studied it or at least knew where it was located." He ran a hand through his thick, dark hair again. A few strands came loose from the band that held them.

The movement caught her eye. She loved long hair on a man, and God help her, Simon had beautiful jet-black hair. The one night she'd kissed him, she'd let it slip through her fingers like water. Without thinking, she reached out to push the wavy strands back but stopped herself when his gaze slipped to her hand.

What was she thinking? She changed direction and grabbed a pencil from the jar that served as a holder to hide the slip.

Simon turned his attention back to her. "As I said, I went to some of the other experts on Greek archaeology, but they didn't know anything about the Eye. Never even heard of it. In fact, all three dismissed its existence, since the only place it's mentioned is in your infamous paper." Rising ire flooded her with heat, but before it bubbled over, her eyes locked with Simon's and she realized the comment wasn't a stab at her career, but the truth. She was unable to turn away, transfixed by the sincerity shining from his eyes. "You're the only person alive who seems to know anything about the Eye, Veronica. I need you."

The muscles in Veronica's jaw relaxed now that she knew what he needed, and she wished she could help him, but reality made that difficult if not impossible. "I never studied it. Never got the chance. And I have no idea where it is."

Barely perceptible disappointment shimmered through his eyes. "Damn."

A twinge of pity moved her at his obvious disappointment, but she quickly reminded herself that he was a jerk. He might need her and she might even be interested in what he offered, if anything, but that didn't mean he deserved her sympathy.

Pushing her chair back toward the window, she paced the few feet behind her desk. If Simon wanted her help, he needed to do better than act disappointed. He was going to have to convince her that he was worth her time.

She glanced at the watch. His five minutes had ended five minutes ago, but he'd snagged her curiosity and there was no turning back until her interest was satisfied—her great gift and her great failing. She put her watch back on, tightening the Velcro strap and turning it until the face was on the inside of her wrist. "But I know where to get the information concerning its location."

"Where?" Simon almost leapt from the chair.

She appreciated and envied his enthusiasm despite her intentions to remain as neutral as possible. "Not yet." She set the folder down. "If this is all you have, you'll be ignored or worse. It's not proof. At least not enough."

He hesitated, but then gave a quick nod. "Hard proof?" A

small metal case rested on the floor at his feet. He picked it up and set it next to his pack. Turning it around so the clasp faced Veronica, he pushed it toward her. "Open it."

A part of her itched to open it and see this proof he offered her. The other half screamed that this was the first step to the same fool's journey she'd been on before, and she'd do better to toss both the metal case and Simon out the door.

As usual, curiosity won. It always did. She flipped open the clasp and opened the case. It was filled with dense foam. The kind reserved for a photographer's lenses. In the middle lay a cloth-wrapped object smaller than her fist. It was heavy. Solid in her hands. She set it on the desk with a *thunk*.

Simon grinned. It was a knowing grin. The smirk of someone who was about to win. "Go ahead."

She peeled back the cloth.

In front of her sat a mouse made of gold.

She picked it up and noted the sturdy weight. It was perfect in every detail, from the tiny, closed eyes to the texture on the tail. The creature was posed as if it were caught cleaning itself, one delicate paw held against an ear and its little nose wrinkled while it turned its head.

Was Simon trying to tell her that this mouse was gold because of the Midas Stone? That it was once alive?

Intrigued, she turned the mouse over. There was no flattened area where an artisan or smelter might have set the statue down to cool.

Perhaps the artist crafted it in two parts and welded them together. She took a magnifying glass from her drawer, then went over the surface area, searching for a seam. After a few minutes, she set it down. Nothing. Whoever made this was incredibly skilled, or Simon was telling the truth.

Despite her suspicions, she wanted to believe, but it would

take more than a cursory five-minute exam to convince her of his sincerity. "Where did you find it?"

"On a dig in southern Italy." Sitting on the edge of her desk, he propped a knee on her desktop and turned to face her. Beneath the black T-shirt, his broad shoulders relaxed, clearly more at ease now that she'd seen the mouse and hadn't tossed him out of the office. "It was a field study for some graduate students. I didn't think we'd find anything of value, much less this."

"Yet here it is," Veronica murmured. She touched the stub of a broken whisker and pricked her finger.

Simon continued. "I didn't know what to think when I found it. It didn't match any styles of art I expected. The site's location next to an artesian spring, coupled with a marble statue of a huntress, led me to believe the site was associated with Artemis. A statue of an animal associated with her, like a stag or a bear, might be expected. But a mouse? Rodents were not included in the lineup of animals she associated with."

"Could one of the students have placed it there?"

Simon's dark brows pinched inward at the suggestion. "And contaminated the site? I'd think they'd know that kind of joke is unacceptable." He hesitated, and she could see him come to some kind of conclusion as his face relaxed once again. "Besides, none have the kind of income needed to pull a trick as expensive as this."

"Good point." She set the mouse down. "Were there any more?"

"No. Just the one."

"What was the focus of the dig?"

"We were excavating the cellar in a church. Digging for pottery." He picked up the mouse and held it at eye level. "This little guy was part of a burial."

"Do you know who was buried there?" She couldn't drag her eyes away from the mouse. How could anything be this perfect?

Reaching into a side pocket of his pack, he pulled out some photos and handed them to her. "Judging from the plainness of the tomb, I think the burial was a lower-level acolyte, but they weren't usually buried with something of this value. If she was Aphrodite's acolyte, I might believe it, but since she was burned in a shrine to Artemis, I can only concede she worshipped the virgin goddess."

Veronica examined the pictures. Other than the location and the mouse, this looked like a simple burial.

When her parents had dragged her all over the Mediterranean, taking her from one dig to another, she'd seen the unusual and the ordinary, but never anything so out of the norm. Unless it was someone of significant importance, no one was buried in a temple, much less with something of this value. And then there would be more burial gifts. Urns of scented oil. Idols to Artemis. A statue of a stag.

None of it made sense. While it peaked her curiosity, it wasn't enough to support Simon's claim or start the whole myth-is-reality fiasco again. She took a deep breath. "It's not enough."

Simon's jaw dropped in shock. "What do you mean, not enough?" He glowered at her, mouse clenched in his fist. "Can you think of a better explanation?"

She shook her head, but the scientist in her knew that the story, and the mouse, was not enough. She took a slow, deep breath, then exhaled. "It's a good story, and the mouse is well crafted, but neither one proves anything about Midas or his gift or your story. Where's the connection?" She reached across the desk and wrapped her hand around his clenched one. The rigid muscles shifted beneath her touch but didn't relax. "Prove to me that this was once alive and maybe you'll have a case, or at least the beginning of one."

His eyes locked with hers, and he pulled away. Setting the mouse on the desk with a thud, Simon grabbed the envelope from her desk and opened it, pulling out what, she thought, were MRI pictures.

He handed them to Veronica.

She turned on her desk lamp and held one up.

It was the inside of the rodent.

If it were solid—a chunk of thick metal—she'd know human hands had crafted it. Smelted and molded it at a forge. It wasn't. Veronica's pulse sped up, and her hands shook with excitement.

Instead, there was texture. Delicate gold bones. A tiny, golden heart frozen in time. Tissue-thin lungs turned to metal in mid-breath.

It was as if someone had indeed turned a mouse to solid gold.

It was gruesome, fascinating, and completely impossible. "Son of a—" she whispered.

"My words, exactly."

A smug smile curved his lips upward. She couldn't blame him. Hell, she'd be smug if she had a discovery of this magnitude sitting in her lap.

The mouse glittered in the artificial twilight. She set the slides down. "This could still be one big hoax. I want to send the mouse out to a lab for my own test."

Simon's lips thinned, and his dark eyes narrowed. "No. You've played with me enough. Just tell me where to find the Eye of Artemis."

"No." He wasn't taking this opportunity away from her. Not yet. Not ever. Even if he didn't know it. "I test the mouse, then we talk."

He frowned and held out his hand. "Unacceptable. I won't let it out of my sight."

She ignored him, set the mouse back in the case and closed the lid. "You don't have a choice. You came to me. Not the other way around. You want to know more about the Eye? You want to know how and where to find it? Then it's my way or you can leave. Trust me, there isn't anyone else who's even seen a picture of it, much less believes it exists." She crossed her arms, daring him to pick up the case.

He didn't.

"I don't like this."

She shrugged. "Too bad, Dr. Owens. I won't risk my reputation for anything less, and certainly not for you."

"It's not your reputation at risk," Simon growled. "It's mine. I'm not asking you to be part of this."

"Then why come here?" she asked. "Why tell me all this?"

"For information." He mirrored her, crossing his arms over his chest, only his expression hardened, as if daring her to defy him.

She smiled. Defy him? She'd do more than that. He might think he could leave her behind. Might think he still had that choice. But in reality, that choice fled when he walked through her doorway.

Her smile spread into a grin of success. "You'll get your information, Dr. Owens. All that and more."

His eyes narrowed, but she knew she had him and he knew it as well. She pointed toward the case. "Now, do I take this for study or do you take it and walk away?"

Slowly, he uncrossed his arms and reluctantly pushed the case across. "Take it."

Trembling with the possibilities, Veronica set the case on her lap. If he were right, she'd be able to prove her theory was true. Her reputation would be redeemed.

And no one could laugh at her again or accuse her of pandering to the masses. She glanced up at Simon through her lashes. He wasn't forgiven for what he said, not even close, but this was a start. "You won't regret this."

He sighed and once again ran a hand through his hair. "I doubt that."

Chapter 3

Veronica's backpack, heavy with Simon's mouse and the MRI pictures, rested between her shoulder blades as she wove her motorcycle through traffic to Alyssa's lab.

She hoped her sister would be excited at the prospect of such a new, unique artifact, but knew it was doubtful. Alyssa was like their parents, a traditional scientist who did not deal with the supernatural, and on more than one occasion she'd fought with her sister over their differing theories.

But despite their competitive natures, she was also the one person Veronica trusted with a discovery of this magnitude.

Turning the corner, Veronica screeched to a halt and parked her bike in the front of the renovated, ten-story brick building. Taking off her helmet, she massaged her scalp and glanced upward to the eighth floor and her sister's archaeological lab.

When Alyssa married the wealthy owner of Bates Pharmaceuticals, Ian Bates, she and her parents thought it was a mistake, especially since Ian was fifteen years older than Alyssa. Veronica smiled, glad that for once, she'd been wrong. Three years later, her sister and Ian were still a "honeymoon couple."

For their first wedding anniversary, Ian had even bought Alyssa her lab with state-of-the-art equipment, wanting to please her and give her the opportunity to prove herself in the highly competitive archaeological-scientific community.

Alyssa was brilliant, with an uncanny intuition that complemented the precision steel-and-glass lab equipment.

Veronica stepped through the antique double doors and pushed the button to call the elevator. Punching in her pass code, she rocked back and forth on her heels as she rose to the eighth floor.

The lab took up the entire floor, and the elevator opened up directly into it. Alyssa sat across the room under the Bright-Bates Archaeology Laboratory logo that was painted on the back wall. Her head bent over a microscope, she managed to appear both professional and cute in her spotless white lab coat and fitted black slacks.

Veronica touched the scratch that ran across her cheek. No matter how she tried, she would never look cute. Professional was doable as long as it involved dirt, beat-up jeans and a trowel.

She and Alyssa were different in almost everything, especially looks. Alyssa took after their English father—pale skin contrasted by espresso colored locks that were sleek and shiny despite any amount of rain. Her eyes were a dark green that some called emerald, and her figure was willowy.

Veronica looked more like their Greek mother—her hair was almost black, her lips full and her body curvy. The only thing that she took from her father's side of the family was her eyes. A bright hazel, they were startling when viewed against the naturally dusky skin of her Greek heritage.

But the real dissimilarity was in how they approached archaeology. She went with her gut while Alyssa was a hardcore believer in the "seeing is believing" theory.

But the differences didn't matter. Regardless of how annoyingly adorable and scarily brilliant her sister might be, Veronica couldn't be jealous of her. Growing up on the outskirts of the Mediterranean, they rarely had other kids to play with, and so they'd always been best friends—and become closer as they got older.

Looking up, Alyssa waved her over, tucking her shoulder-length, espresso-colored hair behind her ears. "Hi, what brings you here?"

Relief rippled through Veronica. Nope. She felt no jealousy. Just pride at her sister's accomplishments.

It would take more than a few tablets and a letter to convince her skeptical sister to believe in the myth theory or get her to help. But she had to try. More than two years ago, her gut told her she was right, and she'd presented her paper based not just on her evidence but also on her instinct that she was on to something. Something important.

Anger, betrayal and shame had made her walk away... until Simon walked through her door. Now every fiber of her being called to her. Begged her to continue the work she'd abandoned.

There was no way she could ignore the call. Not now. She only hoped Alyssa would help her. Prove that, for once, her instincts were right.

Then, there'd be nothing holding her back but Simon and his desire to search for the Midas Stone without her.

And she didn't plan to give him much of a choice in the matter. He needed her and she'd use that to her advantage.

"This." Walking over to Alyssa, she handed her sister Simon's leather backpack. "There's something I want you to see."

Alyssa's green eyes flared with curiosity. "Okay." Opening the pack, she pulled out both the files and the metal box.

"Start with that." Veronica pointed toward the container that held the mouse. No point in delaying the inevitable argument. Despite the energy running through her body, she forced herself to remain immobile while Alyssa unwrapped the artifact with deft fingers.

Her sister's eyes widened as the mouse glittered under the fluorescent lighting. "Wow. It's beautiful. Where did you get it?"

Veronica took a deep breath, knowing that her sister would not approve of what was coming next. "From a new associate. He claims it was once alive. Turned to gold by an artifact called the Midas Stone"

Alyssa's jaw tightened, and the wonder left her face. "Really."

Veronica continued, ignoring the doubt and sarcasm that tinged her sister's voice. "If he's right, it'll prove my theory."

"About myths, reality, and all that nonsense?" Alyssa dropped the mouse back into the foam padding, closed the lid and shoved the box back into Simon's pack. "Take it somewhere else."

"I can't."

"Why not?"

Veronica clasped her hands together, frustration and patience warring inside her for control. "I'm still rebuilding my career. If he's wrong, my reputation will never recover. I need someone who can keep this quiet until I know the truth."

Alyssa crossed her arms across her chest, unappeased. "Then let it go."

Frustration won and Veronica slapped the tabletop with the flat of her palm. "Damn it, Alyssa. This is big. Bigger than your preconceptions. For once, can't you just believe?" she asked, her voice thick with emotion.

Alyssa flipped her hair over her shoulder with a sharp jerk of her head. "For once, could you stay grounded in reality?"

"Reality? Ha! What do you—" Veronica cut off the retort before she said something she couldn't take back. Slowly, she took a deep breath to calm herself, held it, then let it go, all the while ignoring Alyssa's hostility.

For once, she wished she could make her sister feel the ache that consumed her when her gut told her she was onto something big—something that could astound the science community and set the world on its ear.

She massaged her temple with her hand. Alyssa was not about possibilities. She was about facts. In her world, little room existed for a stone with transmutational abilities.

But there was room for a sister in need of help.

"Alyssa, I know you don't believe, and I'm not asking you to. But I need your support. Please. You're the only one I trust."

Alyssa gave her a sharp look.

Veronica met her steady, unflinching stare with one of her own. "Just run the tests and let me know. That's all. There's more in the folder."

She spun on her heel and headed for the elevator, leaving the pack behind, knowing her sister would do as she asked despite her protests. They might disagree, but they never let each other down. Not when it came to the important issues.

"You leave and I swear I'll pitch it out the window," Alyssa threatened.

Veronica stopped midstep. Alyssa might be three years younger than her own twenty-nine years, but she was just as stubborn.

"If this *associate* is telling the truth, what do you plan to do? Go with him on some harebrained expedition in search of some legend?"

Veronica turned back around.

The backpack straps clenched in her fist, Alyssa waited for a reply.

Slowly, Veronica walked back to the cold, dark lab table that separated her from her sister. Alyssa could be so frustrating, and the childish urge to bait her was almost overwhelming. "Considering? Yes. Decided? No. That'll depend on what you find."

Giving Veronica a sideways glance, Alyssa dropped the backpack onto the table. It landed with a dull thud. "You know Mom and Dad wouldn't approve of you running off to prove a theory that's unsound, at best."

Veronica rolled her eyes at the undisguised admonishment. When her parents were field archaeologists, they were a bit more open-minded. Then four years ago, when Veronica began her graduate studies, they both settled down, taking professorships at Columbia University in the Department of Art History and Archaeology. It was a good move. A smart move. A financially sound move. But it had changed them. Made them more cautious—especially when Veronica had a penchant for working in the more uninhabited regions of Turkey. More than once, her father had asked her to take a stateside job.

Sometimes, when the thought of a twelve-hour trek to reach civilization made her want to cry, she wished she was in the U.S. Maybe even staying in a nice hotel that was close to a site. But it wasn't in her. The U.S. was too…safe.

"Nice try. Did you learn the 'guilt Veronica' trick from Mom?"

"It's not guilt. It's true."

"Which is why you won't tell them."

Alyssa cast her another narrow, green-eyed stare. "If they ask, I will."

Veronica wondered if Alyssa was as serious as she sounded. As much as they argued, they'd always covered for each other. Kept each other's secrets despite the occasional war of wills. She hoped that this would not be the exception.

Then tell Alyssa about last night, her conscience whispered. Veronica ignored the nagging urge to blurt out her encounter with Michael. If Alyssa knew about it, her mothering instinct would kick into overdrive and there'd be no way she'd help.

"They won't. Unless you mention it. So don't. At least until we know for sure and I make a decision. Until then, there's no reason worrying them over nothing."

Alyssa raised a brow then yanked the container back out of the pack and pulled out the mouse. "I'll think about it."

Veronica tried to hide her displeasure, but knew that if Alyssa said she'd think about it then that was what she'd do, and there would be no dissuading her. There was simply the waiting to hear the decision.

Veronica frowned. "Fine. Do me a favor? Let me know ahead of time if you decide to tell them. I don't want to get ambushed at dinner."

"Agreed." An oversize magnifying glass was bolted to the table, and Alyssa swung it over, using its extendable arm. Holding the metallic rodent on her palm, she scrutinized the tiny statue. "He says this was once alive?"

"That's the story." Veronica pushed the envelope with the CAT scan film toward her. "You might as well see these now. It should help."

Alyssa pushed the magnifying glass away and set the mouse down. Opening the envelope, she slid out the film sheets and held them up to the light. Her eyes widened again, but she made no more comments.

After a few minutes, she waved the images at Veronica. "These might be forged."

Veronica picked the mouse up again, still stunned by its complexity. A part of her wanted this to be real. The other part, probably the smarter half, wanted it to be a lie. "I know. That's why I need you to run whatever tests you can to either prove or disprove its authenticity."

"Fine." Alyssa gave a curt nod.

Exhaling in relief, Veronica let her shoulders drop. "How long before you know if the mouse is an exquisite piece of ancient art or if it were once a living, breathing creature?"

Putting the slides back in their envelope, Alyssa sat in front of her computer. "Let me check my calendar. I can move some things around," she said grudgingly.

"Thanks."

Impatiently, Veronica waited as her sister punched in numbers and talked to herself. She glanced around the room. It was a well-equipped facility. There was no denying the fact. Spectrometer. An imaging room big enough to fit a mummy. Five kinds of microscopes.

After a few minutes, Alyssa pushed back from the desk. "I'm analyzing some pottery shards for the Incan project being run out of the University of North Carolina, but I'm ahead of schedule so I can move it back a day or two. If I work this weekend, I should be able to get you results by Sunday."

Veronica tapped her foot with impatience. "Can you get me the basics faster? Just an internal imaging-and-density test?"

Alyssa leaned back in her computer chair, arms crossed over her chest. "Why even bother with this? You lost your chance at a Ph.D. and destroyed your reputation because of this theory. Wasn't that enough? Why dredge it all up again?"

Why bother? "You did your graduate thesis on the Mayans. If you had the chance to prove that one of their legendary artifacts was real, wouldn't you jump at the opportunity?"

"No, and this isn't about me. It's about you going off on some half-assed adventure with a man who showed up at your office this morning." Concern shone from her eyes. "Do I have to remind you of Brazil?"

Veronica's cheek heated with embarrassment and frustration. It was bad enough being a fool for Michael but worse that Alyssa brought it up, reminding her of her bad judgment. "Even you thought Michael was a good guy," she replied, defensive before she could stop herself.

Alyssa continued. "That's my point. We knew him for years, and he fooled us. You just met this man." She tucked her hair behind her ear. "I know how bad the prison was."

"It was a jail. Not a prison," Veronica corrected.

Alyssa rolled her eyes. "Call it whatever you want. You can lie to others but not me. You were half out of your mind when I got you out." She took Veronica's hand in hers. "I can bribe jail officials. Money is not the issue. If this artifact is what you say, it's more valuable than money. Don't go with him. Please."

Veronica squeezed her fingers, knowing Alyssa worried because she loved her, but that didn't change the circumstances. "I can't turn down projects because they might be dangerous."

"This is more than dangerous." Alyssa let go and sat back, her expression stern. Veronica knew she was going to get a lecture. "You're the older sister. You're supposed to be the sensible one. I shouldn't have to wait by the phone every time you go on assignment, knowing that if it rings, it's you, caught up in some disaster. I don't want to keep saving you."

Veronica held her temper. She loved Alyssa, but she could be so frustrating when she got safer-than-thou. "I haven't talked myself into going, and you saved me *once*. That's it. It's not as if I walk into disaster on a regular basis. I'm not some screwup that you have to keep tabs on in case I need rescuing."

"Once was plenty for me. I thought it was enough for you as well." Alyssa took a deep breath, but her jaw tightened. "Do you ever think about what would have happened if Ian hadn't given me the money to buy your freedom?"

Veronica squeezed her eyes shut for a moment, remembering the fear. The humiliation. Waking up at night, wondering if the guard was going to do more than touch her breasts. She'd considered herself lucky she wasn't raped. It was probably only a matter of time.

Damn Michael!

She blinked open her eyes, refusing to give in to the memories. "Every day."

Unappeased, Alyssa shook her head. "If this is real, you're going, aren't you?"

She couldn't lie. Alyssa would see through it. "Yes."

Alyssa sighed with resignation, her jaw softening. "Promise me that you'll think about what I've said."

"I will," Veronica promised, managing a small smile. It was hard to stay angry when she knew Alyssa's reaction came from love and worry.

Once, or if, the mouse was authenticated, they'd be arguing again. Until then, there was no point in being angry at each other. She turned away and pushed the button to call the elevator back. The doors slid open with a chime.

"Veronica?"

She hesitated.

"Even if it's all true. If the mouse is real. The legend. Everything. You won't be able to trust him. Not with this kind of potential power at stake."

"I never said that was part of the bargain." Veronica stepped inside the elevator, and the doors slid shut.

"This is about the dumbest damn thing you have ever done," Veronica muttered.

She stood on Joseph Connelly's porch, arguing with herself. After leaving the mouse with Alyssa, she meant to go home, drink a glass of merlot, unwind her thoughts from the events of the past twenty-four hours and catch up on much-needed sleep.

Instead, she had driven to upstate New York and now stood here wanting to speak to her ex-colleague and mentor. What was happening was important, and while Joseph might decide to walk away, he deserved the right to choose.

Blinking back sudden tears, she wished Chris were alive so she could offer him the same opportunity.

Nervous, she clenched and unclenched her hands. God, she missed them both. Missed their friendship. Couldn't count the times she'd wanted to talk to them. Get advice. Give it.

She remembered their parting. Joseph and Chris had met with her at the Columbia University lab and told her about their decision to stop the research on the myths. Joseph was getting old and could not risk his tenure. Chris had a wife and small child and couldn't risk their security.

She was so angry. She'd said some terrible things. Didn't understand. Still didn't, but now she respected their decision. Which was why, despite the fiasco and the self-enforced silence, she was here.

She raised her hand to knock and stopped herself, remembering her heated words. Accusations. "Stupid," she muttered again. He wouldn't want to see her. Not now.

"Just stupid."

She turned to go. The door opened.

Joseph Connelly stood in the doorway, much as she remembered him. Steel-gray hair cut short and over his ears. Deep furrows on his brow and wrinkled hands revealed his seventy-plus years. But his blue eyes were still young and still twinkled with a curiosity that made him the legend he'd become.

The speech she'd rehearsed on the way over fell out of her

head. Veronica asked herself why she had waited so long to return.

Feeling as shy as her first day at the University of Columbia, Veronica took a step forward and stopped. What did you say to someone you both loved and hated? How did you bridge the anger?

Her hands felt useless, and she jammed them into her jeans pockets.

He gave her a cursory nod. "I was beginning to wonder if you were going to stand out here all day, so I thought I'd save you the decision and invite you in."

Of all the scenarios that had run through her thoughts, this was not one of them. Words fled her. The return of the Prodigal Daughter was complete.

"Thank you," she whispered.

He moved aside, and she slipped past him.

"Veronica."

She stopped. He opened his arms. Without hesitation or thought, she slipped her arms around his thin shoulders and the foolish, painful past fell away.

She had needed this. Needed Joseph's approval. In that brief instant of contact, she knew she'd never lost it.

"I'm glad you decided to come back," he said, patting her on the back.

A few thumps and she stepped way, taking a moment to wipe her eyes. She hadn't expected this. This unconditional acceptance.

He motioned her to follow. Feeling both relieved and blessed, she walked through the house toward the kitchen and noticed that some things had changed. Her mentor now walked with a pronounced limp and used a cane.

"What happened?" she asked.

"This?" He wiggled the cane. "The dig last year—the one

outside of Venice. The ground was too wet and the pit too deep. We let excitement override our good sense." He hesitated. "And Chris paid the price for our stupidity."

Veronica swallowed hard at her mentor's self-recrimination, knowing nothing she said could fix the past or the guilt that accompanied it. She wanted to say she was sorry. That she wished she'd been there to help.

More important, that she'd understood why they'd pushed themselves beyond what was safe. The consequences weren't worth it, not when she thought of Chris's wife and son, but she understood.

She managed an inept, "It was a Peloponnesian ship. I would have done the same thing."

With a sympathetic glance, he told her that he understood the meaning behind the words. Then, he always had. He understood her like a father and a friend. Sometimes he understood her better than she did.

"Probably," he replied, his voice bitter. "But it wasn't you. It was me. It was Chris and our damned ambition."

And as always, he refused to grant himself the same forgiveness that he offered her so freely.

She pressed her lips together and didn't comment again— just thanked whatever force that watched over intrepid archaeologists that she hadn't lost Joseph as well.

They reached the kitchen, and she took a seat at the same small cherry-wood table she'd sat at for so many years.

He set his cane on the countertop and patted his thigh. "Broken in three places." Opening a cupboard, he took out two mugs. "Never healed quite right." Settling into the chair across from her with a small grunt of pain, he handed her one of the mugs. "Black?"

"You remembered," she said, pleased.

"You were my favorite student. Of course I remembered."

She warmed at the words. She'd met Joseph her first day on campus. She flushed, remembering her know-it-all attitude and the way she'd dismissed the other students' opinions when they argued over prehistoric Greece. All the other archaeological graduate students had had field experience, but she'd *lived* the archeological life. Was steeped in it from the moment she entered the world. Had spent her formative years traveling throughout the Mediterranean while her parents traced ancient trade routes and wrote papers on the mariners' influence among the cultures that circumvented the turquoise sea.

The same opportunities that gave her more practical knowledge also gave her a kind of diffident insecurity when it came to social interactions. Her companions growing up were the other team members. Her only true confidant was Alyssa.

Granted, there were some summers when hers and Michael's parents partnered for a project and she and Alyssa spent their time with Michael. During those hot, sultry summer days, all three spent hours playing in the warm surf, collecting shells and pestering both sets of parents to entertain them.

It wasn't until she was fifteen, and she saw Michael for the first time in three years, that they took to leaving Alyssa behind while they walked the white sands, holding hands.

But other than that, she'd never led the kind of life that most teens did. There were no sleepovers. No groups of girlfriends to discuss the all-important issue of boys. No prom. No first date with her trembling on the stairs while she waited for the doorbell to ring.

She didn't own a dress until she was fourteen. Her first kiss was from Michael when she was fifteen. Camping out was a way of life.

By the time she was eighteen she'd grown interested in pursuing archaeology as a career, and her parents encouraged her interest by giving her lead on a team. When her crew uncovered a temple to Aphrodite on the island of Cyprus, her interest in archaeology became a passion. The site was the best-preserved of its kind, and she fell in love with both the knowledge it imparted and the excitement with making her own find.

She couldn't see leaving the field to pursue a traditional college education. Instead, she tested out of most of the core courses, like English and psych, then took the rest through correspondence. She graduated in two years with a B.S. in archaeology, and since she spoke Greek, Turkish, Italian and a smattering of Russian, a minor in languages.

However, she couldn't earn her Master's through correspondence. The day she walked onto the campus of Columbia University was her first real opportunity for interaction with people her own age for a significant length of time.

She'd been terrified. Scared witless the first day she walked into the white-walled lab and twenty eyes all looked up to greet her. Fearful of not being accepted by her peers, she appeared arrogant rather than friendly.

By the end of the day, she had met no one and was questioning the wisdom of a traditional education. Then she met with Joseph—her adviser and head of the archaeology department. Years wiser in both practical experience and in social interactions, he'd understood her fear—even if she didn't—and paired her with Chris on a project. Chris's extroverted personality and wicked sense of humor soon loosened her up. One day she woke up and realized that she liked graduate school. Her friends. Her new life.

And they liked her. Respected her. Listened to her.

She'd never been happier. She liked being a part of something bigger than herself. Enjoyed her classes and the attention her experience gained her.

It only took one symposium and failed presentation to destroy her hope for proving the impossible and writing her name into the history she loved.

Her stomach constricted at the memory. She sipped her coffee, content in the silence broken only by the ticking of the clock over the stove.

Finally, Joseph set his mug down. "I tried to contact you about the funeral, but…" He stopped.

He didn't need to finish the thought. They both knew why she didn't attend the funeral. She'd been on her first assignments as the owner of Discovery Inc.—stuck in the middle of nowhere in Turkey. Contact was limited—even with cell phones.

A legitimate excuse and one she knew he understood, but it was still an excuse in her heart. Her chest tightened. "I wanted to go," she replied, her voice coming out softer, sadder, than she intended.

He continued. "I wanted you to be there. Chris would have wanted it, too."

Veronica focused on her hands. "I stopped by the grave when I got back." She swallowed hard, forcing her voice to remain steady. She'd gone in the evening, right when the first stars came out, leaving roses when she walked away an hour later in the dark.

"Good. He missed you." He looked down at his feet then back up. "So did I."

Why had she waited so long to come here? Now that she was here, any reason seemed foolish. "I know. I missed you both." She sniffed hard, remembering when she got the news. The pang of regret. The burning desire to celebrate her ex-partner's life and mourn his death.

Even now, she saw him in her thoughts. Thick brown hair. Teeth like those in a toothpaste commercial. If there was a practical joke in progress, Chris was always the mastermind behind it.

"He knew, Veronica. He was used to your temper and knew that one day, you'd be back." Joseph patted her hand. "Do you want to tell me why you're here?"

Shaking off her sadness, Veronica took another sip of coffee, suddenly nervous and not wanting to tell Joseph about the mouse. Would he tell her, again, that her proof wasn't enough? Would he be sorry he invited her in? "Someone came to me today offering proof, good proof, that our theory about myths was true." She blurted the words out before anxiety changed her mind, then held her breath as she waited for his reply.

Joseph gave a thoughtful grumble. "Tell me more."

Veronica breathed a sigh of relief, and the rest of the past fell away while she told her story and he waited with familiar patience.

When she finished, she put her hands in her lap. There. It was said. She waited for his response.

"You'll need more than the mouse. What's its provenance?"

Just as she remembered—get to the science. "It was found with a burial, but not of a priestess. No other burial artifacts were located other than part of a codex that mentioned the Eye of Artemis," she said, and waited for the inevitable reaction.

"The Eye?" Joseph straightened.

"Yes," Veronica assured him, the excitement in the room growing.

Joseph rose halfway out of his seat, arms braced against the table for support. "Then you know where you have to go."

Goose bumps rose on her arms. It was like old times. They were almost reading each other's thoughts. She knew where this was going. Where it had to go. "Back to the Vatican to get the other half of the codex."

He nodded in agreement and lowered himself back into his chair. "It won't be easy. The Vatican officials didn't want you to read it before. I doubt much has changed." He tapped his cane against his leg. "I wish I were going with you."

Veronica took his hand in hers. He was smart. Her mentor. She wanted his advice and his company. "Then come. This is as much your mission as it is mine."

"I'd slow you down." He squeezed her hand with surprising strength. "I suspect you're going to need your wits about you for this trip."

Veronica squeezed back. His hand was cool, and his skin was thin with age beneath her fingertips. She hated to admit it, but he was right.

Joseph continued. "I'm too old for this kind of adventure, but not too old to dream. If the Midas Stone is real, find it. Prove that we were right."

"I will." She shut her eyes, remembering Chris's headstone. *Husband. Father. Adventurer. Now on to the greatest journey of them all.* "For all of us."

Chapter 4

"It's a hoax." Alyssa handed Veronica a thick plastic folder, her face impassive.

Veronica stared at her sister, stunned into silence. It was Saturday afternoon, and after two days of restless waiting, Alyssa had called, telling her that her analysis was complete.

Two days of barely contained impatience, hoping and praying that the mouse was real and she'd be on her way to offering the archaeological community irrefutable proof that her myth theory was fact. The waiting would not have been as nerve-racking if she were the type of woman who went out with friends. Shopped. Or even did the "brunch" thing.

But she wasn't. Her sister was her best friend, and she couldn't pester *her* since *she* was doing the analysis.

Everyone else either fell into the co-worker or employee category. Besides, when she was this antsy, she knew she was horrible company.

So it was two days of work, hit the gym and gun range in a vain attempt to relieve her mounting tension, return to her apartment in Chelsea, watch a few movies, and then back to work.

All that, just to be told the mouse wasn't real? The revelation stunned her. "What do you mean it's a hoax?" she asked, her voice cracking as she tried to wrap her thoughts around what her sister was telling her.

Alyssa reached out, her fingers smooth and cool as they touched Veronica's shoulder in sympathy. "It wasn't alive. It's a beautiful statue. I don't deny that. But that's all it is. Nothing more. Nothing less."

Veronica jerked away. Her hands shook as she undid the metal clasp that held the folder closed. Alyssa had to be wrong. Had to be.

But a tiny voice in the back of her mind reminded her that Alyssa was never wrong. Not when it came to hard science.

The report was a quarter-inch thick. Veronica flipped through the pages until she found the imaging scans and density tests.

The mouse was solid. Not even a hint of texture that might indicate internal organs. According to Alyssa's notes, it was smelted then carved. Her sister was right. It was a beautiful statue. Nothing more. Nothing less.

Veronica set the folder down, fighting the urge to fling it across the room. The find of a lifetime, and it wasn't real. Disappointment overwhelmed her, making her tired. Making her angry.

She massaged her forehead, feeling as lost as when she separated from Joseph and Chris and founded Discovery Inc. "Is it at least real gold?"

"Yes."

"Thanks," Veronica replied, tempted to keep the tiny statue as payback to Simon for leading her on. But it wasn't in her.

She worked her hand to the back of her neck, rubbing the stiff muscles.

Alyssa laid a hand on her shoulder. "Are you okay? You look a little green."

Veronica shrugged her off, as the lab suddenly became too small and the smell of disinfectant too strong. "All I wanted was a chance," she murmured, holding her anger in check. "Why would Simon even agree to give me the mouse knowing that any tests I ran would prove it a hoax?"

"He might not have known," Alyssa offered, glancing at the door behind Veronica and then back again. "Perhaps someone played a joke, not realizing how far it would go. If they confessed now, well, I doubt they would. Or perhaps he was buying time and thought he'd get the Eye from you while you waited."

"He can't." Veronica ran a hand over her forehead. She felt flushed. Hot. "Joseph and I are the only archaeologists who know where the book is that shows the Eye. And I found that by accident."

She held the mouse in her palm. Perhaps Simon would be as disappointed as she was—not that it made a difference. "The chance to do something great. Prove something to the world. And it's not real."

"I know you're disappointed, but there will be other chances. Other opportunities," Alyssa consoled.

For me? Maybe. But not for Joseph and Chris. Her stomach flipped at the thought of letting them down.

She should have waited until after Alyssa ran her test to speak to Joseph. Now she'd have to break the bad news to him. "Damn."

Setting the mouse back down, Veronica picked up the folder again. Who would do this? Lead people on? A glimmer of anger flickered again, and this time she grasped it with a fierce determination. Anger she could deal with. It was straightforward. Strong. The disappointment made her weak.

She couldn't take feeling weak.

Alyssa took the folder from her, flipped it closed and twisted the metal clasp, sealing it and shoving it in a drawer. "Let it go. It was dangerous, anyway."

Veronica eyed the evidence with contempt. "I can't. At the very least, I'm taking the evidence, or lack of it, to Simon and getting to the bottom of this."

"Why bother? This is his problem now." Alyssa retrieved her cell phone from a drawer. "I'll call the courier. Let's get this over with and get on with our lives."

Veronica took the phone from her. "No. I have to do this."

"No. You don't."

"Yes. I do," Veronica replied. If Simon had set her up, he'd pay.

Alyssa tried to snatch the phone from Veronica's grasp.

Taller by five inches, Veronica held the phone out of her sister's reach.

Alyssa made a halfheated jump, then flopped into her chair, eyes narrowed and legs bouncing with agitation. "Why do you have to do this? Act like a child?" She twisted a strand of hair around her finger. "Just walk away. Let it go, for pity's sake."

"What is wrong with you?" Veronica snapped. "Why do *you* care if I personally want to tell him to take his mouse and stuff it? He came to me. It's not like he can hide…?" Veronica paused, staring at her sister. For a moment, she was ten again and Alyssa was seven. Alyssa had taken her favorite doll, denying the theft. The entire time she denied the theft, she'd twisted her long hair around her finger.

She'd always done that when she was caught in a lie or when she was trying to hide something. Most people wouldn't even catch something so minuscule and common, but she wasn't just anybody. She was Alyssa's sister, and she knew the signs.

Alyssa captured another strand and wound it around her finger.

Veronica froze. Someone was hiding something and it wasn't Simon. "What are you not telling me?"

"Isn't it clear?" Alyssa replied, her tone defensive. "This is a waste of your time. Let it go." Her eyes skated across Veronica's face, then she glanced away and out the window.

Veronica frowned. When Alyssa had taken the doll, Veronica had sat on her, pinning her to the ground until she confessed the theft and returned the doll.

Unfortunately, she couldn't do that now.

She pressed her lips together, reining in her rising anger to a manageable level. "You always did suck at lying. Now, tell me what's going on. What have you done?"

Alyssa focused on the folder in Veronica's hand, her green eyes dark with guilt and a sharp anger of their own. "Nothing you wouldn't do if you thought it was for your own good."

The urge to shout rose in Veronica's throat. She held back. This was Alyssa. Family. She set the cell phone down before she flung it at her sister and waited, her hands clenching the file so tightly it crumpled in her hands.

Cheeks blazing red, Alyssa opened her desk drawer and shoved a thin folder toward Veronica. "Here. These are the real results."

Neck muscles screaming with unreleased tension, Veronica threw the false file to the floor and jerked the new file from Alyssa's hands. She flipped it open. Familiar images greeted her. A tiny heart. A tiny brain. All solid gold.

The attached density test confirmed the findings.

It was true. The mouse was once alive.

The Midas Stone might be real. An artifact from the past that had the power to transmute living tissue into metal.

Her knees suddenly weak, she sunk down onto one of the backless, chrome lab chairs. All she could do was gape at the proof and know that from this moment forward, her life might change, forever.

"Happy now?"

"Very." Veronica nodded, knowing she was grinning like an idiot and not caring.

"Good for you," Alyssa replied, her jaw tight.

Veronica stuffed both mouse and file into her backpack and zipped them in. She could scrutinize the details later. Right now, she had a more pressing problem. "Why, Alyssa? Why hide this from me?"

"It's not professional jealousy, if that's what you're thinking." She walked over to the window.

"Jealousy?" Veronica shook her head. Alyssa had the respect of the archaeological community, something she craved for herself, and sometimes that rankled her, but jealousy? She searched her soul. "No. I don't think that. You want to tell me the reason?"

"Not really."

Walking up behind her sister, she wrapped her arms round her, hugging her close. Alyssa stiffened under her touch. "Come on. Tell me."

"Does it matter? You figured out the lie," she replied, her smaller frame taut.

Veronica leaned her chin on Alyssa's shoulder. "Of course it matters. You lied to me, Bobble. You haven't done that in a long time."

She caught a glimpse of Alyssa's smile at the nickname and felt her sister relax. A little. She backed away, knowing Alyssa would need space now that she was ready to talk.

"I worry for you," Alyssa said, breaking the silence. "I couldn't take it if something happened to you."

"Lying to me was not the answer," Veronica chastised gently.

"Lying to you was the only answer," Alyssa countered. "I knew that once you found out the mouse was real, there would be no stopping you from going with Simon. Hell, he could be Simon Legree, the slave trader from *Uncle Tom's Cabin,* and you'd go."

Veronica couldn't deny the accusation. It was true. They both knew it.

Alyssa shifted. "If something happens to you…" She shuddered. "Seeing you in that jail. Hurt. Scared." She leaned against the windowsill, one hand pressed flat against the glass. "I'm not as strong as you are. If you needed me, like that, I'm not sure I could do it again."

Veronica crossed her arms. "It's okay. I don't expect you to, and I don't expect to land in jail in a foreign country again. Or this country, for that matter."

Alyssa whirled to face her, her normally controlled demeanor darkened with angry passion. "Can't you just ignore this? For me? Do a nice, normal excavation?"

Veronica hated to hurt Alyssa, but knew there was no other choice. "It's not just about me. Not anymore."

The emotion in Alyssa's eyes shuttered closed, shutting out both her rising emotions and Veronica. She walked back to her desk, as poised as if the conversation had never happened. "Call me when you get back?"

"Of course." Veronica flung the backpack over her shoulder, knowing a dismissal when she heard it. Alyssa would want to talk after she took a few days to process the facts, mull them over, and massage them, but until she was ready, there was no point in pushing her.

"Veronica?"

She stopped and glanced over her shoulder.

Alyssa sat at her computer. To a client, she looked professional. Poised.

Only Veronica would notice the strain around her eyes. "Will you at least have Rebecca run a background check on Simon?"

"Good idea," she agreed as she pushed the button to recall the elevator. It dinged and slid open, waiting. She stepped in and turned to wave goodbye, the door sliding shut.

"Veronica!" Beyond the door, Veronica saw her sister jump to her feet. Quickly, she stuck her foot in the closing door, making them slide back open.

"What?"

"If something did happen, you'd call. Right?" She whispered the question.

Veronica smiled. Her sister was stronger than she thought, and their bond stronger than Alyssa's fear. "Of course." And she let the doors slide shut.

With his hair still damp from a shower and wearing only snug jeans, Simon looked better than Veronica remembered. Not even the overkill of the bed-and-breakfast's floral décor could detract from a body honed by years of fieldwork.

Her eyes glanced downward of their own accord.

She liked his feet. Most men had ugly feet. Yellow nails. Hairy. Simon's were smooth. And muscled. She wondered how he managed to do that.

Slowly, she perused his jeans-clad calves, then his thighs, only slowing when she came to his naked chest.

Nice.

His muscles were the kind that came from digging excavation pits—not from a gym.

He had a nice swatch of hair on his chest. Not too much, just enough to catch her attention and hold it. She remembered his chest pressed against her at the party. Even then, he'd had a six-pack. She'd loved it. Laughing and tipsy in the corner, she'd pulled his T-shirt from his jeans and let her hands roam beneath the worn cotton, tracing his muscles with her fingertips until his breath was ragged against her neck.

She inhaled and her eyes continued upward. She met his gaze. Dark. Deep.

And laughing at her as he toweled his hair dry. "See something you like?"

Heat rose to her cheeks. "Nice feet," she muttered as she pushed past him and into the room.

"And nice room." She'd thought it was bad from the hallway. The bed was an antique four-poster with a canopy. The rest of the decor was just as feminine. She counted three varieties of rose-covered wallpaper from where she stood. One was flocked with velvet.

"This must be the I-love-roses-and-I'm-not-afraid-to-show-it room," she commented as she made her way past an overstuffed pink chair with a matching ottoman.

"I didn't come for the decor." Simon folded up the towel and set it inside the door to the private bathroom. "I'm betting that you didn't, either."

He slid past her, opened up the French doors and took a seat out on the balcony at a small white wrought-iron table.

Veronica took the chair across from him, setting her backpack next to her chair. It was a sunny afternoon. Baskets filled with jasmine and ivy hung from the balconies with matching white wrought-iron railings. The air was warm and the scent clean—a welcome change from the stuffy bedroom.

Trees protected the redbrick home from the sounds of the

city, and they could almost be in another world instead of a boutique hotel on the Upper East Side of New York.

His eyes locked with hers, and Simon ran a hand over his still-unshaven, rough chin. "I take it you got the proof you needed?"

No games. She liked that. It would make convincing him to take her with him that much easier once he realized he didn't have a choice. "Yeah. I did." With her sneakered foot, she pushed the backpack to him. It scraped across the tiles. "We need to talk."

He gave a long, deliberate nod.

She held herself still, silent, like a Roman gladiator just before he crossed the threshold to an arena filled with waiting lions and surrounded by the cheering populace. The blood pounded in her ears with such force that it threatened to deafen her. It was foolish, but she wondered if Simon could hear it or if he noticed how her veins throbbed. She crossed the threshold and presented her offer. "I'll tell you what I know about the Eye of Artemis, but there is a condition."

He didn't flinch. "Not a shock. How much?"

She inhaled slowly, keeping herself steady. Then took another deep breath as she prepared for the explosion of anger she knew was coming once Simon heard her terms. "No money. I'm going with you."

He smiled, showing white, even teeth. "No."

Simple. Precise. And without a hint of emotion. Veronica cocked her head, surprised he wasn't angry at her challenge. She'd be furious if he tried that with her. "You might know Europe, but the Stone is in the Mediterranean. My bailiwick. You need me."

"No." Again. Simple. Precise. Firm.

And infuriating. "I don't think you understand. It's not negotiable."

He drummed a beat on the table with his fingertips—the

only suggestion he might be growing angry. "I do understand, but the answer is still no. I knew you might propose this—"

"It's not a proposal. It's an ultimatum," Veronica said, cutting him off, then putting her hands in her lap to keep them still. If he could maintain calm, so could she, even though her inner self wanted to stand up and make her case by pounding on the table until Simon reacted.

His expression remained impassive, but the drumming stopped.

And Veronica noticed that he didn't say no this time. Her lips twitched as she reined in her relief—she hadn't won yet. She leaned toward him, the edge of the tabletop pressing into her chest. "You can try to find another archaeologist who knows something useful about the Eye, but you won't. Believe me, I tried. There's only me and Joseph and he's not going to help you."

He leaned forward to meet her. She ignored the way his muscles bunched. He exhaled. His breath smelled minty and caressed her skin with its warmth. "It's too dangerous. I don't need the added responsibility of taking care of you." He leaned back, one closed fist on the table, the other resting against his denimed thigh. "Now, keep your part of the bargain and tell me where I can find the Eye."

He could argue, try to bully her into doing what he wanted, but it all came down to one irreconcilable truth—she had the information he needed and wasn't giving it up until she got what she wanted. She leveled her stare, defying him even before she spoke. "No."

"No?"

"Uh-huh."

He didn't break their visual lock but held it. She knew what he was doing—the same thing she would do if she were in his shoes. He was weighing the need to find the Midas Stone with the advantages and disadvantages of bringing her with him. "If it helps," she commented, breaking the silence, "My dad made sure I could take care of myself in a fight. You won't have to take care of me."

"Do you think we're walking into danger?" Simon asked, his voice stony.

Veronica bit her lip realizing that she'd just made it more difficult for Simon to accept her ultimatum. Still, there was no taking it back and if they were partners, then he needed to know that potential danger was very real. "Possibly."

"From whom?"

She shook her head. She wasn't going to tell him about the Vatican. Not yet.

"Fine."

His mouth set in a grim line, Simon pushed his chair back and rose. "Show me."

Her face betrayed her confusion before she could mask it. "Show you what?"

He looked down at her in patent disbelief. "You say you can take care of yourself? Prove it."

She hadn't expected that. "You want to fight me?"

His brows rose, and his eyes mocked her as if he felt assured of his own success. "Unless you're all talk. Yes."

Heat made its way up her neck and to her cheeks. Veronica stood. *All talk, my ass.* She raised her chin to meet his eyes. "I do this and you agree to take me?"

He hesitated and uncertainty briefly sketched his face before disappearing. "Agreed."

Idiot. He didn't know what he was in for—which worked for her. The element of surprise was always an advantage.

Veronica followed him into the bedroom. Together, they pushed the floral-covered furniture to the sides of the room, opening up a bare patch that was roughly ten feet in diameter.

Picking up a black cloth hair-tie from the bedside table, Simon ran a hand over his still-damp hair, smoothing it down before he tied it back. "You sure you want to do this? You might get hurt," he said, his tone more sincere and less arrogant than she expected.

"I'll take my chances." Veronica stuck her hand out. "Good luck."

He took her hand in his. It was warm, calloused and strong. Her body instinctively remembered his touch and raced into overdrive. *Useful.*

"You, too," he said.

His words were like a fight bell and the signal she needed. Bracing her feet, she yanked him toward her and kneed him in the groin.

Carrying a half-full pot of coffee and two mugs, Veronica tapped the door open with her foot and walked back into the rose room.

Simon waited in one of the overstuffed chairs, trying to get comfortable.

She tried not to seem too pleased. Served him right for doubting her. She'd warned him that she knew how to defend herself.

And as much as she hated to admit it, it was a nice little payback for not believing her myth theory when she first proposed it. A few more hits like that and she might even forgive him.

Her eyes zeroed in on his crotch for a split second before she caught herself, then flickered upward.

He glared at her. "Let's hope I can still have kids," he muttered.

She handed him a cup of coffee, trying not to appear too pleased with herself. After all, he'd wanted her to prove her worth. It was his own fault. "I'm sure your swimmers will be fine."

He rolled his eyes and took the coffee. "Thanks."

"No problem. *Partner.*"

He hesitated, and for a moment, she wondered if he was going to renege on their deal. It wouldn't be the first time he'd screwed her over—the thought was bitter in her brain. If he did, she'd go after the Midas Stone herself. Without his half of the codex, it would be more difficult. Take longer. Possibly years.

But it *was* possible. She wouldn't let him take this away from her. Not again.

But instead of showing her the door, he assessed her with his piercing eyes. His frank examination gave her the distinct impression she was being judged the way one would judge a quality Thoroughbred. Heat rose in the pit of her stomach, then spread through her body like a flash fire as his intimate assessment took in her thighs. Waist. Chest. Arms.

Finally, he dipped his head to sip the hot coffee, the break in visual contact effectively dousing the fire he'd started in her body. Veronica picked up her own cup, took a deep breath and waited for his decision.

"You win. Partner it is."

Her shoulders relaxed, releasing much of the tension she'd been holding in since Alyssa's report.

Once again, his eyes locked onto her. "Unlike *some people,* I keep my word."

Instantly, her hackles rose at the criticism. "If you'd agreed to take me, I wouldn't have had to push the issue."

He grunted. "As I said, I keep my word. Now, I have to ask, where were you raised that you had to knee men in the balls on a regular basis?"

She leaned back into the pink-velvet chair, forcing the hackles down. If he were willing to play nice, she'd do the same. "All over the world. Some of the regions were less, let's say, *hospitable,* than others. My dad thought it would be best if my sister and I both learned how to defend ourselves. He taught us to do whatever it took."

Simon shifted with another grunt of pain. "I'll remember that next time."

She snickered, despite her attempt to hold it back.

To his credit, he didn't glare at her. Instead, he gave her a look that was almost admiration. Maybe he wouldn't be so bad as a partner.

He templed his hands in front of him. "Do you want to tell me about the Eye now?"

"Sure. I read about it in the other half of your codex."

"You have the other half?" Simon almost jumped to his feet in excitement, but fell back with an "oomph" and a pained expression that told her his crotch was far from recovered.

She didn't laugh this time.

He shook his head, clearing it. "Where is it?"

Veronica took a sip of coffee. "I never said I had it. I've read it. Or part of it. It's in the Vatican."

"How do we see it?"

"That's the more difficult part." She set her cup down and leaned toward him, her forearms resting on her thighs. He wasn't going to like what she had to say, but he needed to know the degree of difficulty involved. "I have a friend, Sylvia, who worked there. She specializes in holy relics. She told me about the codex and got me in to view it. I was partway into my translation when she was fired, and I was denied access."

Simon remained silent.

"I was never told the reason and neither was she, but I can assume that once they realized the basis of my theory, they didn't want the knowledge proven and made public. They told her that her services were no longer required. I tried to get in again but was unsuccessful."

One hand resting over his flat abdomen, Simon rubbed his

chin. A gesture that Veronica knew meant he was taking in the info and drawing conclusions.

"I have some connections." He said, his voice hesitant. "I might be able to get us a viewing."

"Don't be naive." Veronica snapped before she thought to hold her temper.

"Excuse me?" His eyebrows arched in surprise. "Naive? Naive is not mentioning the codex in your presentation. If you had, you might have been more credible, and I'd be in Rome by now."

Veronica rubbed the back of her neck. She was doing this badly. "You don't understand. What was I going to say about the notes to back it up? The Vatican was, and I'm sure still is, in full denial." A deep sigh of frustration escaped her lips. "It wasn't just that I was a nuisance. It was more. They had armed guards escort me from Vatican City. They confiscated my work, and when I got back to the hotel, my room was ransacked. My notes stolen. Luckily, I'd left a few with Sylvia, and in the end, that was all I recovered."

Simon leaned back and Veronica knew he was studying her. Alyssa had that same look when she was evaluating one of Veronica's wilder claims. "What do you suggest?"

Veronica relaxed. "I have a plan. One that will get us into the room where the relics are kept." She hesitated. Simon might appear as analytical and cynical as Alyssa, but his belief in the Midas Stone told her he had an adventurous side. She hoped she was right. "If you're up to doing something that is a tad outside the law."

His eyes lit up, and Veronica knew he was hooked. "What do you have in mind?" He asked, his voice equally interested.

Veronica sent a silent prayer of thanks to the crazy gods that blessed even crazier archaeologists. "How do you feel about breaking and entering?"

Chapter 5

Veronica watched the city pass by as Simon zipped through Rome in their rented Peugeot 307 Coupé. After drawing money from her business account and his savings account to fund their quest, they'd spent the last eight days getting their travel documents in order, going over her notes and the scant evidence from the ill-received myth paper and reassuring both Alyssa and Rebecca that they would be fine.

Now they were driving through Rome in a convertible with the top down. Veronica breathed in the air that was a combination of rich food, marble warmed by the midday sun, exhaust and spring flowers.

A teenager in ripped jeans, headphones covering her ears, and looking very American, bopped past them as they waited at a red light. If not for the plethora of historical artifacts, they could almost be in a city in the United States.

Simon turned the small car into the Piazza Navona where

Bernini's Fontana dei Quattro Fium, fountain of the four rivers, caught her attention with its human representation of the Ganges, Nile, Danube and Rio de la Plata Rivers carved in marble and flanking a Roman obelisk that reached skyward.

Around the fountain, people milled about drinking coffee, taking pictures, gawking and talking.

She grinned. This was definitely not New York. In New York, someone would probably be fishing for change.

It still seemed surreal. She and Simon certainly weren't in the United States. They were in one of the most historical and beautiful places on the planet, planning to break into one of the most well-secured places on the planet. Another day or so and she'd be well on her way to committing a felony.

She'd never done that before.

Correction. It was never *premeditated* before.

Except for Michael's home, and she didn't consider that a felony or wrong in any sense of the word.

It was justice.

They zipped out of the Piazza and toward Via dei Serpenti, a district in the heart of Rome, where they had reservations at the Hotel Apollo.

She pushed her sunglasses back up the bridge of her nose and leaned into the leather seat, letting the sun warm her face.

"Where did you stay the last time you were here?" Simon asked.

Veronica didn't open her eyes. "I rented an apartment for a month. Much easier than a hotel." She yawned with the inevitable jetlag that came with traveling to Europe. "Have you ever been here before?"

"My honeymoon a few years back."

"Hmm. How long were you married?" She asked, then almost bit her tongue. He hadn't told her he was divorced. She only knew it from Rebecca's background check. Unfortunately, that was about all her assistant had found out. It seemed that Dr. Owens was a bit of a mystery. He graduated high school in Seattle, then disappeared for twelve years. Resurfacing when he got his master's in an archaeological investigation of Colletière, a medieval site that was beneath the waters of Paladru Lake in France.

Then the stint at Columbia University, where she met him and he earned his doctorate.

All his degrees were completed in record time, and according to Rebecca's background check, he had just finished excavating the site in France where he had found the golden mouse. So, his story checked out in that regard.

But what had he done for those previous twelve years? Studied to be a monk? Doubtful. Military? With his muscled physique, possibly. Missionary? No. He wasn't the type. Somehow, she couldn't envision those decadent lips chanting a prayer.

Who was Dr. Simon Owens? She wanted to know, and unfortunately, Rebecca had found nothing. Whatever he was hiding, it was a professional scrub job. Otherwise, Rebecca would have uncovered more.

She yawned again, reminding herself that she'd have time to find out all about him. She'd simply watch him. Be careful. Whatever he was, he was her partner unless he proved he wasn't trustworthy.

But had her partner noticed her slip? She gave him a sideways glance.

"Two years," Simon replied. His tanned hands were relaxed as he guided the car through traffic. There was no indication of suspicion in his tone or actions.

Relieved, Veronica settled back again just as Simon whipped the car around a corner, catching her off guard. She grabbed the side of the seat before she fell into his lap. "Jeez, a warning would be nice," she growled.

"You and my ex are a lot alike," Simon continued, seemingly oblivious to her comment. "You'd get along quite well."

Wonderful. Grappling with the seat belt, she pulled herself back. She reminded him of his ex-wife. Was he being sarcastic or genuine? As always, his expression was unreadable. "Is that going to be a problem?" Veronica asked.

"What?"

"Me being like your ex?"

Simon gave her a sideways glance, his eyes unreadable beneath his black sunglasses. "No. Sam's great."

"Then why the breakup?" Veronica asked, curiosity popping the question out of her mouth before she could wonder what he might think of her asking something so intimate.

Simon shrugged, broad shoulders stretching the buttery-soft cotton of his T-shirt. "The usual. Distance. Work."

The silence stretched. It wasn't much of an answer, but she sensed it was all she'd get. He was nothing if not closemouthed. Well, he got points for not verbally slamming the woman.

The light ahead turned red, and traffic came to a stop. "How about you?" Simon asked. "Ever married or come close?"

Veronica stiffened. Was he as uninterested as he sounded? His tone was nonchalant, but his left foot tapped a soft rhythm against the floorboard of the car. Did he know about Michael and Brazil? She'd run a check on him. It was possible he'd run one on her and was playing her, trying to see what she'd reveal.

Peeking at him through her lashes, she could see he looked relaxed, but that left foot told her otherwise.

Did he know about Michael and what happened? She couldn't ask without giving her secrets away. She glanced at his foot again. He wanted to play?

Then so could she.

"No."

He didn't comment, but his foot stilled. Veronica relaxed an iota. If he wanted to know more, he could ask. For now, she'd put her concerns about Simon's suspicions on the backburner.

Traffic moved, and they crept along the northern edge of the Piazza Venezia and finally into the Via dei Serpenti district.

They rounded another corner, and the Hotel Apollo came into view. Constructed of redbrick and with twenty-four private rooms, it was smaller than most hotels in the area. But it was only a few blocks from the secret entrance to the Vatican.

Simon pulled up to the front of the hotel and cut the engine.

"Break a leg," she murmured, preparing herself for their "act." She'd insisted on going undercover while in Rome—which was why it had taken so long to get their travel documents. In today's tightened security, false documents were difficult to come by. Considering they were here to steal the rest of the codex that she'd worked on, it seemed best if they were incognito. Simon had thought her paranoid, but he hadn't seen the suspicion and annoyance on the Vatican guard's faces when they'd *escorted* her off the premises or the way they'd touched the weapons at their sides when she tried to return.

If the Vatican knew she was in town, she would be the first person pegged as a suspect once they discovered the codex was gone.

It might have been her idea to go undercover, but it was Simon's idea to pose as a couple. She had fought the idea at first, but relented after he pointed out that of all the personas she could assume—a happy honeymooner was the last one people would suspect.

Besides, Rome was expensive and one room was much cheaper than two. So, they were checking into the Hotel Apollo as Mr. and Mrs. Blackwell. Honeymooners.

He opened his car door. "Ready, Mrs. Blackwell?"

She took a deep breath and plastered an "I love this man so much I could just eat him up" smile on her lips and gazed into Simon's eyes with what she hoped was adoration.

They carried their backpacks while the bellman retrieved their small amount of luggage. Simon took her hand in his as they entered the lobby. His strong fingers and broad palm were warm and not the least bit sweaty.

They waited at the counter, and Simon wrapped his arm around her shoulder. She leaned into him. He smelled of clean sweat, cotton warmed by the sun and just a hint of cologne. Damn him.

The clerk came out to greet them. Small but voluptuous, she was a pre-Raphaelite beauty. Her blond hair was styled into a French twist and her hips swayed beneath her short skirt.

"Mr. and Mrs. Simon Blackwell checking in," Simon said, pulling her closer and putting his hand up the back of her shirt.

The clerk gave a nod and punched their name into the computer. "Ah. The newlyweds."

Leaning down, Simon gave Veronica a peck on the lips, taking a moment to gaze into her eyes with adoration. "That's us," he murmured. He kissed her again. This time, it was longer. His mouth was firm. Hot. His tongue pushed against her mouth, parting her lips.

It's just the charade, she reminded herself. It meant nothing.

But her every nerve vibrated with unexpected need. It had been too long since a man had touched her, and she didn't care if the kiss was real. She only cared that it continued.

With a sigh, she leaned into him, her hands resting on his hips. Her body remembered his taste. His touch.

With a groan, he cupped her face with his hands and held her captive. It was brief but fierce.

"Ahem," the clerk said.

They pushed away from each other like charged magnets, both breathing heavy, chests heaving. Veronica touched her mouth with her fingertips, wondering if he made love with the same intensity.

She shook herself. *What was she thinking?* He could be another Michael for all she knew. The kiss was definitely a mistake. And not a small mistake. This was the mountain variety, since it woke up the libido she thought was asleep, if not deceased. He didn't know it, but at this rate, he'd sleep on the floor.

The clerk placed the keys in Simon's hand. "Enjoy the suite, but do not forget to take time for the city. Even newlyweds must eat."

Veronica's cheeks blazed. Oh, yes. A *big* mistake.

"We'll try to remember," Simon replied, fingers closing around the key. He kissed the curve of Veronica's neck and she shuddered as a shiver shot down to her toes. "No promises though, right, Mrs. Blackwell?"

"Uh, right," Veronica replied unsteadily. Another kiss like that and she'd be pulling back the sheets and patting the mattress.

Exiling him to the floor wasn't far enough.

She needed a different room.

The honeymoon suite was small but a fairy-tale room, and Veronica was almost sorry she and Simon weren't really newlyweds. Floor-to-ceiling windows were framed by lush, dark blue velvet curtains. Antique mirrors on the wall and gilded picture frames reflected Old World beauty. A small cherry table was opposite the bathroom door.

A king-size bed dominated the far end of the room. The headboard and footboard matched the cherry table and were as equally polished.

On top of the overstuffed mattress were two FedEx boxes. One was an elongated tube.

Lily.

Dropping her pack at the door, Veronica almost sprinted to her weapon.

"Out of curiosity…" Simon locked the door and brought both their packs over to the bed, dropping them on the mattress with a *thunk*. "How did you get her into the country?"

Sitting down, Veronica picked up the long box and yanked the tab to open it. "Private courier. I try not to depend on the postal service. Have you seen what can happen? I got a fruit-cake once that looked like it was thrown against a wall and beaten to a pulp, and I thought those things were indestructible."

Covered in bubble wrap, Lily slid out of the box and onto her lap. Veronica ripped the plastic off. Perfect and pristine, the short-barreled shotgun shone in the overhead light. A note taped to the black stock caught Veronica's attention. There was a familiar happy face drawn on the outside of it. *Rebecca*. She flipped the violet-scented paper open. *Told you she'd be fine.*

"Don't you worry what will happen if the shipping company found out what you were shipping?" Simon asked.

"If they x-rayed everything, yes. But they don't." He didn't look convinced, but Veronica didn't care. She hugged Lily to her chest. Lily might be stiff, cold and dangerous, but she was also the best security blanket Veronica had ever owned.

"I hate to break up the reunion," Simon said, clearly disturbed by her showing of emotion. "But isn't that taking a big chance? What if the ammunition went off?"

"If it were dangerous shipping either her or the ammunition, I wouldn't do it."

She stroked the shotgun's black barrel. "Besides, I'm more comfortable with Lily. I know what she can do, and if it comes down to it that—" she shrugged with an indifference she didn't feel "—then I want to be prepared."

Simon sat down, the bed sinking under his weight. "Fine. For now."

For always, but she didn't voice the thought. Between the kiss and jet lag, she wasn't in the mood to fight.

Simon shifted until his back pressed against the headboard. Stretching his long, muscular legs out, he held back a yawn. "Why did you name her Lily?"

Setting her weapon on the bed, Veronica peeled away the tape that sealed the smaller package. "We lived in Africa for two years when I was about ten. There was a small village nearby, and my mom hired a woman to watch us. She took care of us. Even killed a snake once when it came too close. We couldn't pronounce her real name, but Lily was close." She upended the box and three small cartons of shells fell out and into her hand. "So when I got Lily, it seemed somehow appropriate."

"Do you plan on taking her with you to the Vatican?"

She knew what he was thinking, because she was thinking the same thing. Lily was insurance against any unforeseen problems, but despite her comment, if they were caught, she wasn't even sure she would use Lily against another person— other than maybe Michael. She'd used the shotgun as a threat a few times when she was on some of the more remote digs, but generally, the sound of a shell ratcheting into the chamber was enough to drive away potential thieves. She'd never had to actually fire the weapon in defense of herself or a dig.

The question was, would the sound of a chambered shell work as well on Vatican security guards?

"I'm not sure," she sighed. "But she's saved my life on more than one occasion, and I'm getting the feeling that this might be another one of them."

Standing in a deserted alley a few blocks from the Vatican, Veronica tugged at the Lycra tank top that stuck to the small of her back and yanked her leggings upward. It had rained the rest of the day, and though the summer storm had passed, the night air was damp and warm as a result. Her clothes made the perfect outfit for robbing, but felt tight and sticky in the humid air.

Her eyes adjusted to the dim light that filtered in from the streetlights until she could make out Simon's large frame. Dressed in form-fitting black cotton chinos and a black T-shirt, chosen from his endless supply of black T-shirts, he looked sexy, relaxed and annoyingly comfortable. But there was also caution and curiosity in his steady gaze.

She frowned and tugged at the Lycra one last time. Next time, she'd wear cotton. She set her backpack on the damp ground. It didn't contain much—Lily, a crowbar, gloves, plastic bags, Rebecca's code-breaker and two pairs of goggles for viewing lasers. Her hands pressed against the small of her back, she gave one last stretch and surveyed the lights coming down from the surrounding buildings. Rome resembled New York in that it never truly slept, but after midnight, it did calm down. She and Simon only had to be careful of the apartment houses that bordered either side of the alley. Most of the people were asleep, since tomorrow was a workday, so as long as she and Simon were quiet, she didn't think anyone would bother to look out their windows.

Veronica tightened the rubber band that held her dark hair in its braid. Then they both slipped on black leather gloves, completing their ensemble.

Unzipping the duffel bag, Veronica hesitated. "You sure you're up to this? This is almost the point of no return."

"Completely."

She pulled the crowbar out from underneath Lily and handed it to Simon. "Enjoy."

Using it, he lifted the edge of the sewer cap, got his fingers under it, picked it up and set it aside. It made a *clink* against the cement, but otherwise, all was silent.

The round black hole looked like it could go forever and to anywhere. Veronica shuddered. As safe as she knew the sewer system and catacombs were, she hated going underground. Especially at night. Granted, it was dark in the tunnels no matter what the time was, but at night, her imagination ran overtime, and she invented giant rats and reptiles akin to the legendary alligators of the New York sewer system.

"Just catacombs," she murmured.

Looping the handles of the duffel over her shoulders, she let the bag rest against her back like a long backpack. "Let's do it."

She searched for the ladder with her foot and found metal rungs in the wall. Lowering herself into the hole, she climbed down ten feet, her feet landing on rough cement covered by a half inch of water.

The air was dank. Wet. There was the faint smell of plant decay but nothing too horrible.

Simon followed, stopping long enough to pull the sewer cap back over the hole.

Veronica clicked on her flashlight.

The sewer was surprisingly clean. Other than the water and the occasional soda can, it was devoid of debris.

A rat ran past her, and she yelped before clamping her hand over her mouth. Even though she encountered them on almost every dig, she hated the creepy little rodents.

"As long as there aren't any alligators," Simon said, pulling the sewer cap back on before coming to stand beside her.

She grinned, glad to discover she wasn't the only one with an overactive imagination.

Simon clicked on his flashlight, running the beam up the modern cement walls. "These are the catacombs?"

"No. This is the sewer system. It connects to the catacombs if you know what to watch for."

After the Vatican fired Sylvia from her position as an ancient relic curator, she had told Veronica about the secret catacombs one afternoon. She'd never blamed Veronica for getting her fired. She blamed the Vatican and its rigid patriarchal ideals.

The Vatican catacombs were an anomaly within Rome. During early Christian times, Roman law made it illegal to bury Christians within the walls of the city, so the catacombs that were constructed prior to the Roman law were abandoned and forgotten until they became fodder for the tourist trade.

With the exception of this one. Apparently, the Vatican was exempt from the rules that applied to everyone else since these catacombs contained bodies and were used by the Vatican as recently as the early 1700s. According to Sylvia, these tunnels were known only by a few Vatican officials.

Veronica ran a beam of light over the walls. She'd considered contacting Sylvia to ask for her assistance but decided against it. She'd taken a chance showing Veronica the hidden catacombs. If she and Simon were caught, it was better to involve as few people as possible.

So it was up to her and years-old memories. Luckily, she'd been fascinated at the time of her tour and thought she knew where to go. She started walking in the direction of the Vatican.

Simon followed, his feet sloshing through the water. If she remembered right, it wasn't far. Perhaps ten minutes to the catacombs, then they'd be right under the Vatican.

They continued in silence, following the main line and passing by lesser tunnels that branched off into other directions. She turned a corner and three branch lines came into view. Veronica stopped. "This is it."

"You sure?" Simon stood beside her, the beam from his light steady against the wall.

"Yes," she replied, relieved her memory had proved accurate. She pointed toward the smaller tunnel on the left. Five feet in height, it was cramped, but doable. "We go that way."

Leading the way, she hunched down and began walking down the long passage, her duffel scraping the ceiling when she wasn't careful. With her legs bent at the knee, walking was almost a waddle. She wondered how Simon was faring behind her. She was tall, but he was over six foot. He must almost be crawling.

She swung her flashlight side to side, watching the floor. Five minutes into their walk, a metal plate embossed with Italian words bounced back a reflection. "That's it." She stood on the far side and waited for Simon.

Within seconds, he stood on the opposite side of the metal plate. Light bouncing off the walls created deep shadows across Simon's face, giving him an almost sinister expression. He raised a single, dark eyebrow and the ominous expression disappeared with the arrival of a familiar one. "Do you think I'll fit?"

Veronica tried to visually compare the size of the metal plate against Simon's broad shoulders. The plate was, perhaps, two feet by two feet. It was going to be tight. Very tight. She grimaced. "There's not a lot of choice unless you plan on staying behind."

"Not a chance."

"Good." She was glad he wasn't the kind of person who backed away from a problem—no matter how challenging it seemed. She'd known men like that. The slightest bit of difficulty and they bolted, leaving someone else to take the blame or clean up their mess. And not just Michael. Budding archaeologists who discovered recovering artifacts wasn't like in a movie. There weren't walking mummies, pharaohs' gold or a telephone line to God. Fieldwork was about dirt, sweat and determination.

Going after the Midas Stone was the exception, not the rule.

The crowbar still in his hand, Simon handed it to Veronica with a get-even grin. "Enjoy."

She rolled her eyes, but took it and wedged the curved end under the lip. Using the side of the wall as leverage, she lifted the heavy iron plate.

Simon grabbed it as it came free and put it on the floor of the tunnel.

If she remembered right, this opened into the ceiling of the catacomb with a drop of roughly six feet to the floor. Veronica took a deep breath and shone her flashlight in the hole. Black water covered the floor like a lake. The catacombs had been damp those years back when Sylvia gave her a tour, not like this, and until she dropped into it, there was no way to judge how deep the water was.

"Damn."

"What?"

She felt, rather than saw, Simon tense next to her. She rocked back on her heels, letting the duffel slide from her shoulders. "There's water. A lot of water."

"Is it still passable?"

She rubbed the back of her neck. "Yeah. It doesn't come up to the ceiling." She nodded toward the duffel. "I'll go first, then you can hand me the pack and follow."

Assessing her with his cool, dark eyes, Simon seemed steady and unmoved. "Be careful of the rats."

"Don't *say* that," Veronica responded. She knew she must have stared at him like he was out of his mind because a smug grin broke his composure.

Taking a deep breath, Veronica lowered herself through the hole, landing with a splash.

The water came up to her hips. She sniffed. The ancient air smelled musty. Like damp mummy dust and granite. She shone her lights on the walls. Mummies hung on the wall in various poses. In the past, higher-ups in the Vatican were given their final rest in these unknown catacombs. Their bodies were dressed as they were in life, hung on the wall and placed in various quasi-natural poses.

A bishop from the early 1700s, with nothing left but clothes and bone, had his hand raised as if giving a blessing. Across from him were the remains of a priest, an open Bible tied to his hands, and what was left of his feet floating on top of the water.

She hadn't warned Simon about the mummies. It wasn't something you could describe, and in case he did turn out to be a good guy, she didn't want to spoil the surprise.

"Heads up," Simon said.

She grabbed the duffel as Simon lowered it down. A minute later, he followed. Angling downward, he managed to get one shoulder through and then the next. He also knocked his skull against the edge of the opening with a distinct *thunk*. Veronica cringed, but despite the slight mishap, he slid into the water like a seal and causing not a ripple.

"You okay?" she whispered.

He rubbed his head. "Fine. It was a tight squeeze."

He shone his flashlight on the walls, the beam glancing off white bone and what was left of robes woven with gold threads. For a moment, Simon simply stared in awe. "This is amazing," he finally said, his hushed voice holding a reverence that Veronica recognized. It was the tone that all true archaeologists took when confronted with history. "Any idea who they are?"

"Sylvia did some research but there wasn't much information. Mainly men who were high up in the Vatican or had done something special for one of the popes. And it gets better." Veronica started wading down the narrow corridor, the duffel perched on her shoulder. Interspersed between the bodies were carvings of battles, saints and sacrifices.

"How did she find this place?" Simon asked.

"She found an old map and, being curious, she investigated. But she's also smart and, with the exception of showing me the tunnels, I don't think she told anyone else. Honestly, I think this place was forgotten ages ago."

Behind her, Simon oohed and ahhed.

She slogged forward, enjoying herself despite their reasons for being here. The catacombs were a slice of history. To view the contents was like sneaking downstairs on Christmas Eve and catching Santa.

Under any other circumstance, she'd spend months, even years, down here, digging into the past—mummies and all.

The catacombs began to slant upward, and in another twenty feet, they left the water behind.

"Any thoughts as to why this is kept secret?" Simon asked as they passed an intricate carving depicting the martyrdom of Pope St. Sixtus II—his severed head at his feet.

"Other than the fact they were forgotten?"

"Yes."

"I have my thoughts. These are holy men, and holy men are generally buried with expensive relics. My best guess is that they didn't want to take the chance that the graves would be robbed."

They turned a corner, and the catacombs ended at a thick wooden door.

Veronica's heart rate bumped up and she jogged the last few steps. Almost dropping the duffel, she laid a palm against the wood. It was smooth and damp to the touch. The hinge and lock were almost rust free—someone was keeping it up but not on a regular basis. *Good.* And if her memory served her right, it opened up behind a tapestry in one of the smaller sanctuaries.

She turned to Simon. Once they crossed the threshold, they were legally felons and there would be no turning back. They would be partners until the end of this journey—whatever happened. "This is it." Her voice quivered in excitement.

He gave her shoulder a squeeze. "Any second thoughts?"

She shook her head. After all the planning, trepidation and anticipation, they were here and taking the first step toward proving her hypothesis and reclaiming her place in the archaeology community. She took a deep breath. "None. You?"

He didn't hesitate. "No. Let's do it."

Her eyes slid to the duffel on the ground. Should she take Lily?

"Well?" Simon asked, as if reading her mind.

As much as she hated to leave her, it was too risky to take her. Besides, stealing from the Vatican was bad enough. There was no way she was going to add armed and dangerous, and possibly murderer, to her impending rap sheet.

No career was worth an innocent life.

Veronica zipped open the bag, pulled out the shotgun and set her and the crowbar into one of the niches.

For a brief moment, she and Simon stared at each other, keenly aware that if there was a chance to walk away, it was now.

There was no way she would back off, but what about Simon?

The corner of his mouth quirked in a half smile, and with a flourish, he motioned toward the ancient door that was their entry into crime. "Ladies first."

She returned the smile, took a deep breath and thumbed the ancient, hammered brass handle.

It was locked.

Chapter 6

"**S**on of a—" Veronica yanked at the handle. It didn't budge. She braced herself and tried again. Still nothing. How could she not have realized the damned door would be locked? Alyssa always said she never thought ahead. That she focused so hard on the big picture that she missed important details.

She'd be laughing her ass off over this.

But then, Alyssa would have researched ancient locks and brought a skeleton key.

Frustration burning, she strode over to Lily, wishing she could shoot the lock off. The sheer weight of the gun in her hand was, sometimes, enough to take the edge off her anger. But the last thing they needed was to announce their presence. Instead, she grabbed the crowbar, strode back to the door and wedged it under the handle. "Lock me out? I don't think so."

Simon's hand, muscled from years of working with a trowel and shovel, gripped her arm, stopping her. "Don't."

Her eyes burned with anger. She twisted around. "What do you suggest?" The question came out sharper than she intended, and she reminded herself that the locked door was not Simon's fault. She was angry with herself for not knowing this would happen.

"I can pick the lock."

Veronica's jaw dropped. "Excuse me?"

He looked at her as if she were simple. "I said that I could pick the lock." Reaching into his front pocket, he pulled a small case from the side pocket. Unzipping it, he took out two slender tools that were about five inches long. He held out his flashlight. "Hold this."

Incredulous, she set the crowbar down and took the light. Squatting, he worked at the lock with a calm reserved only for the most mundane of tasks.

Veronica watched over his shoulder. She hated to admit it, but this skill intrigued her on one level and worried her on another. Normal people didn't pick locks. Thieves picked locks. People who could not be trusted picked locks.

What had he been for those missing twelve years? She wanted to ask but knew that any indication she knew about them would only make him suspicious.

But to not ask about this would be suspicious. "Simon?"

"Yes?"

"I have to ask—"

"Where did I learn to do this?" He finished the sentence for her.

"Yeah."

He gave an I-know-something-you-don't-know smirk at her over his shoulder. "A guy has to have a hobby."

She knew her expression betrayed her disbelief and was glad he was busy. "Uh-huh. Picking locks is yours?"

"Yes," he replied, nimble fingers still working. "One of them."

She looked down at him, interested more than she wanted to be. "What're the others? Ninja fighting? Car racing?"

He chuckled. A deep sound that she realized she hadn't heard until this moment.

"How did you know to bring it with you?" she asked as she watched him manipulate the ancient piece of equipment. He didn't swear or hurry. Just maintained that calm persona that both intrigued and annoyed her. He and Alyssa would get along splendidly.

"We're breaking in to the Vatican—the main part being 'breaking in.' It seemed appropriate."

He sounded sincere. She ran a hand over her braid. And it made sense. She only wished she'd thought of it.

The only sounds were the metallic clicking and scraping as Simon worked to open the lock and his slow, steady breathing. From what she understood, picking locks was both a skill and an art. He might joke about this particular skill being a hobby, but she was willing to bet that, at one time, it was much more than that.

She moved to the side. His brows were drawn together in concentration as he worked, totally absorbed by the job. Like she was when she was excavating a particularly interesting artifact.

There was a *click*. "That's it." Simon straightened and took a step back while she handed him back his flashlight.

Veronica breathed deeply. After they got the codex and escaped, she'd talk to him about his "hobby" and find out if he had any more "hobbies" she needed to know about. With his past being such a mystery, they might give her some idea as to what he did during the missing years.

Now it was time to concentrate. Adrenaline pumped through her body, her skin tingled, and her muscles twitched with the need for action.

The beam from her flashlight remained steady despite the

fact that she was ready to jump out of her skin. Her mouth curved upward, pleased with her control.

Running her hands over her skintight outfit, she squeezed out as much water as she could. "Shoes," she said, and slipped hers off. Running around barefoot wasn't appealing, but neither was leaving a trail of wet footprints.

Simon did the same, his cotton pants still dripping. She'd envied them on the street, now they were a liability. "What are you wearing under there?" she asked.

His eyebrow shot upward. "Why? Interested?"

Hands on her hips, she glared at him. "Very funny. But unless you thought to pack a blow-dryer in your other pocket, you're going to leave a trail that damn near anyone can follow."

The eyebrow relaxed, and he kicked off his shoes as he unzipped his pants and slid the damp material over his hips and down his thighs.

Veronica gawked, unable to drag her eyes away. At first, she thought he wore black boxer-briefs since the material hugged his skin and left little to the imagination. In the beam of light, every well-developed muscle stood out.

She felt herself flush.

When he stepped out of the pants, she realized they weren't underwear but black biking shorts. Lycra—like her top.

"What were you? A Boy Scout?" she asked, exasperated that he seemed to be prepared for every contingent.

He chuckled in reply.

She turned back to the door. "That's twice now. Be careful, you might actually break into a laugh." And she opened the door before he could retort.

It swung inward, squeaking and rasping on the hinges. She cringed, hesitating. Silence. No voices. No shouts of alarm. Nothing.

Carefully, she opened the door the rest of the way. Covering the opening was the backside of a tapestry. On silent feet, she slid along the wall behind the cloth and poked her head out.

They were at the front of one of the small private chapels that Sylvia had said were in the pope's private quarters. Chandeliers gave off a dim light. There were, perhaps, twenty pews and a single confessional in the back of the room. In the far right corner was a statue of the Virgin Mary. In the left, a detailed sculpture of the crucifixion.

The chapel wasn't occupied, but a rack of lit votive candles indicated that people were recently here, perhaps this evening.

Crooking her finger, she motioned Simon to follow. She heard him shut the door behind them and skim the tapestry as he came to join her, carrying the duffel bag. Veronica pointed toward the door at the opposite end of the room and they moved in unison. The chapel was warm and dry and smelled of incense, a sharp contrast to the catacombs. He reached the entrance first and thrust his hand out, motioning her to wait. Veronica reached the door and stopped. Ears pressed against the wood, they both listened. Beyond the door was only silence.

He turned the doorknob and stepped through with her on his heels. Her feet hit the cold marble of the hallway and another surge of adrenaline rushed. By the time this was over, she was going to be so pumped up she'd be able to run a marathon.

Dim with whitewashed walls, it seemed that Vatican City was asleep for the night—which was just how she wanted it.

"Prima dobbiamo spegnere le candele?" A man's voice, raspy with age, caught her attention.

Simon turned to her and pushed her back into the doorway. *"Uno momento."* A second voice as ancient and shaky as the first, replied.

"Hide," Veronica whispered, seeing a shadow round the

corner even as she shut the door after Simon. There was no time to run down the aisle and back into the catacombs. The confessional caught her eye. As if reading her mind, Simon sprinted the five feet to it with her following. Simon tossed the duffel in, and they jammed themselves into the small space, shutting the door behind them. Simon's chest pressed against her back. She shut her eyes and listened to herself breathe. Deep inhale. She held it. Quiet, slow exhale.

The door to the chapel creaked open. She thought she felt Simon's heart beating, each pump pressing into her back and then relaxing again.

The booth was small for two and tight with a man as big as Simon behind her. He twitched and wrapped his arms around her waist, pulling her tight against him. His breath was warm and even against her neck.

She leaned into him. It was a childish fear, but a part of her was terrified that if she opened her eyes and saw the men, they would see her. The other, more mature and curious half of her psyche wondered who the men were and why they were awake, wandering about the Vatican when everyone else was asleep.

She opened her eyes.

Through the wicker window of the confessional, Veronica made out the figures of two men as they entered the room. Both wore robes—one in white and the other in cream—and were hunched over with age. They genuflected, then shuffled past the confessional on slippered feet to the front of the small chapel, passing the confessional.

They were so close Veronica could touch them. She willed her breathing to slow even further, her body to relax and for the men to do their job and get the hell out.

Behind her, Simon shifted his weight from one foot to another. The duffel scraped against the back wall of the confessional. It wasn't a loud noise, but to Veronica's adrenaline-hyped body, it might as well have been a marching band playing John Philip Sousa.

She tensed, and for a moment she was sure her heart stopped.

Her eyes remained locked on the two men. Did they hear it? The one in cream stopped and said something to the man in white.

Her eyes widened and she held her breath. This was it. What would they do when the men opened the door and caught them? Her mind raced over possibilities. Tie them up? Abandon the codex?

Instead, White laughed and put out the candles that dominated the front altar. The room dimmed, and the unmistakable scent of snuffed candle reached her nose. Shuffling back toward the confessional, the men turned out the last lights and left her and Simon in utter blackness.

Veronica's heart slowed and she pressed a hand to her chest. White and Cream hadn't heard Simon.

The whole episode lasted just over a minute, but she felt as if she'd been in the confessional for hours. Her breath came out in a whoosh. She raised her eyes to the ceiling and said the only appropriate thought that came to mind, "Forgive me, Father, for I have sinned."

Behind her, Simon groaned at the weak joke, and she was sure if the lights were on, she'd see him rolling his eyes. But it was dark and the confessional was too small to turn in.

It was so confined, Veronica realized, that Simon touched every part of her body. Thigh to thigh. Chest to back. His lips against her hair.

She sucked in a breath at the intimacy. "That was too close." Her voice broke. "Next time we are stuck in a confessional, or any kind of situation where we might be discovered, you might want to try holding still. If those men had been younger they would have heard you."

"You have the ears of a bat, and I doubt anyone would have heard that." He shifted his hold on her, and his palm rested against the flat of her stomach, his fingers splayed outward. "But just in case you're right, we might want to wait a few minutes before we proceed."

She shivered at his touch and tone. His voice deeper than normal, he sounded as if he wanted to wait a few hours. Alone. With her. Veronica knew what he could do given a few hours to kill. She inhaled—damn, he smelled good—reminding herself that he probably rode the same adrenaline high, and that it was dangerous.

"No time," she gasped, opening the door and breaking his grip.

The air in the chapel was cool compared to the heated environment of the confessional, and Veronica almost sighed in relief. If they managed to get out of this alive and without being caught, she was going to need a long, cold shower.

They entered the library five minutes later after a swift trek though the halls of the Vatican. Simon closed the door behind them and the scent of parchment and musty air wafted over Veronica.

She ran her flashlight's beam through the darkness, almost feeling at home. It was much the same as she remembered. Tables and chairs were placed with precision every eight feet, and the walls were lined with book-packed shelves that rose from the floor to the top of the ten-foot ceiling.

"Let's get this over with and get out of here," Simon whispered, his flashlight tracing the opposite wall.

"Agreed." The longer they were here, the better their chance of being discovered.

Veronica wove through the furniture toward the back wall, praying that whoever was in charge of this area was overconfident in his security system. If so, then it was likely the codex was in the same place. If not? The search for the Midas Stone would be delayed.

Possibly finished.

Stopping in front of the bookshelf that lay farthest to the left, she reached for the wide book in the upper left-hand corner of the six-foot shelf and pulled it out, revealing a keypad. "Hand me the code-breaker."

Sliding his pack off, Simon fished it out.

Grabbing a chair, Veronica pried off the faceplate, stripped the wires and let Rebecca's machine do its job.

A minute later, the bookshelf slid backward on tracks, and there was a whoosh and a hiss as cool air blew past them.

"Wow," Simon said in awe.

"Yeah." The room was nothing like the library. White, sterile and climate-controlled, it resembled something from a James Bond movie.

"They let you see this? I'm impressed."

Veronica shone her light in the room. Roughly twenty feet in depth and width, it was empty with the exception of a bookshelf standing against the back wall. "Don't be. The codex was always out on the desk, waiting for me when I got here. This little secret was courtesy of Sylvia."

"Damn, she was a good friend."

"*Is* a good friend," Veronica corrected. "She didn't agree with the Vatican's policy of nondisclosure and had no qualms about breaking rules she saw as useless."

"Thank God for that." Simon edged past her.

The hairs on Veronica's neck rose in warning and she grabbed his shirt, yanking him to a quick stop before he stepped onto the white floor. "Wait. Not too close."

"What?"

She cocked her head, surprised at his slip and her gut reaction. "Goggles," she reminded him. "Just in case."

"Of course."

She was sure if the room were well lit, his cheeks would be tinged red with such an amateur assumption. It was also something for her to remember. He might be able to pick a lock, but when a new discovery caught his attention, all that mysterious and useful knowledge seemed to desert him.

Perhaps it was childish, but it made her feel better to know that he wasn't perfect. Up until now, she was beginning to wonder.

Setting the duffel on one of the tables, he retrieved the goggles, handing her a pair. Made of specially coated glass, they were heavy in her hands.

She slipped them over her eyes, the elastic band that held them snapping the back of her head. Looking through them, a grid of lasers in the secret room came into view. Viewing the lasers through his set, Simon gave a low whistle. "It's a spiderweb." He turned to her, lips pressed tight. "Even after we broke the code?"

"They were supposed to turn off," she said, her lips pressed tight in frustration even as she inwardly sighed in relief for her accurate gut instinct.

She understood his frustration, but was also aware that the Vatican was nothing else if not paranoid. "There might be another keypad elsewhere."

But a quick, two-minute search revealed nothing. It must be pure luck or bad management that the other code worked. "There's probably a remote or something." Veronica sat on the closest table, goggles dangling from her fingertips, but inside, she was anything but calm, knowing what she had to do.

Simon's hands clenched into tight fists. "Damn it. And we were so close."

Veronica "tsked" at him, surprised for the second time in five minutes. It seemed Dr. Owens had a temper when he didn't get his way. "You might think we're done, but I don't."

"How do you propose we get past the lasers?" he shot back, his mouth pulled down in a frown and his voice tight, teetering on the tight edge of anger.

She stepped toward him until she was just outside the edge of his personal space, daring him to disagree with her. "There's only one way. I go in."

His frown deepened.

She returned the frown. He might not like the suggestion, but it was the only way unless they wanted to give up the quest before it barely began. "I'm smaller than you, so I can get through the lasers without tripping them. Plus, I know what to look for, and the last thing we need is me shouting directions."

He hesitated and she was sure he was weighing the odds. After a few heartbeats, he managed a curt nod. The frown never left his face. "Just be careful."

"Of course."

With flashlight in hand, she slipped her goggles back on, took a deep breath and stepped into the darkened, high-security, laser-guarded room.

It really was a spiderweb. When she went over one beam, she had to watch that her head didn't break another. Within seconds, sweat pooled between her breasts and down the middle of her back. A drop worked its way out of the edge of the goggles and fell onto her arm. She exhaled in relief. If her arm had been a fraction over, the drop would have crossed a beam.

Would a single drop of sweat be enough to trip the alarm? She didn't want to find out.

She glanced up. Halfway there.

Now two beams came down on either side. Veronica held her breath and edged through them, wishing she were an A-cup instead of a C.

There was no way Simon could have managed this, not with his physique.

Once more, she went up and over, the beam almost coming to the top of her inner thigh. *This is worse than yoga.*

How did people in movies do this? They made it seem so effortless. Easy.

Damned Hollywood.

One more beam to cross over and she came out on the far side. She took a deep breath, letting it out gently. She glistened with sweat, but she'd made it through. She gave Simon a thumbs-up.

He gave it back and pointed at his watch.

Pulling the flashlight from her waistband, she propped the goggles on her forehead and started searching for the text.

Nothing looked familiar. She pulled one down that was the right size from the shelf and opened it. It wasn't the codex. Too early and the pages were made of parchment. It was a sketchbook filled with da Vinci's work.

Unknown da Vinci, as far as she could tell.

"Cool," she murmured, tempted to take it. But if she took something like that, then she would be as bad as Michael.

At first glance, stealing the codex wasn't much better than his taking the Turkish urn, and when compiled with breaking into the Vatican—the most holy of cities—she was not one to preach about morality.

But she planned to return the codex after they recovered the Midas Stone. Not keep it.

And certainly not take anything else, no matter how tempting.

She put the da Vinci back in its place. Still, it pissed her off that the Vatican kept such treasures for itself.

She glanced upward, and the familiar broken-bound pages caught her eye. "Thank God." Grabbing it, she flipped it open, memories rushing over her.

The ancient Greek text. The careful writing. The scent of the ages. *The codex.*

Relief surged through her in a wave.

Slipping the codex inside her waistband at the small of her back and under her top, she started making her way back through the maze of light with a reminder to take her time. She might have the codex, but that didn't mean she couldn't be caught.

Five minutes later, she was standing next to Simon.

Without a word, she took the book out from under her tight shirt and handed it to him.

Simon accepted it with the same reverence that some had when taking a wafer from a priest. She noticed that his hands had just a hint of tremble, and she couldn't fault him. Now that she was through the labyrinth of lasers, she felt the same way, excited and barely contained within her skin.

He examined the binding. Shrugging his pack off, he pulled out the other half of the text and put them together. They fit—two halves of a whole. He put both in the duffel.

"Thank you," he said, his voice filled with unexpected and sincere gratitude. "You're amazing."

Veronica's lips parted in surprise at the sincerity in his voice. That was number three in surprises for the night, and she shifted, uncomfortable in his praise. "You're welcome." She punched the code back into the keypad and the bookshelf slid forward, once again hiding the secret room. "Now, let's get out of here before our lucks runs out."

As if on cue, a siren sounded.

Veronica and Simon stood in a janitor's closet, listening while two men talked outside the door in rapid Italian. She and Simon had exited the library and had been trying to make their way back to the chapel for the past ten minutes. Once there, it was doubtful they'd be followed.

The smell of bleach stung her nose. She prayed the men would leave before she sneezed. Instead, they continued to talk. She listened harder, trying to make out what they said, but with the heavy wooden door, all she could hear was the occasional word and their tone. One man sounded eager. The other annoyed.

The air was displaced as Simon leaned toward the door, the small duffel held against his chest. She assumed he was listening as well.

The word *falso* caught her attention. It was the "annoyed" one. Did he think this was some kind of false alarm?

Please! She hoped her luck had returned. Even now, she wasn't sure what had tripped the alarm. Perhaps the secret door was set on a timer? Perhaps all the doors? With the Vatican, it would be impossible to tell. The men who ran security for the City were suspicious, Old World autocrats who believed not just in God but also in keeping their piece of the world safe from all outsiders.

If they caught her and Simon, she suspected that they would not be turned over to the Italian authorities. The Vatican was a country unto itself, and as such, she was sure they dealt justice in their own fashion.

What kind of justice would it be? She remembered the bodyguard who escorted her from the city those years ago—the chill in his eyes and the tight grip of his hand on her elbow. She shivered. Whatever their method of justice, it probably wasn't being licked to death by puppies.

Another smattering of rapid, irritated Italian caught her attention. It was the man who sounded eager.

The locked doorknob rattled. Veronica tensed and Simon

leaned back. She held her breath and heard Simon automatically do the same.

A key clicked in the lock. She and Simon flattened themselves against the wall behind the door. Adrenaline pounded through her veins. She was sure they would hear her heart beating if they listened.

The door opened, barely hiding them behind it.

Veronica held her breath. *Don't come in. Don't turn on the light.*

"*Niente.*"

The speaker sounded irritated and a little disappointed as he slammed the door shut.

Veronica relaxed in relief as the speaker relocked it, thanking God for underpaid, half-asleep workers. Simon's hand squeezed hers, and she squeezed back, not realizing until then that they'd been holding on to each other.

Who grabbed whom?

She couldn't remember.

She hoped it wasn't her. The last thing she needed was Simon seeing her as fragile or needy—especially when they were in danger.

She let go of him. "Give them another couple minutes to clear the hall, then let's get out of here," she whispered in his ear, her mouth brushing against his skin. He tasted like sweat.

Several minutes later, they cracked the door open. The hall lights were on—both a blessing and a curse. They could get to the chapel faster, but it would also make them easier to spot.

But it would be worse to wait much longer. Veronica and Simon stepped into the empty hallway. She paused, expecting more alarms to sound or someone to come around the corner and point a finger at them.

Their luck held. Nothing but silence announced their presence. Staying close to the walls, she led him back to the small sanctuary.

Sanctuary. She almost smiled at the aptness of the name. More voices came from behind them.

She glanced at Simon. He pumped his fist up, then down, like a train engineer puling on the train's horn. *What?* She mouthed. What the hell was that supposed to mean?

He rolled his eyes and grabbed her hand, pulling her into a run. *Oh. Move it.* Taking the lead, she let go of him, running as silently as possible through the halls. The chapel door came into view.

Almost. Almost. Veronica sprinted to it and pressed down on the handle.

It was locked. One of the guards must have done it while they were searching for her and Simon. Panic rose like bile in her throat. She wished she had Lily. If she did, she could blow the lock off and silence be damned.

As it was, they were going to be taken while standing in a hallway. Quickly, she scanned the area for a potential escape and spotted a small stained-glass window at the end of the hall. If needed, they could break it out and make a run for it.

Without a word, Simon shoved her out of the way, opened the duffel, grabbed his lock-picking tools and dropped to his knees.

But would he be fast enough for them to evade discovery?

The world dissolved into slow motion, and it was almost as if she watched Simon from outside her body. She saw the details of his world, the way his fingers manipulated the slender tools. The sweat beading his brow. A wayward strand of hair sticking to his neck.

She felt as if they had all the time in the world and none at all.

Simon rose. Time resumed at a normal speed.

The voices grew closer and were almost upon them.

Veronica almost flung the door open in her hurry to get through. Simon followed, shut the door and they ran for the catacombs.

Chapter 7

Forty minutes later, Veronica locked the hotel room door behind them, and every muscle in her body relaxed.

They had robbed the Vatican and hadn't been caught, seen or struck by lightning. And until someone needed to borrow the codex for research, it was doubtful anyone would even notice that it was gone. "We did it!" she whooped, grabbing Simon around the neck. He really *could* be Simon Legree right now and she wouldn't give a damn. They'd done it. He'd done it.

With a shout of his own, he lifted her off her feet and swung her in a victory circle before setting her down on her feet.

Breathless, Veronica smiled up at Simon. He returned it, the smile going up to his eyes.

Setting the duffel on the bed, he unzipped it, then stopped. "You sure you want to do this?" He teased. "We can always take it back."

She shot him a halfhearted look of exasperation and crossed her arms. "Try it and you'll be having a conversation with the open end of Lily."

Chuckling, he held the now-complete codex up like a trophy or the Olympic torch.

Electricity sizzled through Veronica, making her feel more alive, more joyous, than she'd ever felt in her life. Simon seemed almost giddy and she was sure that didn't happen often.

Sheer joy washed over Simon's face, and he handed her the codex with a flourish. Even though she felt able to fly, she wrapped her fingers around the artifact and weighed it with her palm. The completed piece was lighter than she imagined. Thin with the ages.

Yet heavy with history.

Her hands shook. She set the codex on the small table. "Do you feel it?" she whispered. Her voice shook as hard as her hands, but she didn't care if Simon noticed. He was an archaeologist. He understood the sheer joy and energy that ran through her veins. Something a layman could talk about but never truly understand. "The energy of a thousand hands touching its pages. The history of a thousand years."

"I feel it," Simon whispered back.

She recognized the masculine, sensual tone in his voice and knew he wasn't talking about the codex. Slowly, she raised her head.

Reserved, he watched her, their eyes locked while the energy between them changed. Transformed from the thrill of escape to the desire that came with success.

She realized she wanted to kiss him. Just once.

Bad idea. She reminded herself. *Very bad idea.*

But even as she thought the words, her legs drew her closer to him, closing the distance between them.

The voice of reason whispered to Veronica that the heat

rushing through her was fleeting. Sexual desire brought on by adrenaline.

Her legs brought her another step closer to Simon. A hand's width apart, his breath blew over her skin.

"This is a bad idea," she whispered even as she wrapped her arms around his neck.

"I know," he replied, and his mouth came down on hers, hard and demanding.

He tasted like wine. Like adrenaline. Rising on her toes, she pressed herself against him. Hip to hip. Chest to chest. Let one knee lift to wrap itself around his hips and pull him closer.

Simon dragged his hands from her shoulders, down her arms, and stopped at her waist. Kissing a path to her neck, he slid his hands under her top, and traced her spine with his strong fingers, giving her goose bumps and making her shudder.

She turned her head to catch her breath and remind herself that this was her partner, for God's sake, and probably not even a trustworthy one, but instead, she found herself biting his neck. The tang of sweat drove her further and she pushed him toward the bed, the ache between her legs growing with each pulse of her heart.

"Veronica." He groaned her name. "We shouldn't do this." But his hands slid from her waist to her buttocks, cupping them as he lifted her and spun her so the bed was to her back.

She silently agreed but couldn't bring herself to care. "Shut up."

He kissed her again, his tongue tasting, probing. Tangling with hers. He kissed as if her mouth and being were the entire focus of his world.

He left her mouth and began working his way down her throat with an overwhelming combination of strength and gentleness. She tried to turn him back to the bed but he resisted, fought her. "I'm on top," he growled.

"You wish," she replied. Sex wasn't usually a competitive sport for her, but with Simon, it seemed to be the natural path. Retreating, she circled around to his back. He didn't turn to face her, but waited, his hands at his side. Every muscle in his back taut.

Inhaling his scent, Veronica ran her hands up his back and then around to his chest, stroking until his nipples hardened under her fingertips.

"Nice try, but you won't win," Simon said, his voice husky.

"I already have," Veronica retorted.

Rumbling low in his throat, Simon whirled around and lifted her up in one smooth move until she had no choice but to wrap her legs around him. She felt his erection pressed against her and dragged herself along its length.

"No," Simon moaned. "Not yet." Striding to the bed, he laid her down. His right hand flattened on her stomach while his left played with her hair. As he nuzzled her, Veronica closed her eyes, lost in the sensation of his touch. He reached between her thighs, stroking her through her leggings and the shiver of orgasm started. Her breath loud in her ears, she rocked her hips forward and against his palm. "God, Simon. Please."

She was almost there, the cascade of sensation rippling though her.

Bbrrriiing.

"Son of a bitch!" Simon roared, knocking the phone off the hook and to the floor.

A tinny voice floated up from the receiver. *Veronica. Veronica. Are you there? Are you okay?*

Joseph. Her orgasm came to a screeching halt and died. "Son of a bitch," she said through clenched teeth.

Simon stilled. And she knew the "moment" was over for both of them. Rolling over, she picked up the phone from the floor. "Hey, Joseph."

"Veronica. I was worried. I tried to call earlier but there was no answer."

She glanced at Simon. He was lying on his back, staring at the ceiling. He looked pissed, and from his unflagging erection—frustrated as well.

"Veronica?"

"Uh, yeah. I'm fine. I was getting ready to go to bed—" *isn't that an understatement* "—and knocked the phone off the receiver."

"How did it go?" Joseph asked, his tone curious.

"Good. We got what we came for."

He hesitated, and she heard the clinking of a spoon in a cup. "Good. I wasn't sure you'd be able to, uh, acquire it."

"It wasn't a problem," she assured him, anxious to be off the phone, her own frustration making her edgy and snappish. "But I don't want to say too much on the phone." *And I need a cold shower.* "I'll get some information to Rebecca tomorrow and then we should know more."

"Excellent idea. I'm just glad there weren't any mishaps." He chuckled. "I only wish I could have gone with you."

Frustration ebbed at the truthful comment cloaked in casual jest, and Veronica cradled the phone with both hands. "Yeah. Me, too."

A moment later, she said goodbye and hung up the phone. Still sitting on the bed, she edged toward Simon.

He raked a hand through his mussed hair, but once again, his eyes were unreadable. "All okay in the States?"

"Yeah," she replied, both disappointed and angry at the interruption, but knowing it was for the best. The silence stretched between them, and finally, she rose. What she was feeling was the adrenaline and nothing more.

It would be best if they both forgot it ever happened.

Standing, she started collecting the few research books

she'd brought. Kisses happened, she told herself, dropping the stack on the small table. They hadn't slept together, so there wasn't any harm. Not really.

Simon sat up and the bed creaked. Swinging his legs to the floor, he stood and watched her with unreadable eyes. "Leave the books. Get some rest."

"No," Veronica replied. She'd sleep when she was dead. Besides, her body was still pumped up and there was no way she could close her eyes. Not yet. "You're welcome to get some if you want."

"I'm going to take a shower."

"Fine." She waved him off, but not before a flicker of emotion rippled across his features. Disappointment? Irritation? Whatever it was, it was fleeting, and then the shutters went up.

He didn't say another word as he retrieved a pair of boxers from the drawer, pulled his shirt off and headed to the oversize bathroom.

Veronica watched him walk away, muscles on his back flexing. Her fingertips rested on her lips. He slammed the door behind him, and she laid her head in her hands with a groan. Celibacy for the duration of their expedition would be more difficult than she thought. Much more difficult. A part of her still wanted to strip Simon naked and have her way with him.

This wasn't like her. It was like Rebecca. Even Alyssa. Everyone else she knew.

But not her.

She set the codex on the bedspread. She took off her still-damp leggings and sweaty tank top, then put on clean panties and a T-shirt, and slid between the sheets. Propping herself against the headboard with her pillows, she took a moment to collect herself. Simon was her partner. That was all. Anything more was…irresponsible.

And any more reflection was whining.

With a yawn, she propped her legs up so she could rest the codex on them. She'd have to get a hard plastic container for the book. Granted, it was velum, not parchment, but it could still be damaged.

Picking it up, she ran her hands over the worn cover, admiring its ageless beauty. Wild, uninhibited sex would have been great, but this—she hugged the codex to her chest for a brief moment—in many ways, this was so much better.

Veronica woke up with Simon's arm draped over her waist. Why was he in bed with her was her immediate, foggy thought.

She picked up the clock on the nightstand with her free hand. It read 6:00 a.m. She should get up. Rise and act indignant. Get coffee. Work on translating the codex. Be productive. In that order. It would be the smart thing to do.

Instead, she set the clock back down and snuggled into Simon. Perhaps it was weak-willed, but it had been a long time since she'd woken up with a man in her bed.

He sighed in his sleep and pulled her closer into the curve of his body.

When she opened her eyes again, it was after nine, the bed was empty, and his side was made. Had she dreamed of Simon being in bed with her? Or was it real? She rolled over with a groan.

Dressed and sitting at a small table, her partner was already working. She sniffed, wrinkling her nose. Coffee. Nectar of the gods. A kick-start for her body.

She stretched, arms overhead as she worked the morning kinks from her body. "When did you order room service?" She watched him closely, wondering if there would be any repercussions from last night's terminated tryst.

Simon glanced up. "Just a little bit ago. There're pastries, as well."

Veronica licked her lips at the thought. Caffeine and processed sugar? Perfect. And if he could forget the incident and pretend it never happened, so could she.

Rising, Veronica sat down in the opposite chair, poured her coffee into a delicate china cup and began reading Simon's notes before the caffeine took effect.

She'd made almost no headway last night—barely glancing at the codex before her body came down from the adrenaline rush. The last thing she remembered was resting her eyes. "How much have you translated?"

"The first page of the half you recovered, and that's a rough translation. I suspect I'm a lot slower than you are. As you said, the Mediterranean cultures are your thing, not mine. If we were translating French, I'd be your guy." He sipped his coffee. "How far did you get when you were in the Vatican before?"

"Not far enough. I had it for two days before they took it away." When she'd had access to the second half of the codex so many years ago, she'd been obsessed with making a flawless translation, which was the right thing to do. It was the way she'd been trained.

Now, knowing about the Midas Stone, she wished she'd focused on the potentially more useful information, like the Eye of Artemis. She peeked at Simon to see where he was in his translation. He turned the page and methodically began translating the new text. "Do yourself a favor, skip this bit." She picked up a croissant and used it like a laser-pointer. "Just keep turning pages. You'll know when to stop."

"You have your methodology. I have mine," he said, still reading. "I like to get a sense of what the author was trying to say at the moment they were writing the text. I think it has bearing on the translation."

Ouch. "Trust me. It'll be worth changing your methodology for one moment."

With a sigh of resignation, he flipped the delicate pages over and stopped at a picture of a Greek trireme. He hesitated. "Here's something about the 'stone from the gods' and a priestess who saves it from the men who would use it to further their own glory." He squinted. "Apparently, she's its eternal guardian."

Veronica's right foot beat out a quick rhythm. She hadn't read that bit before, or if she had, she'd since forgotten it without the notes to jog her memory. If they could find out more about this priestess, they might be able to get an idea of where she might have hid the Stone. But first things first. "Keep going."

Simon flipped the page and his eyes widened. "I'll be damned," he whispered.

It was a sketch of the Eye.

Veronica smiled, pleased at his reaction. The expression on Simon's face was familiar, and in a tiny part of her psyche, she was jealous of his excitement. There was nothing like the first glance.

Holding his breath, Simon touched the sketch with a gloved hand. Taking up an entire page, the Eye of Artemis was an oblong piece of what she presumed was metal, pinched at either end, to give it a stylized eye-shaped appearance. The right corner was tipped up while the left was tipped down. The surrounding edges were etched with what were once symbols, lines and pictures, but they were smudged and scratched. In the center was a round stone with the shading and highlights giving it a dark appearance.

It wasn't one of the more intricate pieces she'd ever seen, but it didn't need to be. It was the key to their success. She was sure of it. "What do you think?"

He gave a little jerk, as if being woken from sleep. "I think your methodology, in this case, is worth following."

Pleased with herself, she bit into the croissant.

"Don't get cocky," Simon said, both amusement and excitement in his gaze. "Any brilliant suggestions on how we find it?"

Swallowing, Veronica took another sip of coffee. "Since there's a sketch, it must have been recovered at some point. My best guess is that, since there's nothing else known about it, it's either in a private collection or is being called by a different name. With luck, there's a picture or description somewhere in a database or on the Internet. Otherwise, Rebecca won't be able to locate it."

"Rebecca?" Simon asked.

"Sure. We make a copy of this," she tapped the sketch with a fingernail. "And fax it to Rebecca. If it's out there, she'll find it, It might take her a while since the true name was obviously lost, but she's the best at what she does. If she can't locate it, no one can."

Leaning back, Simon looked at her with curious eyes. "Why didn't you sketch this for her before and have her look?"

Veronica shrugged her shoulders. "I could remember the basics but not the details. Without those, there are thousands of pieces that could fit this description. As I'm sure you know, the symbol of an eye was very popular in ancient cultures. Window to the soul and all that."

Plus, after losing Chris and Joseph's support, she had been too hurt, too angry, to want to try. For a long time, she had wanted nothing more than to forget her disastrous decisions, and that meant giving up on the Eye, too.

Simon didn't respond but ran a gentle, skilled hand over the vellum. "We should send this to her while we work on translating the rest of the text." His hand stilled. "What if it's in a private collection?"

"Doesn't matter." She dismissed his doubt with a wave of her hand. "I told you, Rebecca is the best. As long as she knows what she's looking for, there's little she can't find."

"And if there isn't anything to find?"

She stilled herself, not even wanting to consider the possibility. "I don't know." It was an honest answer but she hated to say so aloud—as if mentioning the mere possibility would jinx their search.

"What if she does find it? Can you trust her enough to not sell us out?" Simon asked, concern shadowing his features. "After all, there's a lot at stake."

For a moment, Veronica stiffened, but she reminded herself that under the circumstances, it was a legitimate question. She didn't question Rebecca's loyalty, but Simon didn't know her. When she first hired Rebecca, she employed her for her computer skills and her ability to run an office. But it didn't take long to find out that her new admin was an even better friend and that she was fiercely loyal to those she cared about. After Brazil, Rebecca had begged Veronica to be allowed to destroy Michael's bank account. And it had been tempting. "I'd trust her with my life."

"Okay. Then I will, too," Simon said, his slight frown disappeared.

"Good." Veronica glanced at the picture again. For her assistant, finding a digital needle in a digital haystack was like her own private excavation. Rebecca was going to love this.

Veronica checked her e-mail for what seemed like the thousandth time. Still no answer from Rebecca. They'd faxed her a photocopy of the Eye and had been waiting three days for a reply.

She didn't log off but stood up with a frustrated sigh. Her hands pressed against the small of her back, she leaned backward, cracking her spine.

"Nothing?" Simon asked. He sat at the table still working on the translation. In fact, it was all they'd done since they'd sent Rebecca the picture of the Eye of Artemis.

"Just spam," Veronica replied. "So unless you need to re-finance your house or add two inches to your penis, I think we're out of luck."

He chuckled, and she managed to smile back.

She couldn't believe three days had passed since the morning after nothing happened. At first, she'd been concerned that their encounter that night would damage their working relationship, but the incident turned out to be a nonissue.

As for waking up next to him, she didn't even broach that subject. A "don't ask, don't tell" policy that worked for them.

There were more important issues than sex. They were on a quest, and if they let every little issue get in the way, they'd have nothing but trouble.

Sitting across from Simon, she poked at the spine of one of the research books but didn't make an effort to open it. What could be taking Rebecca so long? One hand propped up her chin, the other beat out a tuneless rhythm on the book's cover.

Perhaps it was inflated expectations, but she thought they'd have a reply within twenty-four hours. Maybe she should call. But if she did, she'd interrupt, and the last thing she wanted to do was interrupt Rebecca when she was focused on a search. She'd done it once before, and it threw her assistant off her stride, making the hunt even longer.

"Are you going to keep doing that, or are you going to work?" Simon asked, interrupting her thoughts.

"Do what?"

"You're drumming on the book. It's starting to get irritating."

She stilled her fingers. "Sorry. I was wondering what was taking Rebecca so long."

He nodded in understanding. "I know. I'm getting antsy, as well."

"You?" she asked in surprise.

"Me."

She examined him. "Hmm. It doesn't show." She found his ability to control his emotions was a quality that, while annoying, she also admired and wished she could emulate to a degree. But it didn't seem possible. Not on days like today when she was so bored with waiting she'd do anything but sit her butt in a chair.

He stared at her in surprise, as if he thought she'd figured it all out already. "Just because I don't act fidgety or show every single emotion at every given moment doesn't mean I don't feel them."

The comment caught her off guard. He was right. She'd experienced his more human side. Felt the heat of his touch.

And then there was the Vatican. His look of sheer joy when she handed him the codex. The satisfaction that turned his mouth from a grim line to a curve when he picked the lock to the sanctuary and they'd escaped.

Where did he learn that? The search for that truth would keep her occupied if nothing else. "Simon?"

"What?" He kept working.

"You want to tell me about more of your hobbies? The ones other than lock picking?"

He raised his right eyebrow in what she thought was confusion. "What brought that on?"

She leaned forward, pushing the research book out of the way, and used both hands to prop her chin. "Just wondering." And curious as a cat.

He went back to translating the codex. "I'd tell you but then I'd have to kill you."

She rolled her eyes. "Funny, but I'm serious. Where—"

Ding. The tinny sound that signaled an incoming e-mail interrupted her.

She fought the urge to leap out her chair. "Probably an offer to increase my sex drive," she muttered.

As if she needed help in that area.

She sat down.

It wasn't spam. It was from Rebecca. "Simon. It's here," she almost shouted the news.

Quickly, she double-clicked and opened the e-mail.

Veronica,
Sorry I took so long. It was a tough one. You were right—the name was changed. It's now called Golden Vision and all association to Artemis has been lost. Thanks for the picture—without it, I would never have gotten a positive ID on the piece.

The air shifted as Simon walked over and stood over her shoulder.

Anyway, it belongs to a Fakhir al-Ahmed in Turkey. His mansion is just outside Istanbul. I did some research on this guy, and he's not a pushover. He's involved in some questionable activities. I attached a doc that gives a brief bio plus details of his mansion: location, security system, etc. Getting in is going to suck. He's not like Michael. This guy has guards that will shoot you on sight. So, for pity's sake, be careful.

I enclosed a picture of what I found and a close-up so you could verify the identification.

Tell Simon I said hi. Take care and let me know if you need anything else.

Smooches, Becca

"Chatty, isn't she?" Simon said.

Veronica downloaded the attachments. "A little, but she's awesome. I've never seen her fail."

"Never?"

"When she's determined to find something, it gets found. Think of her as a cyberspace archaeologist." She clicked on the first attachment. The plan detailing Fakhir's security system opened up and filled the screen. It contained a blueprint with a legend, plus a detailed report about Fakhir, including his suspected ties with known weapons dealers, his family's rise to wealth and his penchant for parties and beautiful women.

On the last page was a scanned, color newsprint photo of Fakhir at a fund-raiser he gave at his home. The women were dressed in evening gowns and the men in tuxedos. He stood in a large room that was converted to an art gallery of some kind. Columns. Marble floors. She whistled in appreciation. Even Michael didn't have anything that impressive.

There was a red arrow pointing to a glass case in the background.

In the case was an object that looked like the Eye of Artemis.

Simon leaned over her shoulder. "Is that it?"

She clicked open the close-up that Rebecca had attached. It was grainy, but the markings were clear enough.

Rebecca had found the Eye of Artemis.

"It is." Veronica relaxed back into the chair, smug in Rebecca's success. She *knew* her assistant wouldn't let her down. "I told you. She's the best."

"You weren't kidding."

His breath was warm against her bare neck. "Do you think anyone else knows about this?"

"No," Veronica turned to face Simon. Her lips were level with his mouth. She lifted her eyes to his. "No one but you, me and Joseph know the Eye's true purpose and it's association with the Midas Stone. Fakhir doesn't even know its real name."

"And the Vatican?"

She shook her head. "Believing in Greek myths and Gods are too far removed from their beliefs for them to even entertain the idea that some of it might be true. Besides, they didn't have the other half of the codex or the mouse. I can't imagine that the Eye is even on their radar."

He licked his lower lip, drawing her attention. She knew that mouth.

With a quick shake of her head, she swiveled back to the map and began formulating a plan of attack, scrolling back up to the blueprint.

The security cameras were marked with tiny triangles. There were so many. "This place is a fortress."

"It's going to take an army to get in," Simon replied. "We don't have an army."

She glanced upward. "You know, you're a bit of a pessimist."

He frowned at the offhand comment. "No. I'm a realist."

She turned back to the screen, not bothering to reply. *Pessimist.*

His frown deepened. "Think we could get him to sell?"

Veronica shook her head. "Men like this don't sell artifacts." She touched the screen, tracing Fakhir al-Ahmed's image. "I'm not even sure they buy them when taking them is easier. Besides, what if he says no? Then we'll never be able to steal it."

"It was a thought."

Veronica closed the e-mail and turned off the computer. "Ever been to Turkey?"

"Not yet." He stretched, his fingers brushing the ceiling. "I'll make the reservations."

Veronica breathed a sigh of relief. "Thanks. We should hurry."

"Why?" He shot her a confused look. "There's been nothing on the break-in to the Vatican. Why make mistakes by rushing around? Better to take our time and do this right."

In theory, he was right. *In theory.* But the reality was that the people at the Vatican could discover they'd been robbed at any minute. Once they did, they'd start looking for suspects, and her name would be in the top ten if not number one. Unplugging the computer from the data port, she wound the cord up around her hand. "I need to tell you, when they escorted me from the Vatican, I was angry."

"You? No," he mocked.

He chose *now* to get a sarcastic sense of humor? "Anyway, I told them I'd be back, and when I was, the codex would be mine."

"You can't believe they took it seriously, can you?" Simon asked, dismissing the confrontation.

"I don't know, but can we take the chance?" Removing the cord from her hand, she put it and the laptop back in the soft nylon case. At the time, her words were an empty threat. A shrill cry of disappointment more than anything else.

She had never intended to make it truth. And now that they had, she really wanted to get out of Rome as fast as possible. "Right now, we have all the time in the world because they don't know what's gone, but we did trigger an alarm. They'll do some kind of inventory to find out what's missing, and when they figure it out, it'll be that much harder for us to leave." She zipped the case shut with barely suppressed energy. "We can't count on fake identities to keep us safe. This is the Vatican. They have contacts all over, and we're on their home turf. I think we need to get out of here as soon as possible now that we have the information we need."

Simon hesitated, and she knew his silence meant that he was evaluating her plan.

After a beat, he nodded in acceptance. "Agreed."

She sighed with relief.

Simon retrieved a small carry-on suitcase from the closet. "I'll start packing if you want to call and make the reservations."

Retrieving Lily from the upper closet shelf, she laid her on the bed and began searching for the remains of the bubble wrap she'd been shipped in.

"Do you have to bring her?" Simon asked. "We're going to Turkey—one of the last places on earth we want to get caught with a weapon."

Veronica dropped to her knees to feel under the bed. It might be foolish, but Lily was more than protection. She was a good-luck charm. Any dig that Lily was on went well. Artifacts were found. No one was hurt.

No bubble wrap.

Any dig Lily was absent from tended to be less that fruitful. Besides, they might need her for more than luck. She rose. "She goes."

Simon began tossing clothes in the empty suitcase. "You're being unreasonable."

"Have you worked in Turkey?" she asked, sitting on the bed. The wrap was gone and, for that matter, so was the box she was shipped in. The maids must have taken both.

"No."

"I have, and more than once. We're going to need protection of some kind. Trust me."

"I do." But he didn't look like he did. "No box?"

"If there was, I'd have it," she snapped.

"It was just a question," he said, obviously taken aback at her anger.

She fell back onto the bed, her legs over the edge. "I know. Sorry." And she was. It wasn't him. It was the thought of the Vatican coming for her. It wigged her out more than she wanted to admit. She pushed herself up to her elbows. "Would you go get one?" She could use a few minutes to pull herself together.

He sighed. "Sure."

Gratitude flickered through her. "Thanks."

She'd take a hot shower while he was gone. It would work out the tension, and if they were going to be traveling all day, she wanted to get clean while she could.

He waved off the thanks as he headed for the door, appearing uncomfortable with the praise. "Just get ready." He clicked the door shut behind him

She'd have to hurry. She placed the codex in the room's small, private safe. It barely fit but was good enough for now. Stripping, she walked naked to the bathroom and turned on the water. The pipes groaned to life. She lathered her hair and soaped her skin, her mind racing with plans. There would be a lot to do once they got to Istanbul. She'd have to contact Nasim and ask him about Fakhir.

Her parents used Nasim as their lead field technician whenever they had a Turkish dig, and he was practically her godfather. If anyone could get them into the mansion to retrieve the Eye, he was the one.

She rinsed her hair and was done in record time, feeling more relaxed. Wrapping her hair turban-style, she stepped out of the oversize tub to dry herself off.

A small crash came from the outer room.

Simon? Damn. He was quick. She hadn't made a single call.

Worse—she realized that hadn't brought any clothes with her into the bathroom.

She cracked open the door. "Hey, I'm coming out. Can you close your eyes? I'm not dressed."

Another noise and then the telltale squeak of the front door being opened.

Her skin broke out in goose bumps and she knew it wasn't

because of her lack of clothes in the air-conditioned room. Simon wouldn't just leave. He'd simply tell her to hurry up.

Cracking the door, she peered out. Whoever was there was gone but might have left a friend. The room appeared empty. She opened the door farther and gave an inadvertent cry of dismay.

Lily was on the floor. The dresser drawers were yanked out. Her laptop was gone.

Chapter 8

Veronica sat in one of four kitchen chairs and watched Simon pace, while across the table, Sylvia talked on the phone in rapid-fire Italian.

Sylvia sounded pissed.

Veronica knew how she felt. After the robbery, she wanted to break something. Or someone.

Simon's reaction, or should she say, *lack of reaction,* made her feel worse.

He didn't yell. Shout. Didn't even accuse her of dropping her guard. But she knew he was angry. At himself? At her?

It didn't matter. She knew pissed when it stood in front of her. She'd never seen anyone so tight. It was as if his entire body was one single, rigid muscle.

Still, he hadn't uttered a word. He simply began searching to find what else was taken.

That's when they noticed their passports and IDs were

gone. The only bright spot was that while the wall safe was dented, it was unopened.

The codex was safe.

After that, they'd come to the one person in Rome that Veronica trusted, Sylvia.

Sylvia's voice rose a notch, catching Veronica's attention. She leaned forward, once again questioning the wisdom of putting her friend in the middle of this insanity. "Syl. If this is going to cause problems, we can—"

Sylvia silenced her with a raised hand.

Veronica raised her own hand in surrender and backed off. She never argued with Sylvia. She could try, but it always ended in shouts and lost time while they bickered.

And time was not a luxury they could afford.

Sylvia waved to get Veronica's attention, then made a motion that imitated writing. Veronica grabbed the nearest items, a chartreuse crayon and a coloring book.

The fact that Sylvia had children boggled her mind. When they parted, Sylvia was a confirmed single with not one boyfriend, but three.

Now, instead of candles and silk, her flat overflowed with toys for her twin sons, toddler-size clothes and piles of laundry. She had an English husband who worked as a biochemist for a pharmaceutical company. Her long hair was loose, and instead of wearing dusty jeans and a skimpy halter top, she wore cotton shorts and an oversize pink T-shirt.

It all seemed so…normal. From the coordinated, overstuffed living room furniture to the pile of folded laundry sitting in the hallway waiting for Sylvia to put it away, everything about the apartment proclaimed Sylvia's transition from a hottie archaeologist to a hottie mom.

Whoever was on the other end of the phone must have said something Sylvia didn't like because she hesitated, her eyes narrowed, and she let loose a string of swear words in a combination of Italian and English.

Then she snapped her mouth shut. *"Buon."* Flipping open the coloring book, she wrote on the back—one of the few places not covered with multicolored scribbling.

Names? Locations?

Veronica leaned forward again, trying to see what she wrote, but Sylvia batted her away.

"Did she get something?" Simon stopped pacing long enough to appear interested.

"I think so," Veronica replied, distracted when he started walking again. "Could you stop that?"

"What?"

"Pacing. It's right up there with me drumming my fingers."

A brief smile flickered on his lips.

"Merda!"

Sylvia's exclamation interrupted them, and she wrote faster.

Simon came over to the table and stood behind Veronica, his hands resting on the back of her chair.

"Ciao." Hanging up the phone, Sylvia leaned back with a sigh, her mouth pursed in displeasure.

"So, what's the situation? Can you help us?" Veronica asked as Simon took the seat between her and Sylvia.

Sylvia fixed her gaze to Simon. "First things first. Do you know an Andrew Carson?"

Simon's dark eyes narrowed. "He's one of my graduate students."

Sylvia pursed her full lips. "It seems that Mr. Carson cannot keep his mouth shut. He bragged about what was found at your excavation. The implications. The possibilities. Most archaeologists do not believe." She turned to Veronica. "We both know, all too well, that they do not want to consider the notion that history can take odd turns and present ideas that run contrary to our education and what we perceive as reality."

Veronica shifted in her seat. Would she ever get to the point where she didn't want to cringe every time her lack of success was brought up?

Sylvia continued, oblivious to Veronica's sudden unease. Ripping off the back page of the coloring book, she set it on the table so Veronica and Simon could read it. Sylvia's writing was atrocious and made worse with the thick wax of the crayon. "But these archaeologists do believe your bragging student, and they are in pursuit."

Veronica read the names to herself. David Conner. Paul Bowers. Morgan Caldwell.

Names she recognized, but nothing alarming.

Her eyes continued down the page, and for a moment, she thought she must have read wrong.

Michael Grey. *Michael?*

"You know him?" Simon asked.

"Yes," she replied, knowing that her every emotion showed. She didn't care. "You might say that. We grew up together."

Her stomach constricted. Was Michael so greedy that he could go after the one artifact that could redeem her career, her reputation?

She knew the answer even as she asked it. Of course he would.

"Could he be swayed to help us?" Simon asked.

She shook her head. "Not a chance."

"Okay," he replied, and she gave mental thanks that he was smart enough to know when to drop a topic. Her eyes slipped further down the page.

Deacon Gilchrist. Every muscle in her body tensed. Now she knew why Sylvia swore. "Aw, crap."

She traced the crayoned name with a fingertip.

"Another problem?" Simon asked.

"You might say that."

"Tell me," Simon said.

She pushed the paper toward him. Concern and curiosity emanated from him in almost palpable waves. "He's a black-market mercenary. Backed by a lot of money, he's beaten me to more than one artifact. If he finds the Stone, God only knows whose hands it will end up in."

Realization dawned in Simon's eyes, and she knew he followed her line of thinking. "And in the wrong hands, it will be more than a source of unlimited wealth."

Veronica finished the thought. "It will be a weapon."

Suddenly, the length of time they had to find the Stone seemed dangerously short.

Sylvia went down the hallway to check on her napping twins, leaving Simon and Veronica alone in the kitchen to study the list of rivals.

"Any thoughts?" Simon asked.

Once again, Veronica read the names of the archaeologists who sought the Midas Stone and let the implications of Michael's and Deacon's possible interference roll through her thoughts. "I think it has to be either Deacon or Michael who robbed us. The others are good archaeologists, but that's the problem. They're scientists with grants."

"I've met Morgan," Simon added. "Money had little interest for her unless it bought her more time on a dig."

Veronica rose, needing to move. She opened a cupboard, hoping to find coffee. "It *has* to be either Michael or Deacon."

"But which?" He took the crayon and underlined the two names as he spoke.

Veronica shook her head. She wished she knew.

No coffee, but there did seem to be a lot of tea.

She hated tea. She shut the cupboard door, fighting the urge to slam it closed instead. She leaned against the counter, the edge cutting into her hip. "My first instinct tells me that it's Michael."

"Lover's quarrel?" Simon asked.

Heat flooded Veronica's face, but she couldn't deny that her past relationship possibly played a part in Michael's involvement. "Partly, but ransacking our room and stealing our passports is his style. It was cowardly, sneaky and leaves little room for confrontation. Plus, it slows us down, giving him time to break in to my computer."

Veronica massaged her temple with her fingertips. "Deacon is another matter. He might ransack our room, but he wouldn't have left because I was going to catch him. He'd wait for me. For you. With a gun. And he'd get the required information—no matter whom he hurt."

Simon circled Michael's name. "Unless we learn differently. Now, how long do you think it will take him to break in to the computer?"

She shook her head, frustrated that any of this was happening. She knew it was going to be difficult to get to the artifact, but she didn't think they'd be running the proverbial gauntlet. "I don't know. I use different passwords for both the operating system and the e-mail, but the encryption isn't standard. Rebecca created it. It'll take a while for him to figure it out."

Simon doodled a circle on the side of the paper. "So we have time."

"Maybe. He'll break the code eventually. He has the money to hire anyone he wants." She rubbed her eyes with the heels of her hands. When she saw Michael again, and she knew she would, she was going to cheerfully beat him unconscious. "The one thing we have in our favor is that we know where the Eye is, and he doesn't. Not yet. We need to get to Turkey before he breaks the passwords and reads Rebecca's e-mail."

"You forgot one problem. We don't have passports anymore."

"We'll have to get new ones," Veronica responded. "And fast."

"If we can," Sylvia said as she entered the room, her pink top marked by what, Veronica thought, looked like baby spit.

"Do you think that'll be a problem?" Simon asked, turning toward her.

Sylvia sat down across from him and raked her hair back into a ponytail, securing the thick mass with an oversize clip. "I have no idea. I have never had to acquire fake IDs before, so I do not want you to get the impression that I can conjure them up."

Simon took Sylvia's hand in his. "I am betting you can do anything you set your mind to."

Was he flirting? Where did that come from? "He's right," Veronica agreed, trying to wipe the surprise off her face. "Ask some questions. See what you can do. But don't put yourself in jeopardy."

Sylvia gave a brief nod. "I will be careful." She glanced at Veronica. "I wish I could do more. I'll admit I would join you if I could. I'm a bit jealous of this new adventure." Her eyes darted toward the twins' bedroom where her sons lay sleeping. "But there is so much to lose now. Too much."

Sylvia's look of devotion and a wholly maternal, unconditional love spoke volumes. No stone was worth risking her or her children. "Syl, maybe you shouldn't get involved. Not with Deacon in the mix."

"I agree," Simon said.

Sylvia threw up her hands in exasperation. "First you come here for help and now you don't want it?" She waved them off. "I will be careful, trust me. So, put your mutual guilt away. Some discreet inquiries won't do any harm."

Veronica glanced at Simon and in unspoken agreement they nodded. Besides, it wasn't as if they had a choice in the matter. Not if they wanted to get to Turkey before Michael. "Okay," Veronica agreed.

She pushed away from the table. "We should leave. Let you get to work."

Maybe it was being around family, but she found herself suddenly missing her sister and wishing she'd come with them. Granted, Alyssa would hate all this. The intrigue. The sewers. The illegal activities.

But it would be nice to have her input.

She kissed Sylvia's cheek. "You have the number to the hotel?"

"Yes." She bussed the air next to Veronica's cheek. "I will let you know as soon as I have any information."

"Thank you." Simon rose from the chair. "Be careful."

Once again, Sylvia glanced upward, and her expression softened. "Do not worry. I know my priorities." Standing on her toes, she placed a light kiss on Simon's cheek. "I know she is tough as nails, but watch her back."

"Always," he replied.

"Excuse me?" Veronica interrupted. The last thing she needed was these two conspiring—even in jest. "I think I can take care of myself."

"Of course you can," Sylvia teased. She turned back to Simon. "See what I mean?"

He grinned, and Veronica rolled her eyes. "I hope you two are done." She tugged on Simons's shirt as she passed him. "Let's go, laughing boy."

Talking over his shoulder, he waved goodbye to Sylvia. "She might be ungrateful, but don't worry, I won't let that keep me from watching out for her."

Despite the fact that he was still a mystery, Veronica's

pulse skittered and her skin warmed at his words and the knowledge that he was watching her back.

"Do you ever feel like this whole expedition is a game of hurry up and wait?" Veronica asked as she tossed her backpack into the back seat of the rental car.

Behind her, Simon loaded their luggage into the trunk. "Constantly."

Buckling herself into the front seat, she shielded her eyes from the direct light of the setting sun and watched as he finished and came around and joined her.

They'd passed the afternoon going over the few notes that weren't stolen and then gone to a library, seeking any information that might help them, but it was the usual pap fed to the masses. Mythology. History.

They'd both avoided the topic of "what if."

What if Sylvia couldn't get replacement passports?

What if Michael hacked into the laptop?

What if they failed?

When they had returned to the hotel, they found a handwritten message pushed under their door. All it said was "Come over. Immediately. Bring all gear. Sylvia."

Simon pulled way from the curb, and they rode in silence. The codex was tucked in between the clothes in Simon's backpack which was at Veronica's feet.

They passed the Spanish Steps, then cut over a street to pass near the Trevi Fountain as they made their way south to Sylvia's. Streetlights flickered to life, breaking the dusk of sunset.

"Any idea on what we'll do if Sylvia can't help us?" Simon asked, breaking their silence.

"Yes." In her thoughts, she'd run scenario after scenario, and they all came down to one thing—they'd have to sneak in. "We do whatever it takes."

He adjusted the mirror. "Glad to hear we're on the same train of thought."

Simon parked the car at the curb in front of Sylvia's apartment house. Anxious to find out what her friend had discovered, Veronica almost leapt out while the car was still moving.

She was knocking on the door as Simon walked up behind her. Sylvia opened the door almost immediately. "*Benvenuto. Entrato.* We have a problem." She ushered them in, bussing them both on the cheek as they crossed the threshold.

Filing into the kitchen, Veronica stopped. An unfamiliar man sat at the same table they'd sat at this morning. His blond hair was cropped short and his blue eyes were bright despite the thick glasses perched on his nose.

"This is my husband, Thomas." Sylvia scooted past Veronica, taking her by the arm and pulling her forward. "Thomas, these are the people I told you about."

He rose and extended his hand. He was almost as tall as Simon. "Nice to meet you." His British accent was thick. "Syl has told me about you and your little problem."

How much? Was it wise to bring in another person? The questions flickered through Veronica's mind, and she glanced at Simon, who looked equally uneasy.

Their misgivings must have been more palpable than she thought, because Sylvia went to stand by Thomas after Simon shook his hand. "Do not worry. He can help you." Standing on her toes, she kissed her husband. "He married me. He can't be too well-behaved."

"True," Veronica replied, forcing herself to relax. Thomas might not resemble the bad boys that Sylvia used to date, but looks were often deceiving.

All four sat down at the table. "Were you able to find replacement IDs?" Simon asked before Veronica opened her mouth.

Sylvia shook her head, dark curls sweeping across her

shoulders. "No. Getting fake passports is not as easy as you would think. If I had more time, I might be able to do it, but as it is, I have no idea how long it would take. Even then there's no guarantee."

Veronica's stomach sank. "It's a no-go?"

Sylvia took her hand. "In that regards, yes. That is of little consequence at this moment. We have a bigger problem." Her strong hands shaking with agitation, she squeezed Veronica's fingers as if to drive home a point. "The Vatican discovered the codex is missing and that Veronica is in town."

Now she knew why Sylvia had them hurry and bring everything. They were lucky the police weren't waiting for them at the hotel, but in Rome, police procedure was notoriously complicated. If they hadn't gone to Sylvia for help, they would never have known this and might be in custody even now.

"Hell," Simon growled. "How?"

"They were tipped off."

"Michael." Both Simon and Veronica said at the same time.

Veronica clenched her hands into fists. She should have seen this coming. He'd probably followed them. "We've got to get out of Rome. Tonight."

Sylvia rested her hand on her husband's arm. "This is where Thomas comes in."

"Thomas?" Simon asked.

"Me." Thomas replied, cheerily. "When Syl and I met, I wasn't in pharmaceuticals. I was in shipping. Some legal. Some that was, shall we say, a bit borderline."

Veronica leaned forward. She *knew* Sylvia wouldn't marry a goody-goody.

Thomas continued. "There are people who owe me a few favors, and I called one in. I can get you on a container ship that will take you to Istanbul—no questions asked."

A container ship? She wanted to fly out to Turkey tonight.

"How long will it take to get there?" Veronica asked, the familiar excitement that came from a challenge, building in her blood.

"Two days."

"Two days!" The excitement died as quickly as it had sprung to life. A lot could happen in two days. Michael could break into the computer, get the Eye and be halfway to the Stone in two days.

Thomas gave her a sympathetic shrug. "It's all I can do. If you say yes, we have to leave tonight. The ship sails in the morning. You have to get to Catania."

"That's in Sicily. How do you propose we get there?" Simon asked. "The train takes more than twelve hours."

"I have a pilot's license. I'll fly you."

Simon didn't respond, and Veronica knew he was processing the information in his usual fashion. Finally, he gave a single, slow nod, then turned his attention to her.

What did she want to do?

With a groan, she buried her face in her hands. Alyssa had been right. This was getting more complicated than she could have ever imagined. While two days seemed like forever in the race to find the Stone, there was little choice in the matter.

She hoped that Rebecca's encryption on her laptop was as good, or better, than she'd promised.

Resting her hands on the table, she met their individual gazes. Thomas was confident. Sylvia eager and worried.

Simon was as expressionless as ever, letting her make up her mind without distraction.

Taking a deep breath, she leaned back in her chair. "This sounds like the plan of a desperate person. I'd say it's perfect for us."

Chapter 9

It was the second day on the ship, and Veronica was sure that she was going to run screaming down the hallway at any moment.

Not from fear but from boredom. One could only read for so long, and staring at open water through a miniscule porthole held no interest. The container ship passed the occasional island, but without binoculars, she could only see uninteresting blobs of green and white.

Yesterday, there had been a brief flurry of activity when they passed through the Corinth Channel, its sheer vertical walls separating the Peloponessus Peninsula from mainland Greece like a misplaced Grand Canyon.

Now she sat on the floor with Simon and a deck of cards.

Unfortunately, she wasn't good at cards. She'd lost count of how many hands of rummy she'd lost. Then Simon had found a cribbage board and beat her again. And again. And again.

To make it worse, they were betting imaginary money, and she was down fifty thousand.

She hated to lose.

"Want to quit?" Simon asked. She didn't miss the triumph in his eyes. Being beaten was one thing.

Admitting defeat another.

"Of course not. You're not worried I'll win, are you?"

He chuckled. "Uh. No. There doesn't seem to be much of a chance of that, does there?"

She glared at him. "We'll see."

Five minutes later, she'd lost. Again.

"Another game?" she asked, shuffling the cards. It wasn't much, but it was all they had.

Simon rose and stretched. His hands flattened against the low cabin ceiling. "Maybe later."

She let the cards drop to the floor. She supposed winning all the time was probably as boring as losing on a consistent basis, but when it came to cards, she wouldn't know.

Simon paced the length of the small room in three strides, then returned to the porthole. He was as restless as a tiger in a meat locker, and she couldn't blame him. They'd been given the cabin with firm instructions to not leave it. For anything. There was a toilet and a sink, but no shower and certainly no tub.

She sniffed the stagnant air. They were both beginning to smell.

Simon yawned.

"You can grab some sleep if you want," Veronica offered, gesturing toward the small single bed that was the only place to rest. Since they got on board, one of them had stayed awake. Thomas might trust these men, but she didn't and neither did Simon. At least she had Lily. "I'll keep my eyes open."

He shook his head. "Thanks, but I'm just bored out of my skull."

"Yeah. Me, too." She rested her back against the wall. "We could talk about Turkey and the Eye."

Simon sat on the bed. Stretched out, his feet hung over the edge of the small twin bunk. "Is there really anything more to say until we talk to Nasim and have Rebecca resend the information?"

"No. I guess not." Veronica sighed. He was right, but what else was there to do but talk and sleep?

Remembering what she dubbed in her head as *the incident*, in the hotel, she had a few ideas regarding how to pass the time, and she was sure the same thoughts shifted through Simon's brain on occasion. She'd seen him sneak looks at her, his dark eyes heated and anything but motionless, leaving her edgy with an animal need that she both wanted to suppress and explore.

Heated glances and animal need aside, she knew neither of them would act on their desires. They were getting used to each other, and it wasn't Rome, their joint adventure into the Vatican or even getting robbed that inspired certain camaraderie.

It was a full twenty-four hours in each other's company with nothing else to do but deal with each other. They argued. They read. She forgave him for being an ass and calling her Hollywood. He tried to hold a conversation with more than just monosyllables.

Early on, she'd tried to get him to tell her more about his past. He refused. She recognized some of her sister's personality in the way he skirted her questions and changed the subject. She could push for answers, but if she did, he'd dig in his heels and never tell her anything. It would be better to be patient—difficult for her even under the best of circumstances. Eventually, he'd tell her what she wanted to know.

Alyssa always did.

Until he caved, she'd keep her eyes and ears open. In the

meantime, they'd come to an understanding of sorts. Perhaps even a quasi-trust despite his secret past.

She stretched her legs out in front of her and bounced her heels on the cracked linoleum to work the circulation back into her thighs. "I don't know if I can take another twenty-four hours stuck in this hole. It seems more like twenty-four days."

"You can always tell me about Michael."

Veronica sucked in air. What brought that on? The last thing she wanted to talk about was her ex-lover. What was she supposed to tell him? That he broke her heart? "There isn't anything to say. Besides, you won't talk about your past. Why would I tell you about mine?"

Simon rolled over onto his side to face her, leaning his head on his hand, his loose hair falling forward to brush his cheek. "I'm not asking where you went to dinner or if he was any good in bed. What's he like as an adversary?"

"Oh." She pressed her hands into her lap. Of *course* that was what he wanted to know. Even deserved to know if they planned to reach the Midas Stone before Michael. "Every decision Michael makes is based on self-indulgence. He lives an expensive lifestyle and uses his archaeological expertise to maintain it." She used to love his mansion. She'd caress the fine objets d'art and marvel over Michael's fiscal prowess, which gave him the money to afford such objects of beauty.

If only she'd known where he'd gotten his funding.

She continued. "Art. Cars. You name it. He has it, and it's all the best. Unfortunately, he sold God knows what artifacts on the black market to buy it all."

"And you dated this guy?" Simon asked, curiosity and surprise in his question.

She shrugged. "I told you, I grew up with him. What was there not to trust? Once I found out what he was up to, I walked away."

"He was a fool," Simon said without hesitation.

She smiled with pleasure, not sure if he spoke about Michael's black-market activities or losing her. Maybe both. "Thanks."

He rolled back over, his face hidden from view from her vantage on the floor. "Do I need to worry about getting shot?" Simon asked.

"I don't think so. He doesn't carry weapons. He steals, makes good connections and runs when he has to. As long as you're not his partner, you should be safe." Even she didn't miss the bitter tinge to her voice.

"Fair enough," Simon said, his hands behind his head.

That Simon didn't pursue the more obvious line of questioning was interesting but not surprising. One thing she noticed was that Simon's need for privacy spilled out onto other people.

In this case, she was grateful. The last thing she wanted Simon to know about was Brazil. It was embarrassing.

"Veronica?"

"Yes?"

"Can I ask you something personal?"

Her pulse sped up. Was he going to break their unspoken covenant of silence on their personal lives?

"If it came down to me or Michael, would you pull the trigger?"

Her mouth dropped open. She wasn't sure if she should be insulted or flattered that he even considered her capable, but remembering how close she'd come when she broke into Michael's home and he'd confronted her, it was a fair question. "I don't know," she whispered. It wasn't a great answer, but it was the truth.

"Have you ever come close to pulling the trigger?"

Was he psychic? "Why?" she asked, suspicious at the line of questioning.

Simon rolled back to his side again, his expression enigmatic. "I think it's important to know how far you're willing to go to get the Stone."

Her suspicions regarding how much he knew about her past faded but didn't die. She drew her knees back into her chest, wrapping her arms around them. Even if he meant nothing by asking, she didn't like this line of questioning. It delved too deep into places she'd rather not go, but as her partner, he deserved to know the answer. "Yes, I have come close to pulling the trigger, but I didn't." She ran scenarios through her mind, projecting her reactions. "If it were just me being threatened, I don't think I could unless I truly thought my life was in danger, and even then, I think I'd hesitate. Now, if it were someone I cared for?" She took a deep breath, forcing herself to voice aloud one of her traits that she never talked about—her quasi-bloodthirsty nature. "Yeah. No hesitation. I'd do what was necessary to protect someone I cared for."

"So, if it came down to me or Michael?"

She may not have known the answer before, but she did now. "I'd pull the trigger for a partner."

"You sure?" he asked, staring at her as if he could see into her very thoughts.

She set her chin. "Yes."

Seemingly satisfied, he rolled back once again. "Good. Me, too."

Veronica shut her eyes. They'd have to work on getting him a gun.

If she was right, it was twelve hours until they reached Istanbul. Veronica was frozen in the Nataraja yoga pose, her leg curved behind her and her left foot almost touching the back of her head, while Simon lay on the bed reading an old *Sports Illustrated* magazine that he found stuffed under the mattress.

The door creaked open, and they both reacted. In a split second, Simon sat up and was grabbing for the shotgun under the pillow while Veronica dropped her leg and braced herself for attack.

In the doorway stood their host, Captain Armand Garcia. They had met him when they came on board, but it had been dark. He didn't say much then, but when he spoke, his accent was Castilian. Now, in the daylight, she couldn't help but notice he also had the dark eyes and curly hair that went with his Spanish heritage.

She took a deep breath. He seemed harmless enough. No weapon at his side. She glanced at Simon. Lily was already hidden back under the thin pillow.

Thomas had paid enough money to ensure the captain's trust—but Veronica had her doubts. Something told her that this man was more on par with Michael. If he thought he could make a profit by dumping them on some deserted island, he'd leave them to rot.

Sticking out her hand, she smiled broadly and with, what she hoped, was sincerity. "Captain Garcia, how pleased we are to see you again."

The captain returned the expression, showing yellowed teeth, and stepped forward, shaking Veronica's hand.

Simon's hands rested on his thighs, fingers splayed, but Veronica didn't miss the tension in his arms. "What can we help you with, captain?" he asked.

Garcia addressed Simon. "We are making good time and will be getting into Istanbul a few hours early. I thought you might want to know, as I am sure the trip has been neither exciting nor comfortable."

"We're making do," Veronica replied, keeping her tone light. "But thank you for being so considerate."

"My pleasure." He gave a twitch. "I do have a few questions before I let you leave this ship. I have known Thomas for a long time, but in this profession, one learns that trust is best left to others. So I need to know, what is your business in Istanbul?"

Veronica glanced at Simon. Where was this line of questioning coming from?

"Does it matter?" Simon's eyes narrowed.

"In today's political environment, yes." He rubbed his jaw. "If you are terrorists, I do not want any part of your conspiracy."

"You can't believe we're terrorists, can you?" Veronica asked. Terrorists? She'd seen what fanatics could do. She'd been in New York when the twin towers fell. "Look at us." She ran a hand over her dirty hair and her wrinkled clothes. "Would any terrorists put up with this? They'd take over the ship. We're scientists, for pity's sake."

"Scientists?"

Veronica bit her tongue, realizing what she'd revealed. Why couldn't she have said missionaries? Their captain probably didn't care about missionaries. It was obvious that scientists proved otherwise. "Uh, yes."

"What kind?"

Simon glared at her as if he wanted to smack her. She knew if he could speak, he'd be shouting *shut up!*

She swallowed hard. With the partial truth out there, it seemed best to stick to it as close as possible to avoid confusion. "We're archaeologists. There's a dig we're supposed to be on. A very important dig concerning a possible settlement off the coast. Our passports were stolen, and the caravan leaves tomorrow. We couldn't wait for replacements." The story sounded weak, even to her. To a layman, it might be enough. Maybe. *Please, let it be enough.*

"I understand." He took a step toward her, invading her personal space, and she held her breath. His blue denim shirt might appear clean but it smelled like rancid cabbage. "Please forgive my suspicions. You must understand that in today's political environment—"

"Everyone is suspect," she finished.

"Exactly." The captain glanced at his watch. "Now, I must return to work. It has been a pleasure."

He shut the door behind him without a glance.

"What were you thinking?" Simon asked as soon as the captain's footsteps faded away.

Veronica crossed her arms over her chest, angry at herself and wishing she could take it all back. "I don't know. He caught me off guard and I was ticked that he even considered the possibility that we were terrorists. The archaeologist part slipped out." She sat down on the twin bed next to Simon, letting herself fall backward into the thin mattress. "Do you think he bought the rest?"

Simon sighed. "Let's hope so."

She covered her eyes with her forearm. She was a fool, and if the captain found out the Vatican wanted them for the theft of the codex, they were dead.

The container ship glided into the Bosporus Strait and past Leander's Tower, signaling their arrival into Istanbul. Veronica motioned Simon over to the porthole, and both crowded to see the tower, which was situated at the entrance of the waterway. "It's twelfth century. Erected by Emperor Manuel Komnenos," Veronica explained.

"Byzantine? Right?" Simon asked, edging her over for a better view.

"You've been studying?" Veronica said, surprised.

"I know a little," Simon replied.

She suspected he knew more than he was letting on—he seemed too overly prepared to be otherwise. "I have a friend who is a guide there. Too bad we don't have time, he'd take us on a tour that most tourists don't see."

The tower passed to their left, and Simon went back to packing what little gear they carried. Knowing they'd be on the move, they'd left their suitcases and the majority of their clothes with Sylvia.

They were down to Lily, the codex locked in a water-tight Tupperware container Sylvia had given them, a change of clothes, the code-breaker and money. Not much, but plenty if they ended up on the run. He put the codex into his pack. "Is there any country where you don't have a good friend?" Simon asked as he slipped off his rank T-shirt.

Veronica bit her lip. Damn, he really did look good.

Despite two days of not bathing, he somehow managed to look amazing. Flat abs rippled as he moved and his skin gleamed, making her want to reach out and skim her fingers along the tanned surface. He turned away, giving her a view of his well-defined back. She flexed her hands and shivered, wondering what those muscles would feel like beneath her palms.

Casually, he wadded up the shirt and pitched it toward a corner.

She wondered what he'd do if she asked him to whirl the shirt over his head like a stripper. She tried not to giggle at the absurd image, but her lips turned upward of their own accord.

"What?" he asked, tugging a wrinkled but fresher shirt over his head.

"Nothing." She sighed and sat on her hands. "Anyway, yes, there are countries where I don't know a soul. South America. Australia. Antarctica."

"Funny." His mouth quirked up in a small smile.

"But my parents traveled all over the Mediterranean when I was growing up, and now this is my stomping grounds for research. Of course I know a lot of people."

Simon pulled the string on his small backpack, sealing it closed. "I've been traveling through Europe and know a few locals, but none that would sneak me aboard a ship or help me break into a mansion."

Veronica wondered if she should change her shirt as well, not that her spare was much better. "You haven't met the right people, that's all."

"Too much of a Boy Scout, I suppose," Simon replied.

"Nice try. I don't believe that."

"Really? Why not?"

She hesitated. He'd avoided her questions before, but now he gave the opening. There wouldn't be a better time. "I watched you pick a lock in record time. Boy Scouts can't do that." She tucked a strand of hair behind her ear. "And what was with the weird hand thing in the Vatican? Where you pumped your fist up and down? My guess is that it's some kind of military code. Care to tell me about those particular merit badges, Simon?"

Simon raked a hand through his hair. "I surf the Net."

She didn't believe it for an instant. It was too easy. Too glib. And if that were the case, then why try to hide it? She leaned toward him. "You've asked me to be honest with you, and I have. Now give me the same courtesy. Is there something about your past I need to know?"

The engines groaned and the ship began to slow. Simon sat down next to her, the tiny bed creaking under their combined weight. "Nothing that affects what we're doing. I'm an archaeologist. *A damned good one.* That's enough."

But it wasn't enough. What was he before he was an archaeologist?

She'd been patient, but now that she'd started this line of questioning, her patience was gone and only curiosity remained. "Tell me the rest."

He took a deep breath. "I would, but then I'd have to kill you."

She pursed her lips. "This isn't funny. I mean it."

"So do I," he said, scowling.

There was a sudden jolt as the ship rammed the dock bumpers, and Veronica fell sideways, catching herself before she fell into Simon.

He continued, "Any more questioning will have to wait. I think we're here."

She grabbed his knee, trying to hold him down. "No, you can't—"

As if on cue, a knock sounded and the thin wooden door swung open. It was the captain. "Time to go."

He glanced at her hand, and she reluctantly let Simon go.

"Later, then," Veronica agreed, frustrated. What the hell had he meant? What was he before he became an archaeologist? Was it legal? Illegal? Or one of those jobs that treaded the line in between?

He rose, grabbed his pack and followed the captain. Veronica grabbed her own bag plus Lily's cloth-wrapped form and jogged up the narrow hallway to catch up.

They walked onto the deck. After spending two days with nothing but a patch of sun filtered through a porthole, Simon and Veronica blinked at the blinding brightness.

Eyes tearing, Veronica fumbled for her sunglasses, her hands searching for the black plastic. Finding them, she slipped them on. "Much better."

Simon wore his as well. "Amazing."

Over the railing, and on the far side of the waterway, was Europe. To her immediate left and at the end of the gangplank was Turkey. If one had never been to Istanbul, a city that spanned two continents, it was a remarkable sight. Modern ships dwarfed the surrounding buildings—loading and unloading amid historical buildings generations old.

People were everywhere. Filling the streets and sidewalks. Tourists. Businessmen. Workers. The city teemed with life.

She loved it. The energy. The excitement. Couldn't get enough of it when she was here.

"You have everything you need?" Garcia asked.

"Yes," Simon replied. "We didn't bring much."

The captain's smile didn't reach his eyes. "Good. Then it will only take me a moment to go through it."

"Excuse me?" Veronica asked, dread roiling through her gut.

Garcia gestured at her pack while his other hand touched the butt of the gun that was tucked into the waistband of his trousers. "Time to go through your things. I researched you on the Internet. There aren't that many women archaeologists, Ms. Bright. Especially ones with your reputation."

Veronica winced, wishing she were a little less well known.

Garcia continued. "Your exploits are fascinating. You are a woman of many talents who uncovers the most interesting artifacts." His grin broadened. "You must be carrying something of great value if you would choose to sneak into this country instead of entering like a normal tourists. I'd like to have it."

"I told you, we're late for a dig," Veronica said through clenched teeth.

"I seriously doubt that." His fake smile never faltered as his gun went from his waistband to his hand. "Now, let's not make this unpleasant."

Simon stepped forward. "We have nothing. If we had anything of value, we'd be sneaking out. Not in."

"Then you do not mind me going through your belongings, do you?"

"As a matter of fact, I do mind," Simon replied.

Veronica laid her hand on his arm. A muscle flexed at her touch. The codex might not look like much, but they couldn't take a chance on Garcia taking it from them.

"The shotgun first," Garcia said, holding his free hand out.

Veronica bristled. She didn't want to give up Lily, but this man wasn't Michael, and she was sure that shooting her would not trouble his conscience. She set the shotgun on the deck and unwound her from the bright cloth that barely disguised her shape. "You can't have her, but I'll unload her."

Keeping her hands in plain sight, Veronica picked Lily up and pulled back the bolt, showing Garcia the empty barrel and the shell that was ready to be ratcheted into the barrel at a moment's notice. She tipped the weapon upside down and the shell fell to the deck, rolling to a stop against Simon's shoe.

"Fine. Now empty the packs and you can leave."

Veronica handed Lily to Simon, praying he could read her thoughts. *Take him out.* Picking up her pack, she tossed it to Garcia with a sudden force. "Catch."

He caught it in midair.

In that instant, Simon whacked Garcia on the hand and the gun fell to the deck. Dropping to his knees, he grabbed the shell from the deck and loaded it with the speed and skill of someone who used a shotgun on an almost daily basis. He pointed the open end at Garcia and kicked the pistol away. "Drop the bag."

Garcia let go and it hit the deck with a dull thud.

Veronica snatched it and stepped back to Simon's side. She thought he might use Lily as a bludgeon, not that he would actually have had the time to load her.

She glanced around. So far, the crew was busy unloading the ship and hadn't realized that Simon held their captain at gunpoint, but that could change in seconds. "Now what?" she asked. They were at a standoff. If they tried to leave, Garcia would call for help and they'd end up in a Turkish prison. If they put Lily down, they'd be robbed and end up in a Turkish prison.

If Simon shot the captain, it was prison and a firing squad.

None of the choices appeared promising.

"Now we jump," Simon replied, backing toward the railing.

Veronica took a quick glance at the water below them. It looked impossibly far away.

But heights weren't what frightened her. It was the water. Or more specifically, what lurked beneath the surface. "Let's try the gangway," she suggested.

"And have the crew stop us? No. Over the edge."

Reluctantly, she hoisted herself to sit on the edge.

Keeping Lily trained on Garcia, Simon sat next to her.

A shout sounded from across the deck.

Apparently, the fact that their captain was being held at gunpoint had been noticed.

Veronica glanced downward, and once again, her stomach rolled to the same, sickly beat.

"Go," Simon urged.

She swung her legs over. "I don't know if I can." But even as she held on to the railing with a death grip, she knew there was no choice. It was jump or die.

Her fingers refused to unclench.

The sound of pounding feet grew closer.

"Sure you can," Simon replied as he put a firm hand on her lower back and shoved.

Chapter 10

Veronica held her legs together and took a deep breath right before she hit the water. Her right arm clutched the pack and jerked sideways at the impact, forcing her to let go before she dislocated her shoulder.

She extended her arms and legs as soon as she was below the surface, slowing her descent. It was a deep-water port, and there was little chance of hitting the bottom, but still, she preferred to not test that theory. Gazing up through the salty water, she saw Simon hit the surface and plunge past her a few feet before stopping.

Once they were below the surface, the sunlight's refraction was no longer an issue, and she saw that he held his backpack, with the codex in it, and Lily clutched to his chest.

Still holding her breath, Veronica swam toward him and he pointed toward the surface. Her lungs were already burning and she nodded.

They rose in unison, breaking the surface at the same time, gasping for breath. "You okay?" Simon asked, flicking the hair from his eyes with a shake of his head

"Good. You?"

"Fine."

"Lily?"

"Intact."

Thank God.

"The codex?"

He unzipped his pack, peeked in and zipped it back up. "Dry, thanks to Tupperware."

"Ms. Bright!"

Captain Garcia's accented voice called her name. Veronica shadowed her eyes with her open palm and tried to find him through the glare, ready to dive. But something told her it would not be necessary.

Garcia laughed again as if he'd just accomplished a tremendous prank. "Enjoy your swim." With a wave of dismissal, he was gone.

"Think he'll pursue us?" Simon asked, treading water next to her.

"No. Not worth it as far as he knows." Retrieving her backpack, she continued her swim for the dock and tried to focus on getting around the front of the ship without being tangled in any ropes or runaway netting.

But in the back of her head, there was only one thing that truly mattered now that she was in the water. Sharks.

She switched to a sidestroke, increased her pace and tried not to think about serrated white teeth biting her feet. *Faster. Faster. Faster.* It was a mantra in her head, helping her keep the pace.

Something tugged on her foot and she jerked away, splashing in the water, erratic and frightened as panic overrode everything else.

Gasping for breath, she flipped onto her back and kicked out, prepared to defend herself as best she could against an animal that had survived for millions of years.

There was only Simon.

She felt like an idiot. She stopped kicking. *Of course* it was Simon.

"What was that about?" he asked, coming up beside her.

Her heart still hammering in her chest, she scowled at him. "Nothing."

She set back out for the dock. Great, he was going to think she was a big baby.

A few more strokes and he touched her shoulder. She stopped.

"You thought I was a shark, didn't you?"

She glared at him through narrowed eyes, giving him the answer he needed.

"A shark?" He started laughing, sank a little way, swallowed water and came up coughing.

Veronica shook her head. Maybe he would drown. "You think that's funny?" Not even Alyssa would laugh at her over something like this. But Simon wasn't Alyssa.

"No, of course not," Simon replied, trying to appear as serious as possible. He pressed his lips together, but his shoulders shook with barely contained laughter.

She'd never seen him actually laugh, and this, her fear, was what caused it? Disgusted, Veronica pushed him under the water and tried to hold him there.

He slipped away and came up laughing.

She tried to ignore him, knowing he wouldn't understand. There wasn't anything rational about her shark phobia. It just was. All she wanted to do was get out of the water as fast as possible. She didn't mind swimming in the ocean when the water was clear and she could see the area, but the polluted waters of the docking area made visibility almost impossible. Once again, she swam for the dock.

"So, that's your fear? Sharks." His swim stroke was awkward, with one hand clenching Lily and the other his pack. "Where did that come from?"

Veronica shuddered in the warm water, wishing he would shut up. "I don't know, but could we not talk about it while we're actually in the water?"

She pictured a hammerhead going for her feet and drew them up before she could think to stop. Stupid, she chided herself. Forcing her legs to extend, she kept swimming and tried not to envision huge jaws wrapping themselves around her feet.

"Sure," Simon replied, keeping pace with her.

They reached the cement edge of the pier, but it was more than five feet in height, and with no footing, it was impossible to reach the top. "There has to be a ladder," Veronica muttered as they swam down the length of the wall.

"There," Simon said.

Squinting into the sun, Veronica made out a long, dark shape on the wall fifty feet away.

She swam faster.

She reached the ladder and hurried herself up the rungs, water running off her clothes in rivulets.

Standing at the top, she stared down from the safety of land as he came up the ladder. She flipped her wet braid behind her. It was so tempting to push him in.

He arched his neck back to see her. His mouth was still stretched in an annoying grin even as he tried to climb with a pack in one hand and her shotgun in the other. "See any land sharks?"

She reached out. "Lily?"

He handed the wet shotgun to her. Metal never felt so good

in her palm. Then, still smiling, she put her foot to Simon's shoulder and shoved.

His eyes widened as he fell back and hit the water with a resounding splash. Bobbing to the surface, he sputtered. She leaned over the edge. "Shark!"

He raised a wet eyebrow, but she heard the amusement in his voice. "Very funny." And he swam back to the ladder.

"Do you need any help, miss?"

Veronica turned. A young man dressed in a tunic and jeans watched them. He zeroed in on Lily, and his eyes widened.

Damn. "It's not real," she said. "It's a prop." She cringed. God help her, she was the worst liar in the world.

"Could you be more childish, Veron…" Simon cleared the dock wall, his voice dying when he saw the stranger standing next to Veronica.

The man's eyes got even wider at seeing Simon emerge from the water.

Veronica wanted to groan. It wasn't often one saw two Americans, soaked to the skin, and one carrying a shotgun, walking on the docks. Why not just hold up a sign that read, I'm Here Illegally!

Then again, she mused, it was Turkey.

"We had an argument. He lost," she said, pointing at Simon. The man scurried away.

"We better get out of sight," Simon said, pouring the water from his backpack. "You've been here before. Can we get a cab to Nasim's?"

"We can, but we're already conspicuous enough. I don't want to leave a trail to his house."

"Fine. A hotel, then, but we need to do something," Simon said. "We're well past the trying-to-blend-in stage. I think it's best we get off the street as soon as possible."

She couldn't argue. Their soggy clothes and Lily were attracting too much attention. She handed the shotgun to Simon. "Will she fit in your pack?"

He zippered Lily inside the wet material. The butt end of the weapon still stuck out, but it was better than carrying it in plain sight.

"Let's go," she said. Walking back to the main road, she held up her hand and a green car with the word Taxi written in six different languages pulled up to the curb.

"Grand Sun Hotel." She slid over so Simon could sit next to her. The driver gave them a strange look but took off down the street at a breakneck pace.

She closed her eyes, letting the heat of the cab lull her.

In her mind, she didn't see Garcia or sharks or the water or the cargo ship. She saw Simon picking up the shotgun shell and loading Lily with breathtaking speed.

There was so much more to him than he let on.

What was it going to take to make him tell her what she needed to know?

Not caring what Simon thought, Veronica tugged her wet shirt over her head as he shut the door to the room. She'd gone three days without a shower, and now she was salty on top of it. She ran a hand up her arm and sniffed the residue that ended up on her fingertips. Diesel fuel from ships. Yuck.

"Glad I don't smoke," she muttered as she shucked her pants off, leaving them in the middle of the room. She eyed them with distaste. She'd rather burn them than ever wear them again.

"Feeling a little uninhibited today?" Simon stared unabashedly at her half-naked body.

Standing in her French-cut panties and sports bra, she gave an unladylike snort, not even vaguely in the mood for anything other than quality time with a bar of soap. "Think of it as a bikini." Walking past him, she flicked him on the chin. "Give me at least thirty minutes."

He waved her on and flipped on the television.

Standing under the hot spray, Veronica groaned in ecstasy. She felt as grimy as the bottom of the ship they had leapt from, and the hot water was well worth the hassle at the front desk. With no ID, the manager hadn't wanted to give them a room, but she'd pinched Simon's arm and he slipped him an extra million lira. Even in Turkey, money spoke volumes.

She picked up the tiny complimentary bottle of shampoo, untied her braid and began soaping the long mass. Now all she had to do was contact Nasim and get the Eye before Michael did. *If he didn't already have it.* She dismissed the thought almost as soon as it emerged. This team already had a *realist* in Simon. She needed to remain optimistic.

Thirty minutes later, she stepped out of the shower, feeling, once again, human. Wrapping the oversize towel around her body, she walked back into the room.

Simon was asleep on the floor, the Tupperware containing the codex clenched in his fist, his still-damp hair sticking out in every direction and his long legs stretched out.

She stood over him. With his long lashes and full lips, she'd say he looked "innocent" except for the scowl on his face.

She sniffed.

And the smell.

There was no way he was staying in the room smelling like that. She nudged him with her foot, and he bolted awake. "What!"

"Nothing," she replied. "I'm out of the shower."

Setting the codex next to him, he rubbed his eyes with both hands. "I was dreaming about sharks. They were after us, and you were trying to turn them to gold using the Midas Stone."

"Interesting." She sniffed again. "Now, please, go get clean while I call Nasim."

Simon rolled to his feet. Like Veronica, he took his shirt off and let his pants fall to the floor.

It seemed he was a boxer-brief man. They clung to him like the Lycra shorts from the catacombs, but the red cotton material was much thinner and left almost nothing to the imagination.

"Feeling a little uninhibited?" Veronica asked, her mouth dry.

"Think of it as a bathing suit," he replied, walking toward the shower, the snug cloth showing every flex of the muscles beneath.

He shut the door, and Veronica fell back onto the bed, put a pillow over her face and groaned. It wasn't fair. Why couldn't he be ugly? Fat? Covered with boils? Dumb as a post? Something. Anything!

But no. She had to get the sexy archaeologist with secrets, and as much as she hated it, even that appealed to her. Not that she'd give in to her libido, but damn it, it wasn't fair.

She yanked the pillow off her face and flung it to the floor in one swift step. One arm outstretched, she stared at the cracked ceiling. She remembered his answer when she asked him to explain. *I'd tell you, but then I'd have to kill you.* She shivered.

Until he explained that comment, he wasn't to be trusted. At least not fully.

But even that would have to wait. She wanted to leave the hotel as soon as possible and that meant contacting Nasim. Once that was in progress, maybe she'd have the time to press Simon for some answers.

She couldn't wait to hear them.

Sneaking out of the hotel was easy. Getting a cab proved to be harder. Not that anyone was following them, but paranoia was as good a defense as anything else, and the last thing she wanted to do was leave a trail to Nasim's home.

They caught a cab almost a mile from the hotel, and in thirty minutes they were dropped off in front of the two-story, wooden house that Nasim and his wife called home.

"You're sure he can be trusted?" Simon asked as Veronica knocked on the door.

"Absolutely," she said without pause. "He worked for my parents for years. His wife practically raised me, especially since her own children had already left home."

The blue-painted door swung open to reveal an older woman with white hair, olive skin and eyes as green as a cat's. Iamar was still beautiful, Veronica noted, remembering her as she first saw her. Her skin was smoother then and her black hair shot with only a few strands of white.

But even with the absence of youth, she was still stunning in her beauty.

"Veronica!" she cried, moving forward with the grace of a dancer. "We were not expecting you. Why did you not tell us you were coming?"

She kissed Veronica on the cheek, and Veronica wrapped her arms around her shoulders, hugging her. "It is good to see you, too, Iamar." She stepped back. "You have not aged a day."

Iamar put her hand to a wrinkled cheek. "A few more wrinkles, perhaps, but they are worth it. You should meet the grandchildren. They make having children worth the trouble."

Iamar loved her children and grandchildren fiercely. She might make the occasional complaint, but woe to the person who did the same. She'd once watched her give an archaeologist a tongue-lashing worthy of a fishwife for telling her to keep her brats under control.

"Who is this gentleman?" Iamar asked, turning to Simon.

Veronica stepped aside. "This is my partner, Simon Owens."

"Another archaeologist?" she asked, curious.

"Of course."

She cupped Simon's hand in hers. "And a handsome one, as well. Much better-looking than Michael."

"Uh, thanks," Simon replied.

Heat bloomed on Veronica's cheeks. Iamar was never known for keeping her opinions to herself. A trait Veronica both loved and dreaded. "Uh…yes. Anyway, can we come in? I'm trying to keep a low profile."

"Of course. Of course." She ushered them through the doorway. "Nasim is in the study."

Veronica followed Iamar down the familiar hallway. Not much had changed since her last visit. A new tapestry decorated the wall, and as she passed the kitchen, she saw it was painted a bright blue.

Iamar loved bright colors. Sparkle. Glitter. The swish of silk. The texture of satin. She was like a flower in bloom.

Nasim was more like the stem of the flower. Pale in comparison, but strong, sturdy. He dressed in greens, dark browns, or a pale yellow cotton if he was feeling wild.

If Nasim had his choice, the house would be brown and beige, but as usual, when it came to matters of the home, Iamar won out. Veronica ran her hand along the back of a vivid red silk chair as they passed through the living room and into the study—the one room where Nasim reigned.

Decorated in dark wood and white, it was a study in contrasts. Bookshelves lined the wall, and she noticed his archaeological kit sitting on a small table next to the door.

Nasim glanced up from his desk and a broad smile appeared on his wrinkled face. "Veronica, my child." He rose to greet her.

Veronica smiled back. Once as handsome as his wife was beautiful, he was still an attractive man. Even more important, he was the best archaeological field worker in Turkey, with an instinct that was second to none. He knew everything, everyone and every deal that was worth knowing. Crossing the room, she met him halfway. He took her hands in his and kissed her cheek, then glanced past her. "You have brought a friend?"

"My partner, Dr. Simon Owens."

"I have heard of you Dr. Owens," Nasim said. "You did your thesis work in France, did you not?"

"Correct. On Colletré. The sites at Lake Paladru."

Leaning back, he stage-whispered, "He is much better than Michael. Smarter."

"Better-looking, too, from what I hear," Simon replied, shaking Nasim's hand.

Veronica held back a groan. Sometimes it seemed as if Nasim and his wife shared the same mind, but then maybe they did after forty years together, and their common goal seemed to be to get her, their surrogate daughter, married.

Nasim laughed and slapped Simon on the back. "A better sense of humor as well."

He motioned them toward the chairs. "Sit. Sit. I am anxious to hear what brings you back to Turkey."

Veronica sat in one of the two hard-backed chairs that faced the simple wooden desk and drew her unbound hair over her shoulder. Fidgeting with the loose strands, she decided to get to the crux of the matter. "A few months ago, Simon stumbled upon an artifact that proves my theory about myths. It's led us here, and you're the only person I trust in Istanbul."

"The myth theory again," Nasim muttered, sounding unconvinced.

"Yes." Veronica glanced at Simon, but he waited, obviously

allowing her to tell the tale. Reaching into her backpack, she pulled out the Tupperware container, opened it and set the codex on the desk. "We are looking for the real Midas Stone. As you know from mythology, it gives the user the ability to turn whatever he or she touches into gold."

Nasim steepled his hands in front of his lips, unconvinced. "You have proof?"

"Simon brought me a mouse made of gold. We didn't bring it, but I had Alyssa run tests on it, and it shows lungs, heart, bones, you name it. All solid gold and most definitely not made by smelting." He perked up and she continued. "To keep it short, the codex here—" she laid a palm on the book "—tells about an artifact called the Eye of Artemis. It says that it's the key to all that is gold, which we believe is the Midas Stone. But to get to the Eye, we need your help." She took a deep breath and braced herself, knowing that with the next phrase, Nasim was going to slip from interested archaeologist to surrogate father. "It's at Fakhir al-Ahmed's mansion."

Nasim frowned. "Fakhir? He is a dangerous man, Veronica, and not known for letting people into his house to take precious artifacts."

Veronica leaned forward and reached across the desk, pleading. "I know. That is why I have come to you. There has to be a way in, and if there is, I know you are the man to show me the way."

Nasim's frown deepened into a scowl, and his black eyes grew hard. "It is too dangerous. Your father would never forgive me if something happened to you. I hate to think of what your mother would do."

She sat back, hating that it came to this, but he'd given her little choice. "If you do not help me, be assured we will try to get the Eye, anyway."

The small desk clock ticked away while Nasim regarded

the pair. "Are you sure you want to do this?" he asked, addressing Simon. "Even as a child, Veronica was known for getting others into trouble."

"We're a good match, so far," Simon replied, laying his hand on her shoulder in a show of solidarity. "I'll take my chances."

"Fine. Better I should help than let you fail." Anger at the blatant manipulation darkened his eyes, but Veronica knew it would not last long. He loved a good adventure, and soon the excitement would outweigh the worry. Cupping his hands over his mouth, he shouted for his wife.

Iamar opened the door. "What are you bellowing about?"

"Tell Veronica what you will be doing tomorrow night."

"We have a dance demonstration."

"Where?" Nasim asked.

"There is a party at the al-Ahmed mansion. He wants authentic dancing, and I am coordinating the performers as well as performing with my troupe."

"Aw, damn," Veronica muttered. She could see the gears turning in Nasim's head. "No."

Nasim laughed, knowing she had tracked his idea to the outcome. "Oh, yes."

"Am I missing something?" Simon turned to Veronica, curiosity in his eyes.

"Yes, what is going on?" Iamar asked, standing behind Veronica, hands on her hips.

Nasim's hands dropped to the tabletop, fingers interlocked. The anger faded from his eyes, replaced by self-satisfaction. "Our daughter wishes to *borrow* an artifact from Fakhir al-Ahmend."

Veronica heard Iamar's sharp intake of breath.

"And has told me that she will do so with or without our help."

"Nasim," Iamar interrupted. "We cannot—"

He cut her off with a raised palm. "You know she will do it with or without our help."

Behind Veronica, Iamar huffed in frustration.

Nasim continued, "The safest way to get her in is as a dancer."

Veronica scrunched down in the seat. "I haven't danced in a year. How about I go as a dresser? Help the girls prepare?"

"We already have one," Iamar replied, coming around to sit on the edge of the desk, her green eyes flashing with fury. "If you need to get into the mansion, you will have to go as a dancer. At least I will be able to keep an eye on you to some extent."

"Fine." Feeling like a five-year-old girl, Veronica sank even lower. Could this get any worse?

"How about me?" Simon asked. "I can't have her going in there alone."

"Can you drum?" Iamar asked.

"No. I'm rhythm impaired, or so I'm told."

She sighed. "Then you shall go as my assistant."

"No," Simon replied, pressing his lips together. "Too dangerous. If we were caught with you, you'd be implicated."

Veronica turned to look at him in surprise. He'd shown the same consideration for Sylvia—not wanting her to be implicated in their activities. He wouldn't explain himself, but he worried for others. It wasn't much, but it was a good sign.

Iamar tapped a finger against her chin as she considered what to do. "As I said, there are many troupe members. It is doubtful the guards are aware of how many. I have an invitation for the dance. We shall make a copy." She clapped her hands in front of her, pleased with the decision. "With the outfit I find for Veronica, there will be no way they will deny her entry." She turned to Simon. "You shall go as Veronica's assistant. Will that be acceptable?"

Veronica bit her lip. "I don't know. It sounds half-baked." Simon was right. She did not want to jeopardize her friends. But on the other hand, with Michael out there and her laptop in his possession, there wasn't time to wait.

"There will be no better time," Nasim replied, solidifying the decision for her. "We shall have to work fast."

"Good enough," Simon said, clapping his hands on his thighs. "What kind of dancing do you do?" He turned to Veronica. "Classical? Modern?"

Veronica answered the question in her thoughts even as Iamar spoke. "No. Oriental dancing, or what you call belly dancing."

Chapter 11

Veronica stood in front of the full-length mirror and twirled twice, her deep red-and-gold petal skirt flaring out into a perfect circle while the motion made her coin-trimmed halter ring with a hundred tiny metallic chimes.

In the other room, Simon caught Nasim up on all that had happened to them.

She stopped and the material swirled around her ankles. With a frown, she tugged at the top, trying to cover her exposed abdomen until a hand slapped her away. "Leave it. I want to get this finished before you have to go back to the hotel." Iamar knelt at her feet and tugged at the skirt, adjusting the way it rested on Veronica's hips.

Impatiently, Veronica shifted. Were she and Simon insane to think this would work? With her long dark hair and dusky skin, she could pass for a local, but were looks enough?

She might be paranoid, but she felt something about her appearance looked, well, wrong. Maybe it was her eyes.

Finished, Iamar rose to her feet, fluid in movement thanks to her years as a dancer. "What do you think?"

Veronica twirled again, and the multilayered silk petals swirled and floated around her legs. She loved Lily and the occasional brush with death, but there was something about the exotic sensuality of belly dancing that appealed to her. She felt both excited and decadent despite her trepidations. "It's beautiful. Just beautiful."

Belly dancing also had the added benefit of being a great workout. No athlete had stronger abs, or more control over his or her individual muscles, than a professional belly dancer.

Behind her, Iamar brushed her dark hair until it fell into perfect waves down her back. "We should trim the ends. Perhaps henna your hands and feet. It's popular with the dancers right now."

Veronica considered it. Henna took weeks to wash out and while it might be popular, it was memorable. The last thing she needed was to be recognized. She touched Iamar's hand. "Too hard to get rid of."

"As you wish." Iamar agreed, although Veronica heard the disappointment in her voice. "Then perhaps a belled ankle bracelet?"

Veronica nodded approval. "As long as I can take it off after the dance, sure." The last thing she needed was to announce her presence as she sneaked through the mansion. She kicked the dancing slippers off and back into the closet.

Iamar handed her an ankle bracelet covered with tiny brass bells and a matching slave bracelet for her wrist. "Once we add makeup, no one will recognize you as anything but a dancer." She sized up Veronica with her eyes, as if imagining the overall effect, then smiled in satisfaction. "What dance would you like to do? Is there one that you think Simon might prefer?"

Veronica gave Iamar a quick sideways glance. She knew what the older woman was trying to do—open up the "Simon topic" so she could pick Veronica's brain.

It wasn't going to happen.

She put on the slave bracelet, sliding the three finger rings over her index, middle and ring finger before snapping the main bracelet over her wrist. "Nice try, but I am not going to tell you a thing."

Iamar's eyes widened. "What do you mean? It was a simple question."

"Umm-hmm." Sure it was. She held back the humor that tried to escape. The last thing Iamar needed was encouragement.

Putting on the ankle bracelet, she straightened, taking a moment to tug at the halter top. "To answer your question, I thought a veil dance would be entertaining. Plus, it will distract people from my face, which we don't want remembered." She'd been dancing since she was seventeen and first met Iamar, but it had been a year since she'd performed. She'd play to her strengths, and she'd always danced well when veiled.

"What music?" Iamar asked.

"The first track of the *Immortal Egypt* CD, if you have it."

Flipping through a book of music, Iamar put the CD in the player and the Saaidi rhythms of Upper Egypt filled the room. She handed Veronica a red-chiffon circle veil and headed for the door. "We should invite Simon and Nasim to watch. Give you a practice audience."

"No audience." Veronica caught her by the arm. She shook her head in exasperation. "You don't give up, do you?"

Iamar tried to appear insulted, but her green eyes twinkled with mischief. "You are paranoid."

Veronica scoffed and restarted the CD. With a flourish and

a dramatic toss of her head, she whirled the six-yard chiffon scarf in front of her, smiling to discover that veil dancing seemed to be on par with bicycling—one simply had to get back on, or, in her case, swirl a veil.

Picking a dance that she had done before, she tried to lose herself in the music, smiling when an improvisational step succeeded and grimacing when she stumbled or made an obvious mistake.

When she finished the five-minute piece, she was breathing hard. "That wasn't too bad," she said, wiping the thin sheen of sweat from her forehead with the back of her hand. "I need practice but should be ready—"

The sound of clapping interrupted her, and Veronica turned to see Simon leaning against the doorway. "It was perfect from what I could tell," he said, grinning from ear to ear. "I had no idea that you were so talented."

Heat rushed through Veronica, and she knew she blushed from foot to forehead. She crossed her arms over her chest, trying to hide her skimpy costume. "Has it ever occurred to you that sneaking up on someone might get you killed?"

He entered the room and picked up the veil from the floor. "What are you going to do? Beat me to death with this?"

She snatched it from him. "No. But strangulation comes to mind."

He held up his hands in mock defeat.

"I will leave you two to work out your...plans," Iamar said, exiting the other door, but not before Veronica saw the satisfaction in her expression.

Veronica ignored the thin excuse to leave her alone with her partner, but only because Iamar was right. "We do need to make a plan of some sort. Code words. Something." Turning back to the mirror, she was glad to see her skin was no longer red with either exertion or embarrassment. "Unless, of course, you want to stand there and harass me the rest of the afternoon."

"As much fun as that sounds, I'll have to decline," Simon said from behind her. "We have a day to prepare, and I don't want us to get caught off guard like we did in the Vatican."

"Give me a minute to change." She turned and pushed him toward the door. She didn't want to discuss it dressed like a cabaret showgirl.

"It doesn't bother me if you stay in costume," Simon replied, bracing his body against hers.

Suddenly, there wasn't enough air in the room to breathe. It was hot and oppressive and, well, hot.

"You okay?" Simon asked, his attention on her mouth.

Veronica swallowed, unable to tear her gaze away from Simon's eyes and the way they were devouring her. "Fine," she whispered. "Just…uh…need to change. It's…uh…hot in here. Don't you think?"

"Sweltering," he whispered back.

His thigh rested against hers, and she licked her lips, visualizing just how strong his legs were beneath his jeans. How they looked in Lycra shorts. In boxer-briefs.

Naked.

She held back a moan. This was bad. This was very, very bad. She had to get him out of the room before she ripped off his pants to see what he wore underneath. She licked her lips again. "Um, I really should change," she said, tearing the words out of her throat. "I want you to go."

She knew her remark was like cold water. Simon shook himself as if coming out of sleep. "Sure. Later."

A second later he was out the door, nearly slamming it behind him.

Veronica carefully unhooked her slave bracelet, took it off and flung it on the bed.

Composing herself, she emerged five minutes later, dressed in her usual jeans and T-shirt to see Nasim and Simon engrossed in conversation over a small stack of papers. Nasim motioned her over. "Come. We received this from Rebecca."

Veronica pulled up a chair. It was the map her assistant had sent before, but now it was blown up and printed into several sections. For a brief moment, she wondered how Rebecca found such detailed plans, but just as quickly, she decided she was probably better off not knowing. No doubt, it was illegal to a degree. Some things were better left unknown

She picked up the top piece. It showed the east corner of the mansion and all the security measures that were in place in that section of the house. "God love that girl," Veronica murmured, handing Simon the sheet so he could add it to the larger map he was piecing together. When this was all over and the Stone was in her possession, she was going to have to give Rebecca a bonus. *Perhaps a golden apple,* she mused.

When Simon was finished, the map measured four-by-four feet. He taped the pages together, then Simon laid the map on the rug. All three hunkered down to search for the room that contained the Eye.

It was toward the back of the mansion, away from the main ballroom. "It seems that money can buy everything," Simon commented, pointing out the icon that the legend indicated was a pressure-sensitive alarm system keeping the art gallery safe from intruders. If any weight even a few ounces touched the floor, all hell would break loose.

Veronica leaned on her elbows, mentally cataloging the area. "Do you think he'll have this section open to show off his collection?"

"My guess is yes," Nasim replied. "Fakhir is a vain man, but he is also a paranoid one. If the private gallery is open, you can be assured that it will be heavily guarded."

It didn't look as if Simon would be able to do as she'd hoped—steal the Eye while she danced. Standing up, she paced the room while her mind whirled, exploring their now more-limited options.

For what felt like the millionth time, she wished there were another way besides infiltrating the mansion as a dancer. It would be best if they weren't seen at all, but with the time limitation there was little choice. She stopped in her tracks and looked up. "What if we find a place to wait out until the party is over, steal the Eye and leave before daybreak?"

Simon gave a thoughtful nod, then scanned the map. "There's a storage area not too far from the gallery. According to Rebecca's map, it's wired, but the security level is minor compared to the gallery. We should be able to disable it with the code-breaker." His mouth turned down with concern. "If it still works."

"It should." Rebecca had built it to last, but they'd have to test it. If it didn't work…she blanched at the thought.

If it didn't, there was little to be done besides doing a snatch and grab. "But even with it, it's a long shot."

"I know." Simon met her apprehension with concerned eyes. A small smile turned his mouth upward. "You can always take Lily and shoot your way to the Eye."

He was joking but a huge part of her wished she could do just that. She was always more comfortable with her shotgun at her side, but in this case, that was going to be impossible. "Somehow, I don't think I could hide her in my skirt." She managed a small laugh, grateful for the levity. "No, with Michael out there, I think we should stick to the plan."

"Okay," Simon said. "But there's one more issue I think we need to address."

"What?"

"If something goes wrong." Simon's smile died and Veronica gulped a breath of air at the thought. He continued, "We should have a rendezvous point." He pointed to another spot on the map. "This area is a blind spot. The cameras don't quite overlap."

She followed his finger to a spot on the west side of the house, directly under a main window and behind a row of hedges. "Good idea," she agreed, wishing she'd thought of it. "We can meet there and wait until either the chaos dies down or, let's say…" She tried to estimate how long would be safe for either one to wait, but came up with no good time frame so she picked an arbitrary number. If one of them were caught, it wouldn't help to have the other wait until they were found, as well. "Until ten."

"Midnight," Simon countered.

Veronica sighed. Did he have to question everything? She shook her head, but shrugged the irritation off since she didn't plan to be caught, and if Simon were, the last thing she'd want to do would be to abandon him unless she had no other choice. "Midnight then."

"Good," Simon said, but he didn't look pleased.

Veronica turned to Nasim. "There's one more thing. The codex."

Simon's attention veered away from the laptop and back toward her. "What about it?"

"We can't take it with us. If we're caught, have no doubt that Fakhir will confiscate it."

Simon's face darkened but he didn't disagree. She didn't like leaving it, either, but there was little choice. Once again, she turned to Nasim. "Will you watch it for us? Keep it safe?"

He hugged her to his barrel-shaped chest. "Of course. I will treat it like a baby."

"Thanks," she said, relieved. "We'll also need transportation ready as soon as we come back. The longer we stay in

Turkey, the more likely we'll be caught, and the last place I want to end up in is a Turkish jail." She shuddered at the thought.

"It will be dangerous, Veronica," Nasim replied, seriousness overtaking his normally cheerful features. "Is this Stone worth it? You do not even know if it's real."

She laid her hand on his, deep conviction moving her. "It's real. I know it." Finding the Midas Stone was no longer a matter of want. It was a matter of need. The Stone called to her, and she couldn't resist.

Nasim dropped the pair off at the hotel late in the evening. The next day crawled by even though Veronica spent most of it practicing her dance and trying to ignore Simon's heated gaze and occasional comment.

By the time evening arrived and they had to leave for Fakhir's mansion, she was more anxious about her performance than stealing the Eye of Artemis.

Retreating to the bathroom, she skillfully applied her borrowed makeup—kohl to line her eyes, lipstick the color of merlot, gold, glittery shadow on her eyes, and a shimmer lotion on her skin.

Brushing her hair until it fell softly down her back, she slipped on her red and gold dancer's costume, and added a crystal bindi to her forehead before slipping on her wrist and ankle bracelets.

Straightening her posture, she surveyed herself in the small bathroom mirror.

Even she had to admit she looked good.

Taking a deep breath, she opened the door and entered the small bedroom where Simon waited.

"Wow," he whispered. "You look amazing."

"Thanks," she said, feeling more confident. "You look pretty amazing yourself."

Simon was wearing a pair of Nasim's pants. The cocoa-colored cotton slacks were belted tight around his lean waist. A borrowed, cream-colored tunic set off his tan, and brown leather boots completed the outfit.

Slipping into her dancer persona, Veronica didn't bother to hide the fact that she was dressed as a belly dancer as they walked past the night clerk. She even flipped her hair and flashed the startled man a seductive smile. Normally, she'd wear a cover-up, but better if the staff noticed her, then there was less chance that Iamar or Nasim would be implicated in what she and Simon were about to do. They were two crazy Americans acting even stranger than they already were.

"Did he notice me?" She threw a cape over her shoulders once they cleared the lobby.

"The only way a man would not notice you is if he were blind or dead, and even that is debatable," Simon replied, ushering Veronica into a waiting taxi. The white car smelled of cloves and cigarettes, and Elvis blared from the radio.

Veronica blushed at the compliment. It had been a long time since she'd been in full dancer regalia, and while she knew she made a presentable appearance, it was still nice to hear it confirmed.

In Turkish, she instructed the driver to take them to Fakhir's mansion, and to hurry. The small, dark-haired man nodded and simultaneously gunned the car into traffic.

Silent, she watched what scenery she could in the dimming light of the day. From big cities like Istanbul to the quiet villages, she loved Turkey. She'd spent so much time in the country that it felt like home, or as much like home as anywhere else.

But it wasn't the country itself. It was Iamar and Nasim. They trusted her judgment. Supported her despite her somewhat questionable goals.

Not even her parents could say that.

Her parents. She sighed. If they knew what she was doing, they would have a conniption. Sure, they'd loved adventure, but usually the low-risk kind reserved to a dig.

They passed the Blue Mosque. The sun was setting behind it, creating a glow around the edges. "Too bad we can't take a tour," Simon said, glancing out the window.

"Next time," Veronica replied, orienting her thoughts on the dance. If she didn't get mentally prepared, there wasn't going to be a next time.

By the time they reached the mansion, the sun was down, the stars were out, and they were late. "I should have gone with Iamar and the other dancers," Veronica said, wringing the edge of her cape as unfamiliar worry crept over her.

"And leave me behind?" Simon asked, leaning in until his mouth almost touched her ear. "What would you do if something went wrong? Who would guard your back? Another dancer? And what are they going to do? Dance them into submission?"

His voice was tight with irritation, but she also heard the worry beneath the tone.

"I can handle myself," Veronica replied calmly. "You should know that."

"I do," he said. "But we're partners, and we do this together or not at all."

The taxi drove to the heavy iron gates that guarded the mansion and stopped, so Simon was directly in front of the guard. True to the map, cameras were mounted on either side of the entrance and there was a manned guardhouse.

What the map didn't show was that the guard that waved them through carried a 9 mm Glock in a shoulder holster.

"Do you want to go back? Give up?" he asked, his voice low.

"Not a chance," Veronica whispered. "Let's do this."

Simon cranked the window down and handed the guard the fake invitation, printed on a heavy cream paper. Simon had made the forgery himself, which didn't surprise Veronica. Nothing he did surprised her anymore. But the forgery wasn't perfect. She prayed it would hold up if the guard chose to give it an intense scrutiny.

Another car pulled up behind them. The guard handed the invitation back, told them to go to the back of the house and waved them onward. Veronica's breath blew out with a whoosh.

Simon slowed down. "What did he say?"

She'd forgotten that he didn't speak Turkish. "Go to the back of the house. All the entertainment must be off-loading there."

"Thanks," Simon replied. Slowly, they drove past the front of the mansion and Veronica tried to spot any potential hazards they didn't already know about.

"Wow." The modern building was impressive from the street, but up close, it was spectacular. Made of stone and glass, quite unusual for the region, it was four stories tall with a recessed entryway out into the middle of it.

Veronica scouted the layout of the mansion's grounds as best she could in the growing dark. Strategic lighting illuminated the grounds, but less than she thought there would be. It seemed most of the attention was focused on the entrance and the people who entered the oversize portal.

With valet parking and people dressed as if they were attending the Oscars, the modern mansion made an interesting juxtaposition to the ancient city of Istanbul.

There was little time to gawk. The taxi turned the corner and parked, letting them out. Simon handed the driver a few bills and the taxi pulled away, spewing gravel. Iamar was at the back door, waiting.

Show time. Veronica handed Simon her cloak and they hurried in. With Simon following, Iamar led her through the kitchen and down a hallway, chiding her loudly for her tardiness and informing her that if she were one of her dancers, she'd be fired.

Veronica protested in Turkish that Iamar was being too harsh, and her mentor, in performance mode, grabbed her shoulders and shook her. "Do not talk back to me," she demanded, her voice harsh but her eyes filled with worry.

"I apologize." Veronica dipped her head. "Please forgive me." *For asking this of you.*

"You are forgiven," Iamar said, tipping Veronica's chin upward. "I was young once, and not always so patient or proper."

Relief rolled through Veronica. *Thank you,* she mouthed.

Then they were at the entrance to the dance floor.

Beyond her was another dancer finishing her performance.

The ballroom floor served as the stage for the dancer. The rest of the room was dimmed and a small stage light followed the current dancer as she twirled and undulated. Surrounding the dance floor were the guests—a sea of people, dressed in tuxedos and ball gowns, who stood transfixed as the dancer finished her performance and the music faded.

There was a thunder of applause and the artist bowed, leaving the floor in a flutter of blue and silver silk.

Quickly, Simon cut away, and skirted the wall behind the guests, making his way towards the Fakhir's gallery so he could evaluate the situation while everyone was busy watching the dancers.

Veronica followed him with her eyes, but otherwise made an effort to pay him no more attention than she would anyone else.

"Make me proud," Iamar whispered, and pushed Veronica out onto the now dim floor.

Veronica moved smoothly to the center of the space, head held high, took a deep breath and held it as she centered herself. She cast her attention to the crowd and her pulse lurched. *This is just a dance,* she reminded herself, calming the butterflies in her stomach. Nothing mattered. Not Simon. Not the Eye. Nothing.

She took another breath and held it. Just the dance mattered. Only the dance.

With her veil tucked into her waist, she put her arms above her head, creating a graceful frame for her face. The beginning flute began and the lights rose. Veronica emptied her mind of anything but interpreting the music that strummed through her body.

Slowly lowering her arms, she stretched them out to the side, undulating them with the classical snakelike move that the entire world seemed familiar with. Keeping up the supple movement, she moved them in front of her as if beckoning the crowd. The main, stronger beat took over. She added a simple hip shimmy and curved her hands away from the audience as she moved toward them and away.

The music grew, increased in complexity, and the real dance began. Discreetly, Veronica undid the veil tucked in at her hip and shoulder, executing a series of turns, the veil swirling about her like wings, and she was propelled into the music full-force. Arabian beat mixed with South American, driving her onward and filling her with sound until she was oblivious to the audience and there was nothing left but the dance.

The performance felt as if it ended in a blink, and Veronica found herself kneeling on the floor, head bowed, the veil in a puddle about her and the final chords of the music fading.

Then the applause began and a rush of energy surged through Veronica. She lifted her head and smiled at the crowd. Her knees shaking from both the dancing and excitement, she rose, bowed and then exited with a wave, her feet pointed as she almost skipped across the room and out the opposite door.

She slipped through the curtain to find Simon waiting for her. There wasn't anyone else. The other dancers were either preparing to dance or part of the audience. "Did you see?" she asked, knowing she sounded a tad overexuberant and not caring. The applause was for her. Her!

"I've never seen belly dancing before. Well, in bad B movies, but that's about it. This was different. Beautiful. You were amazing." He handed her a towel. There was no sarcasm in his tone, just sincere appreciation.

The praise warmed her more than the dancing. "Thanks, I was hoping you'd see the beauty of the dance."

His gaze skimmed her body. "Oh, I did."

Veronica flushed and patted the back of her neck. The heat of more than a hundred bodies had made the ballroom uncomfortably warm. Or was it the way Simon was looking intensely at her?

"You ready to do more than dance?" Simon asked, admiration gone and suddenly all business.

She steadied herself. "That's why we're here. Did you get a chance to verify the Eye's location?"

"Down this hall," Simon said, nodding toward his left. "I walked down on the pretext of looking for a bathroom and was turned away, but not before I got a glimpse of Fakhir's personal gallery."

"Is there a guard?"

"One."

"And the storage closet?"

"Before the entrance to the gallery."

"Perfect." She tossed the small towel into a corner, pleased. It seemed that something was finally going their way. "I'll try to catch Iamar's attention and let her know we're going for it." She peeked back out through the curtain. Two dancers, both with swords, were performing. Quickly, Veronica scanned the entranced crowd, hoping to get Iamar's attention.

She didn't see her and realized her mentor was probably helping the next set of dancers prepare. Veronica started to turn back, and as she did, a spotlight panned over the mass of people.

It was for a split second, but it was enough for her to make out details. Standing in the front of the throng was a man.

Blond. Tall. Lean. Familiar.

Michael.

"This isn't good." Veronica leaned against the wall, sweating, and it was no longer because of the dance.

"What?" Simon barked, alarmed.

She bit her lip. "Michael's out there."

"Son of a bitch!" Simon growled.

"Exactly." Veronica said, surprised at Simon's departure from Mr. Enigmatic. She stuck her head back outside the curtain.

Michael caught her eye, held it and mouthed the words "Hello, Veronica."

She ducked back in. "He's seen me."

Simon rolled his eyes. "He saw you dance. It was hard to miss."

Veronica's mind ran through several scenarios, searching for a way to salvage their plan. Now that they knew Michael was here, there was no way they could wait until the party ended. He was here for the Eye of Artemis, as well.

"I say we do this now," Simon said, his black brows pinched in an angry frown. "Everyone is busy. We break in, take the Eye, then we get the hell out of here before they know what's happened."

Veronica felt her flesh grow cold. "What about the guard?"

Simon clenched his hands into fists. "I'll take care of him."

"And get shot?" She glared at him. "Don't be foolish. I'll take care of him."

"How?" Simon asked, incredulous.

Men. "I'll seduce him," she explained, exasperated. "Get him to take me to the gallery for a more *private* dance." She rocked back on her heels waiting for the agreement she knew was coming.

"Screwing a guard is not an option," Simon replied.

Veronica crossed her arms indignantly. "I didn't say I'd have sex with anyone, and that you can even think that is beyond me," she said with disgust, surprised that he took the scenario that far. "Is that what you think of me?"

"Veronica, it's not that—"

"You can follow me, and once the alarm system is turned off, we can tie him up, get the Eye and leave before anyone knows the Eye is gone and before Michael shows up." They were following her plan whether he liked it or not.

For once, Simon looked sheepish. "I apologize. I wanted to—" his eyes proclaimed his uncertainty "—protect you."

Veronica ran a hand through her sweaty, stiff hair feeling like a total bitch. He meant well. She should have known that. It was his nature to protect. She knew that from how he tried to keep her friends safe.

If she were any other woman, his gesture would be appreciated. But she was Veronica Bright, and the day she let someone else do the tough jobs because she wore a 36C and had ovaries was the day she'd give up her business, stay home and raise a pack of children.

"Do you really think I need protection?" she asked, her tone softened.

"No. Of course not."

"Then trust me," she implored him. "Don't treat me as if

I'm an amateur who doesn't know what she's doing. I've been retrieving artifacts longer than you. Going into situations that were tenuous at best. Dangerous at worst."

He looked as if he might respond, but he clamped his jaw shut, obviously realizing it was useless to fight the inevitable.

She took a deep breath, reining in her rising temper with another reminder that he meant well, however misguided he was. "Do we understand each other?"

"Perfectly."

She managed a weak smile. "Good. Then let's get this over with before Michael decides to blow our plan."

Chapter 12

Veronica surveyed the corridor that led to the gallery. The hallway was dim, with the occasional spotlight reflecting off the marble-covered walls. And beautiful marble it was—lustrous, white and unblemished.

"Are sure you want to do this?" Simon whispered, leaning over her shoulder.

"Positive," Veronica replied, even though she wasn't as sure as she sounded. She turned to face him. "Besides, it's not as if there's a lot of choice, is there?"

"I suppose not," Simon agreed, moving closer until he was only inches away. He brushed her cheek with the back of his fingers. "But it doesn't mean I have to like it."

She blinked slowly, inhaling his scent. He smelled like warm cotton and spice, and she automatically turned into his touch. Catching herself, she cautiously tried to distance herself. "If it's any comfort, neither do I."

She smoothed her skirt, turning her thoughts away from Simon. It's like dancing, she told herself. Just an act. Giving them what they want to see.

"Be careful?"

She took a deep breath. *Focus.* "Completely."

Simon melted into the shadows to wait, and Veronica began the long walk down the hallway, her bare feet silent on the cold floor. Squaring her shoulders, she forced herself to smile as she increased her pace.

Turning the corner, she ran into the guard. He was solid muscle, she realized as she bounced off his chest and stumbled backward a step. Dressed in black fatigues, he looked like the cover model of *Soldier of Fortune* magazine. She swallowed hard, her gaze sliding to the CZ 75 holstered at his waist.

Damn. She swallowed again, trying to work some dampness into her dry mouth.

"What are you doing here?" He spoke in Turkish, and Veronica cocked her head as if she didn't understand. She twirled a dark curl around her finger, hoping she appeared pretty but dumb.

"I asked what you were doing here?" He looked her up and down, his annoyance faltering as he fixated on her cleavage. "You're supposed to be with the other dancers."

Once again, she played dumb. "I don't know what you're saying. I'm looking for the bathroom."

The guard sighed, and in accented English said, "Go back."

"Okay, but where is the bathroom?" Veronica asked, tossing her head. Looking past his shoulders, she squealed with what she hoped passed as girlish delight and slid around him before he realized she was moving.

Ignoring the guard's protests and the click of his boots on the marble, she hurried across the room to where the Eye of Artemis was displayed.

Out of the corner of her eye, she saw the guard press a code into a keypad on the wall, turning off the pressure alarm before he came to retrieve her.

Ignoring him, she walked around the case. The display was five feet in height and one square foot around. The Eye of Artemis was perched on a glass pedestal so it could be observed from all angles.

The artifact was more beautiful than she had imagined and more detailed than an ancient sketch could ever hope to capture. Solid gold and etched with symbols, it was as large as her hand. The crystal in the center was almost clear except for a silver sheen that caught the light. Fakhir might be slime, but she couldn't fault his taste.

The guard grabbed her arm, jerking her to a sudden stop.

"Oh!" She'd forgotten about the guard in her excitement to see the Eye. *Remember, it's an act.*

Taking a deep breath, she ran a painted fingertip up her sternum, drawing the guard's attention to her cleavage. "It's beautiful, don't you think?" she asked breathily.

His eyes didn't budge from her chest. "Yes."

She leaned toward him, and he licked his lips and relaxed his grip on her arm. She leaned in farther, pressing herself against him. Could he really be this gullible? she wondered. Or that horny?

He ground his hips against her. It seemed he did. A seductive smile still on her lips, she had to force herself not to wince.

Where was Simon?

The guard traced a path from her arm to the small of her back, pulling her even closer. His garlicky breath quickened.

The last thing she wanted to do was kiss this guy. She would if she had to, but Simon was going to pay.

A shadow caught her attention. *Simon.* She tried to discreetly catch his attention, but the guard's bulk dominated her scope of vision.

A thump broke the silence.

The guard whirled about, but not before a strong hand clocked him in the jaw. He fell, his thick body hitting the floor with a dull thud. Veronica dropped to her knees. He was out cold. She'd never seen anyone drop so fast.

"Thank God," she mumbled. "Are you nuts, you might have killed…" Her voice died as she raised her head.

It wasn't Simon who'd hit the guard.

It was Michael. Every nerve in her body sprang to readiness.

"I couldn't have him kissing my best girl, could I?" Michael said, obviously pleased with himself.

She eyed the guard's holstered weapon, but it was on his side that faced away from her. She glanced up at Michael. He didn't have a gun. She edged toward the guard's fallen pistol.

"Don't even try." Michael pulled a Glock from the inner pocket of his tuxedo. "I wouldn't kill you, but I'm not above wounding you if you force me."

Dammit. She eyed the guard again. There was no way she could move that fast. She was good but not that good.

And what was she going to do if she did get the gun? Shoot Michael? That would bring everyone running and she'd never get the Eye.

Her only hope was Simon. Where was he?

"Now, let's get to business, shall we?" Michael held his free hand out to help her up. Veronica ignored it and rose on her own.

"The guard will be up and about soon enough and looking for the person who stole the Eye. Meaning you."

Cautiousness morphed into rage as she realized what was happening. "You set me up. Again."

"No," Michael corrected her, his lips thinning. "Not *again*. There's a difference from last time. Last time was a mistake."

"You bastard," Veronica bit out, her clenched fists at her side to keep herself from pummeling Michael. "There's no difference. It's all the same. Same motivation. Same outcome. Same scapegoat. This is Brazil all over again."

Michaels face darkened. "This is nothing like Brazil, but I don't have time to discuss this." He thrust a manicured hand through his blond hair, mussing the strands into sloppy waves, caught himself and glared at her. "Now, get out of my way," he said, and edged past her, his gun steady and pointed at her chest.

"Why are you doing this to me?" Veronica pleaded.

Michael stopped in his tracks. "You think you're so holy," he sneered, turning on her. "You robbed the Vatican. And now this." He nodded toward the Eye. "Robbery again? We're not that different. Not really. We are both here for the same purpose."

Veronica's skin burned. He was wrong. "I plan to return it all once I find the Stone," she retorted. "That's the difference. I don't sell what I find, and I don't keep what I borrow."

"Borrow? You can say that, but we both know that you're treading the line." His face cleared of all expression. "Sleeping beauty, over there, will be waking soon. I wish I could trust you. If I could, I'd take you with me." He reached into his jacket and took out a center punch—the kind firefighters used to shatter windshields. "Since I can't, I'm taking the Eye, and you get to stay."

"And go to jail for you."

His face reddened, and for a brief moment, she thought he might pull the trigger. Instead, he went to the display case that held the Eye. "You'll be fine if you leave as soon as I'm gone. You're a smart girl. You already have a way out of the country, don't you?"

Her expression betrayed her.

"I thought so," Michael said, a smug gleam in his eyes

declaring him the winner. "I suggest you get to it as fast as possible."

"How do you plan to steal it without setting off the alarm?" Veronica asked, grateful that Simon had Rebecca's code-breaker and not her. The last thing she wanted to do was to make this easier for Michael.

"I don't." He pressed the five-inch, spring-loaded center punch against the glass. It shattered at his feet.

No alarm sounded.

Michael grabbed the Eye and shoved it in his inside pocket. "It's a silent alarm. Most of the guards are watching the dance so you might have a minute before Security arrives. Two if you're lucky.

"Michael, you son of a—"

Grabbing her, he silenced her with a kiss.

She tried to bite him, but he pushed her away, chuckling. "Always the wildcat."

His expression softened, almost saddened, and he tried to touch her cheek. She flinched before he could make contact. "I never stopped loving you, Veronica," he said, drawing away. "If you believe nothing else I told you, believe that." Leveling his gun on her, he backed down the opposite corridor from which they entered, turned a corner and was gone, leaving her to take the blame.

She had to run. Not knowing Michael's route or wanting to be shot if she followed, she started back the way she came.

There was a clicking of footsteps coming toward her. She glanced around, hoping for a place to hide. The gallery contained glass display cases, and the marble pillars weren't wide enough to hide her unless she was a size four.

She turned down the hallway Michael took.

"Stop."

She stopped midstep. This was it. Incarceration.

"Hands in the air and turn."

Slowly, she turned, praying that at least Simon made it out okay.

Her captor wasn't a guard. It was Deacon Gilchrist.

Barely her height, he made up in inches with bulk. Arms that popped with muscles. Pants that rode a bit snugly around massive thighs. It seemed he'd changed his facial appearance.

The last time she saw him he was clean-shaven and his brown hair was military short. Now his head was shaved bald and he sported a goatee.

It was as menacing a sight as she'd ever seen.

Her breath caught in her throat.

He stared at her as if she were a bug. Something to stamp out. His MK-23, equipped with a silencer, was in plain view. "You know too much, and after hearing Michael's little display of affection, you're more a liability than I want."

He raised the gun and shot the guard, blowing a hole through his chest. Blood splattered, speckling Veronica's legs and chest.

Her stomach rolled, but she dropped to her knees before she had time to be sick. The guard was dying. That was not supposed to happen. Applying direct pressure, she tried to stop the bleeding. Within seconds, her hands were covered with blood.

Another set of footsteps echoed behind them. The guards. The real ones this time.

"Why?" she shouted.

Deacon tossed the gun to her in answer.

In reflex, she caught it. In the time it took to realize her mistake, she dropped the weapon, but it was already too late. *Fingerprints.* She had her answer. For a man like Deacon, the thought of her in a Turkish prison was much more satisfying than a quick death. The bastard.

"*Ciao.*" Deacon said, and sprinted back down the way Michael had left.

With a rattling sigh, the guard stopped breathing.

She started CPR on the dead guard.

"Don't move," a voice screamed in Turkish.

She froze.

After her capture, Fakhir's men had hauled her up a set of back stairs to the fourth floor and into what she thought was Fakhir's study. There was a desk, some wooden chairs, bookshelves and little else.

Tying her to one of the chairs, they'd left her with only a wall clock to tick away the time. She suspected there would be an interrogation. Men like Fakhir didn't use police or the law. They were a law unto themselves.

At first, the thought horrified her, and as much as she hated to think it, terrified her. She waited for Simon, but with the security surrounding the mansion, she knew he had little chance of coming to her rescue. Now, it was past midnight and if he stuck to their plans, he was gone.

She hoped he'd escaped. Not even the Midas Stone was worth spending a lifetime in a Turkish prison for accessory to a murder.

The only bright spot was that Iamar probably had no idea yet that she'd been caught. If she had, Veronica knew she'd try to help and she didn't need the worry on top of everything else.

She had plenty already.

Another hour passed, and she was just beginning to wish for something, anything, to happen when the door swung open and a dark-haired man with a bodyguard entered the office, officially ending her boredom.

He didn't say his name, but she recognized him from the pictures Rebecca had sent. Dark skin. Manicured hands. Armani suit. Smooth, dark hair and smelling like expensive cologne. Fakhir al-Ahmed.

Fakhir stood in front of her, hands clasped in front of him. "Untie her," he barked. The other man kneeled down and cut her rope free with one pull from a short knife.

"And the cuffs."

With a frown, he released her. Careful to make no sudden moves, Veronica massaged her bruised wrists. "Thank you."

Much like Deacon, Fakhir looked at her as if she were less than human. "What is your name?"

"Elizabeth." Veronica glanced around the room. Other than the window, there was no way out.

"Elizabeth what?"

"Elizabeth Smith."

Fakhir chuckled, clearly amused and not falling for the lie. "A lovely name, and very unlikely your real one." He stepped forward until he was almost touching her knees. With a rough hand, he grabbed her chin and jerked her face upward. "Now, will tell me your real name, or shall I beat it out of you?" He asked the question the way most people asked if someone wanted cream and sugar with their coffee.

Her mouth felt stuffed with cotton. This would not be like Brazil, she vowed. She would not give in to fear. Would not give Fakhir the satisfaction of breaking her.

"Elizabeth Cromwell," she replied. Her voice dropped but she didn't flinch from his penetrating gaze.

He thrust her away. "Good enough, Elizabeth. Next question, why did you kill my guard?"

She remained steady, unmoved either physically or mentally, and refusing to be anything else. "I didn't."

"The evidence says otherwise. You were found with the gun and blood on your hands, and I have an artifact missing. Did your partner steal it and abandon you?"

"I don't know what you're talking about," she spat.

He raised his hand, and for a moment, she thought he was

going to strike her, but he stopped. "Tell me your version of what happened."

She didn't blink. "I was looking around. That was all. Stupid, I know, but not illegal."

Fakhir nodded in what she hoped was belief. "Continue."

She briefly debated giving him Michael's or Deacon's names, but dismissed the idea. If she admitted to knowing either by name, Fakhir would want to know more. And more would inevitably lead to Simon and her real reason for being in the gallery. "I was talking to the guard and someone knocked him out while we spoke. Then the assailant took the artifact and killed the guard."

"Then how did you come to have the gun?" Fakhir asked, frowning. Veronica knew she was losing the argument.

She plowed forward, hands in her lap, twisting the fabric of her costume. "He tossed me the gun. If you have it tested, you'll find that my fingerprints are on it, but they're not on the trigger. I was trying to save the guard, not kill him." She pointed toward the nameless man who stood at the door. "Ask him. He knows all about it. I was doing CPR when your men arrived."

Fakhir frowned. "Was she trying to save Hadda?" he asked in Turkish.

The bodyguard gave a minuscule shrug.

Veronica kept still, not wanting to give away the fact she understood them. "What did he say?" she asked.

"He is unsure."

Idiot guard. "Ask the others," Veronica urged. "They'll tell you."

Fakhir gave a nod of agreement. "I will do that, but in the meantime, tell me who your accomplice is, and it will go better for you."

She shut her eyes as a wave of hopelessness washed over

her. He hadn't believed a word she said. "Please, there is no one else."

Fakhir raised his hand and this time he didn't stop.

Veronica's head rocked from the blow and her cheek stung. Otherwise, she didn't flinch. That was a love tap compared to being hit with a closed fist by a Brazilian cop. She tasted blood on her mouth and licked it with the tip of her tongue. "You can hit me all you want, but that doesn't change the truth."

Fakhir stared down at her. "Then tell me the name of the one who took the Eye."

"I don't know."

He hit her again, knocking her to the floor. For a moment, the world wavered and spun.

"Tell me who took my Eye!" Fakhir demanded.

"I don't know," she said, wiping her blood from her mouth and praying he'd grow bored or at least too frustrated to continue.

Fakhir glowered at her. "I am not a fool." Swinging his foot, he landed a single kick to her ribs. Veronica curled into a ball and cried out despite her best intentions.

Turning, he motioned the guard to open the door. "Perhaps the police will have better luck getting the truth out of you, Ms. Cromwell," he said. "If that's even your name."

He locked the door and Veronica lurched to her knees, tears in her eyes. Holding her side, she shuffled to the door, wincing at each jarring step. She shook the knob. It was locked. She banged on the wood, but it didn't move and barely made a sound.

Mansions like this were built to last and protect the occupants.

She sank to the floor. She couldn't go through another incarceration. The beatings. The humiliations. Brazil had almost killed her. Turkey would be much worse and not even Alyssa would be able to buy her freedom.

Alyssa. She couldn't give up. Not now. If she did, Alyssa would never forgive her. With a groan, Veronica propped herself against the door and hauled herself to a standing position. Her side hurt, but it felt better than it did a minute ago. She took a slow, deep breath and her rib cage expanded.

Shuffling over to the desk, she opened the drawers. They weren't locked, and she flung them to the carpet one by one, but found they held nothing but papers. No key.

She turned. That left the window.

Which wouldn't be a problem if she weren't four stories above the ground, hurting like hell and running out of time.

Veronica wiped a hand over her forehead. Not wanting to fall four stories, she'd been bent on trying to pick the door lock with one of the pins from her hair. At the same time, she alternately cursed Simon for not being present, since lock picking was his specialty, and thanking God that he'd escaped.

One of the tumblers moved. "Come on." She pressed harder, and the pin snapped off, leaving the tip stuck in the lock. "Damn it!" She kicked the door in exasperation, then winced at the sharp pain in her side

She went back to the window and leaned over the edge.

Four stories. Forty feet—give or take a foot—and there was nothing she could use to make a rope.

She spun about on her heel to survey the room one last time. But it was as useless now as it was thirty minutes ago. The couch was made of leather, the windows lacked curtains, and unless she had scissors, there was no way she could take apart a Persian rug.

She turned back to the opening that represented both freedom and death. Would she survive the fall if she dangled and jumped? "Not unless you've grown some superpowers in the last thirty minutes," she muttered to herself.

Even if she lived, there was no way she'd walk away.

But maybe she could climb down.

She leaned farther out and ran her hand over the outside wall. The mansion was made of cut stone. It was rough. Textured. And there was almost an inch indentation where the stones were cemented together. Getting a good grip would be difficult.

But not impossible. When she was thirteen, she'd climbed up the lava cliffs of Santorini on a dare. This was no different.

She moved fast now that she had a plan. She turned off the lights in the room, breaking the bulbs with a book. The darkness would keep her from being silhouetted to anyone outside, plus would buy her time when Fakhir returned and had to search for her in a dark room.

Standing back at the window, she rubbed the silken costume between her fingertips. It would have to go. Especially the top. The coins that made it beautiful also made it noisy.

Unhooking the back, she let it drop to the carpet, leaving her in a red bra.

As for the skirt…she moved to unhook it and stopped. If, no *when*, she escaped, she was going to have to go through the public streets. She might be able to pass off the bra as a top, but not if she wore only it and a matching red thong.

The skirt stayed. She tied the ends around her waist to keep it out of the way, took a deep breath and flung her leg over the edge of the window. "I can do this," she whispered into the night as she straddled the window casing.

She pulled the other leg over so she was sitting on the edge of the windowsill, both legs hanging over and into the abyss. For a fleeting heartbeat, she wondered if she could make the descent.

She looked down at the dark ground below her. Facing the front of the house, there was nothing to break her fall but landscaped grass and a few shrubs.

"What else are you going to do?" she muttered to herself. "Let them take you to jail?"

Veronica turned over, legs hanging free, and lowered herself over the edge.

Chapter 13

Veronica had only climbed down eight feet when headlights coming up the driveway caught her attention. Her right foot slipped, and she automatically latched onto the stone with the other three limbs. Fingernails tore away from flesh, and her toes scraped the walls as she fought to get a hold with her right foot.

She found a crack and held it. "Too close," she mumbled. "Too damned close."

She knew she wasn't going to be able to make it to the ground—not like this. Already her arms were trembling with fatigue, and her side, where Fakhir had kicked her, was screaming for release.

That meant she'd have to get back into the house. Out of the corner of her left eye, she spied a window below and almost beside her. *Good enough.*

The incoming car stopped in front of the house. Veronica froze. Her section of the house was in shadow, but it would only take a tiny movement to draw attention. As long as she remained motionless, chances were they would not look up. The police? She wasn't going to turn her head to find out, but it was a sure bet. Who else would be coming over at one in the morning?

But if it were the police, then her time was running out. Quickly, her muscles screaming, she climbed down another foot, her grip tenuous. She stopped. The ledge was close. She stuck her left foot out. Not close enough. She inched sideways. One. Two. Three inches. A little more and she'd be able to get her foot on the ledge.

If Alyssa could see her now, she'd have a cow. Her sister hated heights almost as much as Veronica hated sharks.

Below her, the front door opened and Veronica recognized Fakhir's voice. He was telling whoever had arrived that he had the murderer locked safely away upstairs—*that's what you think*—and would they like a cup of tea?

Thank God for Middle Eastern hospitality. She closed her eyes and clung to the stone like ivy. Sweat poured down her spine. *Come on. Take the tea.*

Whoever replied spoke softly and she couldn't make it out. There was some laughter as the door closed.

Then nothing but the sound of the city that lay beyond the grounds and the slamming of her heart in her chest.

If the cops accepted the tea offer, she had, maybe, ten minutes. If they didn't, then ten seconds would be more accurate, and the last place she needed to be found was on the side of the building.

If they caught her here, they'd simply wait for her to come to them and then they'd haul her to prison. And *hauling* it would be. There was no way she'd go without a fight. Not this time.

She moved another inch and her thighs and calves cramped. She gritted her teeth against the pain and eyed the window ledge. Could she make it? Was she close enough? There was one way to find out.

She gripped the stone as hard as she could, every muscle in her back and arms protesting, and extended her leg. Her toes touched the wide stone ledge, then her arch and her heel. *Solid footing.*

She wedged her calf against the side of the sill for stability, and her arm followed the same path, except it gripped the side of the opening. Hanging on, she heaved the rest of her body over, both feet planted firmly on the ledge and her arms gripping the sides of the window.

Oh, God. She faced the window, resting her cheek against the cold glass. Her knees shook, and for a moment, she thought she'd pass out from sheer relief.

But now was not the time. She wasn't safe. Not by a long shot.

She pushed against the closed window with her hand and it swung open. She wanted to sob with relief that something had finally gone her way.

Pushing the heavy curtains aside, she dropped into the darkened room. Her knees gave way as they touched the carpet, and she sunk to the floor, catching herself with her hands before she made a noise.

Rising to her hands and knees, Veronica gave her eyes a moment to adjust. In the dim light that came through the window, she saw she was in a bedroom.

Perhaps even the master one. Or one of them.

There was king-size bed with a massive headboard. A few chairs and a flat panel television.

And there were artifacts. Idols. Standing up, she picked up a box. It was made of alabaster, and she'd bet it was a thousand years old as well. Veronica set it back down where she found it.

What a creep. All of this deserved to be in a museum. Her eyes narrowed as she realized that the artifacts were probably why Michael was at the party tonight. He was one of Fakhir's suppliers.

The scum. She should have given them Michael's name and damn the consequences. That would have been entertainment. Who knew what Fakhir would have done when he found that one of his suppliers stole from him? Maybe then Michael would be here instead of her.

Once again, she'd played the fool for Michael. "No more," she vowed, slamming a closed fist into her open palm, solid as granite in her conviction to escape, find Simon and get the Eye back.

Careful not to knock anything over, Veronica threaded her way past the furniture and to the door on the other side of the room.

Leaning her ear against it, she listened for any noise to indicate that the hallway was occupied.

There was nothing but silence.

She took the sheets off the bed, slit them in half and began knotting the ends together. It was a clichéd escape, but sometimes the oldest ideas were the best ones. The living space of the house was a guarded deathtrap. Leaving by way of makeshift rope would give her a fighting chance.

She started a tear in the satin bedspread, pulling it the rest of the way to rip the expensive fabric into two pieces.

Next came the drapes.

Within minutes, she had her makeshift rope. Quickly, she anchored the end to the bedpost. Hurrying to the window with the rope in her arms, she peered over the ledge. A guard walked below, making his rounds.

A thump came from the room above them.

Her eyes widened in alarm.

"Fakhir!" Veronica murmured, her voice cracking.

A shout sounded and there was crashing and running

about. They were searching the room. Good. It would buy her more time.

Below her, the guard turned the corner, and she dropped the sheet over the ledge.

Adrenaline fueling her, she gripped the rope and went over the edge of the windowsill. She clung to the rope, her arms straining from supporting her dangling body.

Quickly, she slid down the sheet, using it less as a rope and more as something to break her speedy fall. Her feet hit the ground hard, but the grass was soft as she rolled and came up on her knees.

How the hell was she going to escape the compound?

Above her, the window to her makeshift cell opened and Fakhir peeked out. *"Durdurmak!"*

Her heart was like a hammer in her chest, and she ran toward the darkness on the side of the house.

She'd just cleared the bushes and only made twenty feet when a muscular hand yanked her to a sudden stop.

She lashed out, her fists clenched.

"Stop it. It's me," came the urgent, forceful command.

She froze. "Simon? What the hell?" He wasn't supposed to be here. He was supposed to be gone. Safe.

But he'd waited. She warmed at the thought.

"Are you okay?" he blurted out, his hands roaming over her, checking for injuries.

"Fine. Fine. A little bruised." The voices grew closer. She pulled away, anxious to be gone. "Can we talk about this later?"

He grabbed her hand. "Let's go."

"You have a plan?" she asked, his pulse pounding against her fingertips.

"Keep up" was all he said, then he was pulling her along and back toward the front of the mansion.

She didn't know what he had in mind, but there wasn't time to question—just trust that he had a plan.

They reached the police car in the driveway and he stopped. Yanking the door open, he pushed her in. She slid over and he slid in behind her.

Using the butt-end of his knife, he knocked off the ignition switch. Jamming the end of his knife where the key used to go, he turned it and the car roared to life.

Simon slammed it into gear and they sped down the driveway toward the giant wrought-iron gate. "Hang on" was all Simon said as he gunned the engine. Veronica ducked in the seat and braced herself. There was a great bang, and the car jerked and slowed but didn't stop.

When she raised her head, they were on the narrow road that ran in front of the mansion, and there was nothing trailing them but angry shouts that died away as soon as they turned the corner.

Simon cruised down a dark narrow side street while Veronica kept a lookout behind them.

"Anyone?"

"Not unless their headlights are turned off," she replied, twisting around to face the front. "I think we lost them."

"I'd still feel better doing a little more backtracking." He glanced in the mirror, squinted with concentration, then turned way, obviously judging whatever he saw behind them to be a nonthreat.

She gave his thigh an affectionate pat. "We've switched cars three times. I think we've ticked off enough people in Istanbul tonight." She could imagine the headlines in the morning paper: Wave of Car Thefts Terrorizes City.

Maybe not terrorize, she thought with a yawn. But at least annoy. Stretching in an attempt to stay awake, she turned on the radio, but there wasn't much besides static and an early-morning talk show.

"Anything interesting?" Simon asked.

She'd forgotten he didn't speak Turkish. She turned the radio off. "Nothing about us. Maybe later."

"Doubtful. The cop whose car we stole probably doesn't want anyone to know he lost it," Simon mused as he turned a corner. "I can't blame him. He's got to feel like an idiot."

"True," Veronica chuckled. "I'm sure he didn't think you knew how to hot-wire a car, but then, neither did I." She turned in the seat. "Part of the past you won't tell me about?"

He didn't answer.

"Is that also how you managed to hide and make your way upstairs without getting caught?" she asked, not really expecting a reply.

"Yes," he replied, surprising her.

But she didn't miss the way his hands tightened on the steering wheel or the way his lips thinned and his face closed down, locking her out.

She shut her eyes in disappointment and leaned against the window. She didn't want him to close off. They'd been through too much for that.

An inner demon whispered that it was for the best. Simon had secrets and secrets killed. Remember Michael?

But there was another part, a stronger, optimistic area of her heart that forgave the secrets. He had them. Maybe he'd tell her sometime. Maybe not. That didn't matter anymore. Whatever his past was, good or bad, he was a good man now, and that was enough for her.

She opened her eyes and looked at Simon through a new lens. He was beautiful.

He rubbed his hand over his chin, obviously tense and frustrated with the line of questioning.

Granted, he appeared the same. Thick, dark hair. Scruffy chin. Strong hands. Strong shoulders that looked like they could hold the world and, she suspected, sometimes tried.

Oh, he was the same man. But she'd changed. She was no longer the woman who didn't trust.

She trusted Simon. With anything. Including her life.

He ran a hand through his thick hair, catching her attention. She wanted to see what those hands could do. Those hands that picked locks, loaded a shotgun and touched her cheek when he told her to be careful. "Pull over."

"What? What's wrong?"

If he didn't hurry, she wouldn't have the nerve. "Nothing. Just do it."

Simon slowed and pulled into a darkened alley.

The car came to a halt and Simon hung his head. "Veronica, I can't tell you what I was. Who I was. We've had this discussion."

"I know," she replied, pulling her hair to one side and wishing he'd catch on. "I'm not asking."

In the streetlight, she saw the confusion in his eyes. "Then why did you have me pull over?"

Leaning forward, Veronica grabbed him by the collar and guided him to her. "For this." She kissed him. Kissed him hard. She wanted him to see the change in her and this was the only way she knew how.

For a moment, he stiffened, startled. She didn't relent. With a groan, he wrapped his arms around her waist.

She opened her mouth, and he took the invitation with a boldness that surprised and thrilled her. His unique taste flooded her senses, bringing back every memory of him touching her.

Shifting in the seat, she was aware that he had unbuckled his seatbelt. The seat of the Mercedes slid back, startling her. "What are you doing?" she murmured against his mouth.

"Making room."

"For what?" she asked, opening her eyes. She knew what she wanted, but how about him?

"Whatever you want." His gaze was honest. Open. She knew he meant what he said. This was her call.

She knew what she wanted. She rested a hand on his cheek. He was an enigma. His past was a mystery.

She didn't know anything about him, but what she knew was what mattered. He was intelligent. A doer. Most of all— he had come for her despite the risk to himself. He had not thrown her to the wolves.

He was nothing like Michael.

Oh, yeah, she knew what she wanted. She ran her other hand through his hair, winding the long strands through her fingers. His breathing deepened.

"I want you," she whispered.

They met in the middle, a clash of lips warring for dominance. Neither offered quarter nor gave it.

Once again, Veronica opened to him. He tasted like musk and sweat. Like heat. Like deep, dark sex.

He murmured her name and left her mouth, trailing small kisses along her jaw. It felt right. Erotic. Better than her dreams, and while she knew she should savor the moment, she didn't think she could. The need was too great. Gentleness could come later. She wanted him. *Now.* She rose, her back to the windshield, and braced her arms on the back of the seat. "Move over," she demanded, her libido making her hurry.

Simon slid until he was under her. She settled herself on his lap, her thighs on either side of his, his jeans rough against her bare legs.

He unsnapped her bra and slid it down her arms. "Damn, you're beautiful," he said, taking a nipple in his mouth.

Veronica arched backward, her hands searching for purchase and finding the roof of the car. "Yesss," she hissed as almost painful pleasure radiated from where Simon suckled down to her groin. God, it had been too long.

She pushed him away and yanked his shirt over his head. She flung it to the floor, then ran her hands up his thighs until she reached his erection. It was hot under her hand. She rubbed him through the rough material and he arched into her palm.

She squeezed him as best she could. He reached between them and stroked her through the thin panties, sending a shock wave all the way down to her toes. "Simon." She ground her hips into his, wanting more. She craved him. Needed him. Maybe he could take his time, but her patience had already worn thin. "I can't wait."

"Thank you," he groaned. Wrapping her hair around his hand, he devoured her with his lips and pulled her panties down as far as he could. It wasn't far enough. He gripped her right thigh. "Can you lift your leg up a bit? This is really awkward."

She'd only made out in a car before, never actually had sex. It wasn't as carefree as books made it out to be. She extended her leg and a seam ripped as he forced the garment past her knee and over her foot, leaving it dangling on her other calf.

She didn't care. Her hand still on his groin, she unzipped his jeans. He lifted his hips, and she jerked the material down to his knees, freeing him. "Far enough." He crushed her to his chest, and in seconds, he was in her, filling her. She wished she'd taken the time to see him, taste him, but that could come later. After they took the edge off.

And her edge was sharp. Screaming for release.

His hands on her hips, Simon thrust upward and Veronica moaned as he stretched her. "Harder." She needed to feel him. Needed the tension. The torture. Needed to feel alive.

Grabbing the back of the seat, she thrust downward and he wrapped his arms around her waist, grinding her against him. Skin against skin.

"Oh, yes." That was the spot. He held her tighter and thrust. "More."

She rode him, his breath hot in her ear, and his body so close she could feel his pulse.

Her orgasm came seconds later, unexpected and hard, as what felt like every muscle in her body contracted. She screamed in the consuming pleasure even as she heard Simon urging her on. Telling her to ride it out as he stiffened under her. Gritting her teeth, she clenched her muscles around him and squeezed, propelling herself into another orgasm as he thrust himself into her.

Then Simon was chanting her name, and she knew he was close to climax. The veins in his neck bulged as he fought for control. Now it was her turn to urge him onward. With a groan, he pulled out of her and she took him in her hand, stroking him until he peaked.

He shuddered against her for what felt like forever. Finally, he let his head fall backwards onto the headrest, then he drew her to him for a kiss.

"Simon."

This time, his mouth was sweet. Soft and moist as he tasted her. His tongue gentle in the taking. His caress as tender as a first kiss. He was still in her. Not hard but not soft. A satisfying reminder of what had happened.

She leaned on him, enjoying the aftermath and the simple pleasure of making out in a parked car. A shaft of morning light glinted off the hood, striking her in the eye like an alarm clock. The night was over.

"We should go," Simon said, sculpting her jaw with his thumb.

She glanced at the car's clock. Five-thirty. "Nasim and Iamar will be worried."

Simon cleared his throat. "I've been thinking about that."

"What?"

He smiled sympathetically and kissed her forehead. "Do we really want to take a chance on going back? If someone saw us, it would implicate them."

She sighed, disappointed with herself for not thinking of that possibility, and tucked her head into the crook between his neck and shoulder. She didn't even bother to agree or protest since the answer was obvious. "What about the car? Lily and the codex?"

"Lily and the codex are safe. Once we get to where we're going, Nasim can send both to us by FedEx. As for the car, you've been here before. Is there anyone we could trade with? Someone with less-than-perfect morals?"

Leave Lily? The codex? She knew they would both be safe with Nasim, but it just seemed so wrong somehow.

"I don't like this, either," Simon assured her. "But unless you want to go to their home...?"

No. Neither Lily nor the codex was worth the risk to her friends. "Benny."

"Benny?"

"Just this guy we all use," she explained. "No one can pronounce his name so we all call him Benny." She smoothed a strand of hair away from his forehead. "He can get anything we need. I've never asked for anything illegal per se, but I've heard rumors. He'll take the car in trade and give us something a little less obvious. I'm sure of it."

In her head, she drew a map from their current position to Benny's workshop. "It'll take us about fifteen minutes to get there."

He sighed. "Then we better get started."

Disappointed, and wishing the world would stand still for

a while longer, she rolled off him. There was the sound of a zipper, and he was back in the driver's seat.

She tossed him his shirt. Her skirt was bunched around her waist. Her panties were trashed. Her bra had somehow made it under the seat. She slid the straps over her arms.

"Let me," Simon whispered. Her back to his chest, he slid the straps up to her shoulders. Taking a moment, he cupped her breasts before covering them with the skimpy piece of material. Finally, he dotted her shoulder and the back of her neck with feathery kisses as he snapped the back closed.

She breathed a heavy sigh as she buckled herself into the passenger's seat. Others might call her nuts, but that was probably the most erotic thing a man had ever done to her.

Chapter 14

Mykonos was everything a Greek island should be. White
sand. Even whiter buildings. Blue water. Friendly people. A
veritable Eden.

With one snake in the mix: Michael.

Four days ago, they'd traded the Mercedes for a rusted-out,
pea-green, 1985 Volvo, a set of clothes for her and a new Dell
laptop. Afterward, they'd driven to Ceme, a tourist town on
the coast, where stealing a boat at night proved just as easy
as stealing a car.

She hated taking the boat, but with Michael and Deacon after
the Midas Stone, there was little choice. It wasn't just her career
anymore. If one of them found the Stone, who knew what they'd
do—especially Deacon. He was as cold-blooded as they came.

Rebecca had traced Deacon as far as Athens, but Michael
had come here, to Mykonos—the sister island to Delos and
according to the codex, home to the Eye of Artemis.

Veronica leaned back into her pillow, looking up at the white ceiling of their small bedroom at a local B and B, tracing a crack with her eyes. Coincidence?

She hoped so. She prayed there was something on the Eye that told Michael to come here but didn't give any more information.

She prayed hard.

At least she had Lily and the codex back. Both had arrived yesterday evening, courtesy of Nasim, and now she and Simon were ready to enter the next phase of their quest—retrieve the Eye, find the Stone and get the hell out of Greece before they added another country to their list of countries-they-could-never-go-to-again.

The sheet slid off her shoulder as she snuggled against Simon's back. She kissed his bare shoulder. He stretched and turned over, throwing his leg over her and pinning her to the bed. "Morning, Mrs. Adams," he yawned.

"Morning, Mr. Adams," Veronica replied, kissing his mouth and laughing. She and Simon had once again assumed a "honeymooner" persona when they checked in. One thing Veronica loved about the islands, as long as you paid cash and were friendly, identification was not necessary.

He smoothed a strand of hair away from her forehead. "Ready?"

"As I'll ever be," she said. "Think he'll fall for it?"

"Let's hope so. I don't know about you, but as great as the islands are, I'm ready to get on with this," he kissed her again but she had heard the frustration and impatience in his voice. He was a man of action—something she could completely relate to.

Sitting up, she stretched, excited as a kid on her first day of school. She was finally going to get to confront Michael, and this time, she wasn't alone.

An hour later, they sipped espresso in the Blue Waters café, which was right across the street from the Coral café, which was where Michael went every morning for coffee.

Veronica tugged at the short blond wig that covered her hair, her head baking in the heat. "He really needs to hurry," she said, realizing it sounded like a whine and not caring.

"Suck it up," Simon said, glancing over the edge of his newspaper.

"Yeah?" Veronica adjusted her sunglasses. "At least you're comfortable."

"It does appear that way, doesn't it?" he said as he ran his fingers through his recently cropped hair. Even though they weren't sure Michael would recognize him, they hadn't wanted to take the chance, and so Veronica had chopped it off with a pair of borrowed manicure scissors.

Simon sat up in his chair, suddenly more interested in activities across the street and less interested in teasing her.

"What? What?" Veronica whispered. "See anything?" Her back was to the café and she couldn't see a damned thing.

"He's on the move," Simon said, setting his paper down.

Veronica tossed a handful of bills onto the table, grabbed her oversize beach bag and followed Simon to the street.

Staying as close as they dared, they followed him down the street. Dressed in tan slacks, white shirt and a tan cotton jacket, he looked more like a wealthy tourist than a black marketeer.

"Do you really thinks he's dumb enough to carry it on him?" Simon asked out of the side of his mouth. "I wouldn't."

"That's because you're trusting."

Simon grunted in disbelief.

Veronica continued. "And honorable. Michael's not. He's a

greedy jerk who expects everyone else to think like him. There is no way he'll leave it in a vault that he doesn't control."

"What if Deacon has it?"

"He doesn't," she snapped. They'd had this conversation more than once and she was getting tired of it. "Now, do you trust my judgment or not?"

He took her hand in his, swinging their arms as they followed Michael. To anyone else, they looked like a carefree couple. But she felt the tension in Simon's hands and could see the lines of strain around his mouth. "I do," he said.

She heard the sincerity in his voice.

She kissed his knuckles, not caring if public displays of affection bothered him or not. "I know. I'm just…tense."

He squeezed her hand and both refocused on Michael. He turned a corner and they sped up. Rounding it, they saw him unlocking a rental car. It was small but had four doors and tinted windows. *Bingo!*

"Go," Simon whispered. Simon speed-walked to the car and began to speak to Michael. Veronica crossed the street and went up the sidewalk that paralleled Simon and Michael.

Luckily, it was still early and the side road was deserted. She could hear the conversation, Simon asking for directions. Michael trying to help.

Then Simon casually leaned against the car door, making Michael turn and put his back to her.

Her signal.

She counted off the steps, like they'd rehearsed in the room. *One.* She quickly crossed back and came up behind Michael. *Two.* Simon moved away from the driver's door, opening it. *Three.* "What are you doing?" Michael asked, still unaware of her presence. *Four.* Her hand dropped into her bag where Lily waited, loaded and ready. "Hello, Michael."

Michael whirled about, his eyes wide. "Veronica?"

She pulled Lily out just enough so Michael would see her. "Get in the car."

"I don't think so," he scoffed. "We're in broad daylight. What are you going to do? Shoot me?"

She wanted to. Wanted to wipe the smug glint from his eyes. Her hand tensed on the trigger. "It's a thought," she replied. "And might even be worth jail time."

"Or I can break your fingers," Simon offered. Michael jerked backward and Veronica saw that Simon had Michael's hand in some kind of weird grip. "Now, get in the car," he said, twisting Michael's hand for emphasis.

Michael flinched and got in, sliding over so Simon could drive.

Veronica opened the back door, pulled Lily from the bag, slid into the back seat and slammed the door before anyone on the street had a chance to glance her way.

Five.

Simon parked the car on a dirt road that was almost overgrown. They'd found it yesterday. It seemed the perfect spot.

"You realize she's nuts, don't you?" Michael said to Simon as her partner shoved him out of the car. "I don't know what she told you, but if you let me go now I promise not to press charges."

"Shut up," Simon said, his voice low and controlled.

Michael glared at him. "She's angry that I dumped her."

"Dumped me?" Veronica shouted, kicking up dust as she marched toward him. "You abandoned me. Left me for dead!"

Simon grabbed her by the arm as she passed, effectively halting her. "Let it go. He's not worth it."

Michael simply shot her a malicious grin. "It was after I

found out about her record. She's wanted in Brazil for selling artifacts on the black market, you know. I couldn't let her get away with it again."

Heat flooded Veronica's face and she glared at Michael. She had been debating telling Simon about Brazil but hadn't come to a decision. To have him find out from Michael was beyond mortifying.

It was infuriating. Her ex was lucky Simon had the gun, otherwise he'd be minus a limb. "Tell him the truth before I beat it out of you," she demanded, her fists clenched at her side.

"You're a thief and a liar. That is the truth," Michael retorted.

She would kill him. "Let me go," she said, trying to yank herself out of Simon's grasp.

"Veronica," Simon said, holding her back and never taking his eyes off Michael. "I know all about Brazil. You don't have to defend yourself. Not to me and not to him."

Stunned, Veronica froze, and her jaw dropped in disbelief. "You knew? When?"

"Before I ever came to your office. There were conflicting reports on what happened, and that was one of the things that made me hesitant to work with you, but after meeting you—" letting her go, he stepped toward Michael, only stopping when the open end of Lily pressed against his chest "—I knew the truth of who did what to whom."

She tried not to feel too pleased at the revelation. "Why didn't you say anything?"

"It was your story to tell. Not mine."

She couldn't help but smile. Simon didn't simply believe her. He believed *in* her. "I can't believe you didn't say anything."

"I told you. I didn't need to. I know you."

He couldn't have surprised her more than if he'd proposed marriage.

"Excuse me. While I'm enjoying this love fest, can we

please get on with whatever you plan to do?" Michael said, his voice tight. "I have appointments to keep."

Veronica swung her attention back to him. "Meeting Deacon?" she spat out.

Surprise etched Michael's face. "Deacon who?"

"Deacon Gilchrist," Simon said, sinking Lily's barrel deeper into Michael's gut. Michael backed up a step, but Simon followed him. Lily never lost contact. "The murderer who set Veronica up." His eyes darkened. "Seems that birds of a feather really do flock together."

His eyes wide, true alarm showed in Michael's expression. "I don't know what you're talking about."

"Liar," Simon said.

Veronica laid a hand on Simon's arm. While she appreciated his desire to protect her name, she'd fight this on her own. Later. Right now, they needed to stick to their agenda. "Let it go, Simon. We have other things to do."

Simon hesitated, then backed up a step. "You're right." He met Michael's eyes. "And you're lucky." He motioned to the car. "Assume the position."

Facing the car, Michael put his hands on the hood. Veronica patted him down. She didn't feel a thing. Not in his right breast pocket. Not his left. "Crap," she muttered under her breath.

"Trying to cop a feel, love?" Michael said. "All you had to do was ask."

She patted down his legs but felt nothing besides hard muscle. He turned and smiled at her, victory in his eyes, making her bristle. She wasn't wrong. She knew it.

No, he had it.

And she knew where. Dusting her legs off, she stood. Face-to-face with Michael. Inches away. "Ready to concede defeat?" he asked.

"Not even close," she whispered as she cupped his balls in her hand and squeezed.

With a scream of pain, Michael dropped to his knees but not before she felt what she wanted. There was something harder than flesh between his legs. There was metal.

The Eye of Artemis.

Veronica and Simon sat in the back of the café, side by side, where they could both face the door and have some privacy. They'd abandoned Michael and warned him not to show himself again or Simon would let Veronica shoot him.

Taking the time to eat a late victory lunch, they kept uneasy eyes open for any hint of Michael, but it seemed he'd taken Simon's warning and Veronica's anger to heart. There was no sign he was watching them or that he'd paid anyone else to do so.

As for Deacon, there was no sign of him, either.

Still, that didn't mean Deacon wouldn't come or that Michael would take the warning seriously for long. There was no way either man would let her and Simon keep the Eye of Artemis without a struggle. Michael was too greedy. Deacon was just too damned mean.

They'd be hunting them down in the next day or so.

She took a halfhearted stab at the *pontica* on her plate, then set the fork aside. The orange cake was good, but her appetite was almost nonexistent. Cautiously and so no one else could see, she took the Eye back out and searched, again, for any clue on its use.

But any hint was as elusive now as it was an hour ago, and at the rate she was going, it would be as elusive tomorrow as it was today. She dug an ice cube from her glass and rubbed it over her forehead to try to offset her growing tension headache, then slid the Eye across the table to Simon. "Here, you take a shot. If it's a key of some sort, I have no idea what it might fit. There's nothing to even vaguely describe the location of the Temple of Light or what to do once we find it."

Simon ran a thumb over the Eye, then slid it back to her. "You're the one who reads ancient Greek. What does the writing say?"

Trying to ignore the increasing pain, Veronica set the ice cube on her napkin and picked the artifact back up, tracing the letters with a fingernail. "This side is a dedication to Artemis, Goddess of the Moon, and an acknowledgement of the Sea and its role. The Greeks knew a lot about tides and associated the Moon with them, so that's not a shock."

"Nothing about the island or the temple's location in reference to the sea?" Simon asked.

"No. Praise for the virgin goddess and her birthplace—which was why Michael came here in the first place, but that's all."

"We could always take another look at the codex," Simon suggested.

They'd been over the ancient text repeatedly, and while it was written that the Eye of Artemis was needed to find the Midas Stone, it didn't say how.

Either they were missing a page or the author was completely paranoid. Maybe both.

"Frankly, I don't care if I ever see the codex again," she muttered. Flipping the Eye over, she pointed to a selection of letters that bordered the crystal. "Now, here is the interesting bit. It talks about The One Most Favored lying in the womb of Artemis waiting for rebirth."

"The priestess who stole the Stone in the first place?" Simon asked, pushing bits of cake around on his plate.

"That would be my first guess. As for womb?" Veronica flinched as her head gave a particularly hard throb. "Perhaps a roundabout way of saying a *tomb?* Waiting to be reborn into the afterlife?"

"Does it matter?" Simon replied. "It all comes down to the fact that we think we have all the pieces of the puzzle, but we can't put them together." Simon pushed his plate aside, his dessert in pieces, but virtually untouched. "One. We know a priestess guards the Stone." He ticked the points off on his fingers. "Two. The Stone is on Delos. Three. The womb or tomb, whatever, is associated with the Eye. Four. The Eye is the Key to finding the Stone. And five—" he clenched his hand into a fist "—we are missing the connection between these four elements."

"God, you're right," Veronica groaned and rested her head on the table.

His hand gently stroked her hair. "Turn around."

"What?" she said crossly.

He took her by the shoulders and turned her so her back was to him. "I can't stand watching you like this." Unbraiding her hair, he placed the long strands so they cascaded over her shoulder. His strong hands caressed her shoulders for a brief moment then dug in, giving her a deep massage.

She groaned in ecstasy as her trapezius muscle released and, beneath it, the serratus posterior superior. "Oh, God, I knew you had spectacular hands, but you didn't tell me you were a masseuse."

His thumbs concentrated on her spine, working their way down the cervical vertebrae to the thoracic and stopping at the top of her lumbar before he reversed direction. "I like to save some things for later," he chuckled. His hands continued upward until he was cupping her head. The tension in her cranial muscles released as well, and she slumped in the seat.

"Feeling better?" Simon asked, hands slowing.

"Much." And she did. "But I didn't say you could stop."

Again, he chuckled and she settled in, enjoying his amazing therapeutic touch. But her concerns and frustrations with the Eye remained at the forefront of her thoughts. "Simon?"

"Yes?"

"Hand me the Eye. I want to take another stab at it."

"No." His hands dropped to her shoulders and worked her trapezius again, and then her shoulders and arms, massaging her deltoids and triceps as he went to her elbow. "We need to solve the puzzle, I'm not denying that, but you're tired. Whether you want to admit it or not, that little encounter with Michael drained you."

She stiffened and he squeezed her neck.

"Ow," she growled.

"Anyway," he continued as if she hadn't spoken, "it's been a really long two weeks, and neither of us is going to figure it out if we're stressed. Let's forget the codex, the Eye, Michael, Deacon, the whole thing. For tonight, we'll relax. Eat good food. Drink good wine. Maybe even dance."

"It's too hot to dance." She didn't want to wait. She wanted to figure it out. *Now.*

Simon slid his arms around her, linking his fingers to enclose her in his arms. "I know you're impatient" he said, his voice in her ear. "And wanted to have this solved two days ago."

Was he reading her mind now or was she that obvious?

"But you're never going to figure it out if you can't think straight," he finished. He kissed the side of her neck. "Trust me on this. I'm as anxious as you are to find the Stone, but I think it would do us both good to relax."

"It would help if you at least looked stressed," she said.

"Not my style or my nature, but I'll try," he said, chuckling. "If I promise to at least *look* stressed, will you take the night off?

She leaned over so she could see him. "Show me."

He twisted his face into an exaggerated grimace.

Despite the pressure of finding the Stone, she laughed and

leaned back into him again. "One night. I'll give you one night. But I hope it's not a mistake."

He squeezed her shoulders.

And then, she promised herself, it was back to business, before Deacon came after them and tried to finish the job he began in Istanbul.

The sun was rising when Veronica poured another cup of coffee. She and Simon had spent the evening drinking wine, making love, and then he'd fallen asleep.

How like a man.

Unable to keep her promise to relax, she'd risen, lit a candle and despite her comment about never wanting to see the ancient text again, she read the codex by the flickering yellow light. She went back over the Greek, hoping that she'd missed a vital part. A passage that contained a hint of the Stone's location and how to use the Eye of Artemis to find it.

There was a lot about Thalassa, the priestess who'd killed herself to keep the Midas Stone from falling into the wrong hands. According to the codex, she guarded it, waiting for her rebirth into Paradise.

But otherwise, nothing to help her resolve the riddle. Just gut instinct that came from years of experience.

Veronica rubbed her eyes. She'd managed to put together written facts into somewhat coherent information, but it wasn't as exciting as physically finding an artifact. And it wasn't enough. They only knew that Thalassa guarded the stone—not the location of her tomb or how the Eye figured into the mix.

She pushed the codex away.

If whoever wrote the book wasn't already dead by a thousand years, she'd be tempted to kill him herself. The pages were a mishmash of facts with nothing to pull it all together.

Why hadn't they at least made it coherent? Given her a clue to the tomb's location? A picture? Map? Something?

She picked up the Eye again. This was the key. She *knew* it. She turned it over, taking what felt like the hundredth look at the inscription, hoping she'd missed something. A clue. A hint. Something that would provide her an "aha!" moment when she finally discovered it.

But it looked the same as when she'd looked at it ten minutes ago. The dedication to Artemis and the Sea on one side. She flipped it over. The Favored One on the other.

Veronica rested her forehead against the gold metal. They'd come so far. Knew who the favored one was and knew the Stone was on Delos—the birthplace of Artemis. But Delos was more than a square mile in size, and neither she nor Simon had the time or funding to search one of the biggest archaeological sites in the Mediterranean. If they tried to find the Stone with a normal excavation, it would take years.

The secret was the Eye.

And she was at a standstill.

Another sigh and she leaned back in her chair, letting her thoughts wander while her fingers rubbed the Eye as if it was a worry stone. Funny, it was so easy to be caught up in what it meant, she'd forgotten what a beautiful artifact it was in its own right. Silver crystal. Gold. Inscribed.

Blowing out the candle, she held the artifact up to the early morning light that filtered in through the window. The natural flaws found in the center crystal made rainbows on the wall.

She polished the stone on her shirt. When she returned to New York, she'd have to ask Alyssa what the crystal was made of. She didn't think it was a diamond, but she'd also never seen anything like it. Although it was as smooth as glass on the outside, it had interior flaws. Otherwise, it was so clear it could be used as an eyeglass.

An *eye*glass? The *Eye* of Artemis?

The connection hit her with the force of an epiphany. Veronica smacked herself in the forehead.

She held the Eye of Artemis up and peered through it. It offered nothing but a distorted view of the room.

But that didn't dissuade her. She was right. This was it. Her gut told her so.

She opened the codex and started flipping through the pages one by one while looking through the Eye. Still nothing. Just words marred by black spots and lines. Another page and she was at the original sketch of the Eye.

It wasn't a blur.

"Oh, my God," she murmured, running her hands carefully over the ancient page. "Oh, my God. I'm an idiot."

Both she and Simon had thought the picture smudged. Damaged by someone who wanted to hide the true words and to keep would-be treasure-seekers away from the crystal.

It wasn't destroyed. It was exactly what it was supposed to be—a map to the location of the Midas Stone. A map that could only be used if one had the right tool to view it.

The Eye of Artemis.

She didn't blink. Didn't move. Scared the map would disappear.

"Simon." He didn't make a sound. Reaching under the table with her foot, she kicked the bed. "Simon!"

He sat up. "What?" he asked, stifling a yawn.

She held the Eye up. "I found something."

In an instant, he was at her side, wide awake. "Show me," he demanded.

She set the Eye in his palm. "Look." She pointed to the picture. "Through this."

He held it up and squinted, staring through the lens. "I'll be damned."

"Probably," she replied, ripe with self-satisfaction. "But what a way to go."

The defects in the crystal lined up with the smudged picture, creating an outline of the Island of Delos. There were inlets, a darker smudge for the tiny mountain in the center of the island and even the coast of Mykonos, the sister island they were standing on, at the outer edge was represented. More important was what was on the southern coastline. Here, a single flaw resembled a silver arrow—the symbol of Artemis—overlying a circular fleck of gold.

The location of the Midas Stone.

"Aha," she whispered.

Chapter 15

Dressed in fresh shorts and a clean top, and almost inhaling another cup of coffee, Veronica climbed off the small ferry, her sneakered feet sinking in the damp sand of the Delos shoreline.

The coffee in one hand and a guidebook in the other, she surveyed the almost flat island. Ahead of her and the other tourists were the archaeological ruins of Delos. Rubble that was once homes for the wealthy, a temple to Artemis and even a shrine to Isis, the Egyptian goddess.

At one time a great city, Delos was now nothing but a reminder of the precariousness of civilization. Was it the search for the Midas Stone that caused the demise of Delos? Did Menophaneses destroy the town and kill the population in a fit of anger at its loss? It was possible.

"Are you going to be okay?" Simon asked.

"What?" Did she look that pensive?

"You were glazing over."

Veronica followed his gaze to her travel mug. "I'm fine." Taking a last sip, she rinsed the container out in seawater and shoved it into her backpack. "I've gone a lot longer without sleep."

"Ladies and gentlemen!" Their ferry captain shouted over the surf, catching their attention. "The last ferry is at three this afternoon. Please be here. No one is allowed to stay on Delos overnight. If you miss the ferry, we will come back for you, but be assured it will be at triple the cost."

Turning the boat around, he sped back across the small stretch of sea that separated Mykonos and Delos to pick up another batch of tourists.

There were murmurs among the other tourists: a few snide remarks about how triple the pay was outrageous, that eight hours wasn't enough time, and a short blond woman telling her even shorter husband that a bunch of old rocks was boring and she wanted to leave *now*.

"Let's go," said Veronica, trekking across the almost desertlike landscape.

Quickly, she and Simon distanced themselves from the rest of the crowd as they made their way to the south end of the island to search for the Stone. If they were lucky, there would be some indication of Thalassa's burial tomb—an unexpected rise in the landscape indicating that the earth had eroded around a stone sarcophagus or an indentation if Thalassa and the Stone were buried in something less resilient.

Anything out of the ordinary only an archaeologist would notice.

When they found the tomb, they'd have to survey the area as best they could without attracting the attention of their fellow tourists or the archaeologists who were already working on the island, excavating the ruins for the museums on both

Delos and Mykonos. Then she and Simon would return to-night, under the cover of darkness, and excavate the Stone.

Walking through what was once the Theater Quarter, she stumbled as she stepped over a short wall, catching herself with a little hop. She'd told Simon that she was fine, but her legs felt as if there were twenty-pound bricks tied to her feet. Her lack of sleep was beginning to catch up to her.

"Any plans on what to do if we have to make a full exca-vation?" Simon asked, having the same concerns as they trod through the once-great city.

"C4?" Veronica replied. "Think you can get some?"

He hesitated, then chuckled. "I thought you were into pre-serving sites, not destroying them."

"I am," Veronica replied. "Unless I have Deacon Gilchrist and Michael Grey on my tail. Then I'm into preserving my butt and getting the artifact before they do."

"Point taken. Let's hope it doesn't come to that," Simon said.

"What do we do if Michael or Deacon shows up?" Veron-ica mused. The thought had crossed her mind more than once over the last twelve hours. "We can't have them interfering."

Simon didn't answer, but his hand clenched into a fist and she knew the thought had crossed his mind as well.

It wasn't long before they cleared the ruins and left the tourists behind. The land rose as they continued southeast. De-spite the morning breeze blowing over them, Veronica's heart thumped harder the closer they got to the coastline, and she was beginning to sweat.

The problem of Michael and Deacon nagged at her. She and Simon needed a diversion. Something to throw their ad-versaries off their trail. Make them think that she and Simon weren't going after the Midas Stone.

At least not here.

"That's it!" she cried, her voice carrying away in the strong breeze.

"What's 'it'?" Simon asked, not slowing his pace.

She grabbed his arm and stopped him. "We set up a false trail. Make Michael and Deacon think we're going somewhere else to find the Stone. I'll contact Rebecca. Tell her to purchase us tickets to Ephesus."

"What if they're already on our trail?" Simon countered.

"Even better," Veronica replied. "This would really throw them off."

He gave a thoughtful nod, the beginning of a smile turning his mouth. "The big temple to Artemis?"

"Maybe the Eye brought him to Delos, but would the Midas Stone be on a scrubby island or at the mondo, glitzy temple?" It might not make sense to an archaeologist, but to two men who lived in a world where wealth counted more than symbolism and tradition, it made perfect sense.

The beginning smile turned into a full-fledged grin. "I like it. Simple. Effective. Believable." He kissed her hard and swift before they began walking again.

Veronica snuck a peek at Simon out of the corner of her eye. Their relationship was beyond weird. He was a mystery. He'd hurt her by destroying her reputation. And now he was her partner on this amazing journey and she couldn't fathom undertaking it with anyone but him.

Her straying thoughts were interrupted when they crested a short rise in the land and reached the coast. A small segment was indented, just like on the map.

Veronica cried out, grabbing Simon's arm, adrenaline running through her, giving her the energy that caffeine couldn't. *Please be there. Please be there.*

They sprinted to the edge of the cliff and her hormone-fueled high came to a crashing halt as they turned in a circle.

There was nothing but flat land. Scrub. Stone. Not even a hint of a potential tomb.

"Well, damn." Simon ran a hand over his head, making his newly shorn hair stand up on end despite the breeze coming off the ocean below them.

"Double that," Veronica replied. She turned in a circle again. Was the Eye wrong? Had they misinterpreted it?

In her gut, she didn't think so. She *knew* she was right. She let her pack slide to the ground. Tired or not, she was not going to let this mystery get the better of her.

Sitting down cross-legged in the dirt, she retrieved the codex and took another look at the map through the Eye of Artemis. There was the coast. The indentation. And the combined sign of Artemis and the Stone.

"Anything?" Simon hunkered down beside her.

Nothing had changed. "I don't understand," she said, putting both back. "This is the place."

Simon stood and offered her a hand up. "Perhaps it was already excavated, then filled back in."

"No," Veronica said. "If they'd found the tomb, then they should have found the Stone, and there is no way an archaeologist could keep quiet about that, not even with government interference. There would have been some news about it, I'm sure."

"Then we're missing something." Simon took their translation notes from the pack. "Something obvious."

"I can't imagine what. I've gone over this so many times that it's lost all meaning," she said, rubbing the back of her neck as tension tightened every muscle.

Simon flipped through the loose pages. "We're assuming a lot, and I think that's hindering us. Forgive me for sounding like a corporate monkey, but we need to think outside the box."

"Corporate monkey it is," she said. "I'm willing to give it a shot. Let's go over what we know."

"The Stone is on Delos."

"Definitely."

"Thalassa is the guardian and it's buried in her tomb."

"No. Womb," Veronica corrected.

Simon kicked at the dirt, hesitated, then gave her a curious look. "Veronica, this might sound crass, but hear me out."

"Okay. Shoot."

"Assuming *womb* is right—"

"It is."

"To get to a womb, you go between a woman's legs."

Her "what the hell?" expression made him stop short. She smoothed her features over. "Go on."

He raised a guarded eyebrow but continued. "In this case, the womb might belong to a metaphorical Artemis since she's the mother of her priestesses. So what if Thalassa isn't buried in a regular tomb? So why do we assume that *womb* translates into a traditional *tomb*. What if it's something less obvious? Like a cave?"

"An opening into the mother earth, or in this case, mother Artemis since this is her island," Veronica finished, excited by the breakthrough.

"Exactly!" Simon proclaimed.

The question was where? The only known cave on the island was the Sacred Cave and it had already been excavated.

They turned toward the cliff at the same time.

Walking out onto the twenty-foot-wide piece of land that jutted out into the sea, they looked downward along both sides of the fifty-foot cliff. The sheer walls were rocky and broken but there were no signs of any caves.

"Nothing," Veronica groaned, disappointed.

"Wait," Simon said, grabbing her arm and sounding anything but disappointed.

"What?"

"Look."

Across from them, another projection of land jutted out fifty feet into the sea, paralleling the outcrop they stood on.

"What?"

"These two projections…could they represent legs?"

"Possibly," Veronica said, drawing out the reply. "But it would be a stretch."

"Maybe," Simon agreed, but there was a stubborn glint in his eye. "But it does correspond to the map." He glanced up at the sun, then down to the blue waters that slapped the side of the rocks below.

"Have you ever seen the Blue Grotto at Capri?"

"Yes, it's a tourist trap."

"It is," he said. "But what's interesting is that it lies at sea level. The only way to get in is to take a boat at low tide, and even then you have to lie down in the hull of the boat to clear the entrance."

He walked with her until they stood exactly between the two outcrops of land and in the indentation where a symbolic "womb" might reside. He pointed toward the surf. "I think we found the entrance."

Veronica stared, straining her eyes. The waves washed in and out. It was on the third cycle that they both saw it.

A dark spot on the wall peeked about the waterline.

Thalassa. She gaped at Simon. "I'm a woman. You'd think I would have figured that out."

He shrugged, looking exceedingly pleased with himself. "I'm more familiar with the path to a womb that you are."

Veronica felt herself blush and tried not to laugh. She was getting used to his sarcasm. Even appreciated it. But this was new. "That was so crude."

He wiggled his dark eyebrows up and down, leering at her. "I have more. Want to hear it?"

"Not if it's that crass." She threw her arms around Simon's neck and kissed him on the mouth. "You rock, you know that?"

"Yes. I do." He gave her a quick kiss in return.

Untangling her arms, she nodded toward the way they'd already come. "Let's get out of here. There's a lot to do if we plan to finish this tonight."

"Right. Contact Rebecca. Rent wetsuits and scuba tanks. Buy a tide table." Simon ticked the items off on his fingers. "This is going to be tight."

Veronica's heart dropped. "We're going to dive? I thought you said we could use a boat."

Simon shook his head. "This is low tide and the cave isn't above water except on the backwash. It's dive or nothing."

"At night?" she asked. Her voice unexpectedly squeaked.

Simon's right brow shot up. "You can't dive, can you?"

Veronica flushed. "I never said that. I can dive."

His brow lowered, and she saw doubt in the way he looked at her. "Really?"

Her eyes narrowed. "Just because I'm scared of sharks doesn't mean I don't dive."

He didn't look convinced.

"I don't run from my fears, Simon," she explained. "I face them, and in this case, it meant that I had to learn to dive." She tucked a strand of hair behind her ear. "I don't ever want my fears to govern my actions. Can you understand that?"

Admiration replaced the doubt in his expression, and he gently stroked her cheek. "I get it."

"Good." She said, taking his head and squeezing it.

"I doubt there'll be any sharks," Simon assured her. "Chances of us running into one, much less having it harass us, are slim. We stand a better chance of getting hit by a bus."

"A bus doesn't have teeth," Veronica muttered. Big, white, serrated teeth. In her head, she knew he was right. It was the rest of her that wanted to pick another option.

"You can always sit this part out," Simon offered. "I can go alone. Take pictures. Maybe even video. It'll be like you were there."

Veronica glared at him. She knew when she was being baited. Even without his lame attempt at reverse psychology, there was only one answer. "Thanks but no. It's time I faced my fear. *We* go after the Stone. *Together.*"

Simon drove their rental boat while Veronica paced the small deck. Her nerves were still on edge despite her eight-hour nap.

She'd slept the afternoon away while Simon had contacted Rebecca. When she woke, everything was in place. As far as Michael and Deacon were concerned, she and Simon were on their way to Ephesus, and, even better, Rebecca had e-mailed her that Deacon and Michael had purchased airline tickets and were on their way there as well. At least that problem was solved.

Now she just had to get through the dive.

Veronica passed Simon, and he reached out, pulling her to his side. "You don't have to do this if you don't want to."

She shook her head. "I'll be okay." She'd just feel a lot better when this was over.

"Good. Because we're here."

The boat slowed to a stop, and Simon dropped anchor approximately thirty feet away from the cliff—far enough to keep the boat away from the rocks.

Veronica went to the edge of the boat to lean against the railing. Silently, she stared into the water, but there was nothing but blackness. Behind her, she heard the scrape of metal on wood as Simon brought their gear up from the hold.

Ten minutes later, they were ready.

Outfitted in a black, neoprene wetsuit, Simon adjusted his tank by moonlight. With the no-visitors-after-dusk ban on the island, they'd had to cut the lights to avoid alerting the authorities as to what they were doing.

Now it was past midnight and the tide was almost at its lowest point. At this distance from Delos, in the dark, she couldn't see the cave, but she knew it was there. Maybe it was a metaphorical womb to whoever constructed this elaborate treasure hunt, but to her it was more like a giant maw waiting to eat her.

Veronica situated her single tank, settling it between her shoulder blades. Strapped to the tank and wrapped in plastic was Lily. One could never be too careful. "Okay, I'm as ready as I'll ever be." She put on her mask, making sure the seal was firm.

She prayed that once they went through the cave, there would be some dry land. If she had to be in the water for the entire expedition, she'd be a nervous wreck by the time they recovered the Stone.

"Let's do it," Simon said, fins in hand.

She put a small jar of silver greasepaint in her oversize dive bag, between the Eye and the codex still in its waterproof Tupperware container. If there wasn't dry land once they cleared the entrance—please, oh please—then it was possible there was a network of caves below the island. If so, they'd need to mark their path. "Weapon? Shark repellent?"

He flashed her a grin, his teeth brilliant in the moonlight and against his black suit, and flipped over the side of the boat, landing in the water with a small splash. A few seconds later, his head popped above the waves. With his dark hair, mask and wetsuit, she could barely make him out. "Coming in?"

"My kingdom for shark repellent," Veronica muttered. Taking a deep breath, she dropped backward into the water.

The water was warmer than she thought it would be. Kicking to the surface, she fought the urge to reach for the ladder and climb to safety.

Just an excavation, she reminded herself. *A dig.* Putting in her own regulator, she breathed in the oxygen. It was cool on her throat. Simon tapped her on the shoulder and pointed toward the cave. She nodded and they dove deep and swam along the ocean floor. Once under the waves, Simon turned on their underwater light, giving her a view of the ocean that she'd never seen before.

As anxious as she was, its beauty captured her attention. Sea anemones dotted the rocks that littered the ocean floor. Closed for the night, a few responded to Simon's light and opened. She brushed one with her gloved hand as she swam past, and it closed again. Gorgeous.

The ocean floor rose as they grew closer to the cave, and all too soon, Simon's light found the entrance to Thalassa's tomb. Perhaps three feet across and three feet high, it looked ready to swallow them. The urge to turn back grew stronger.

Knock it off, she told herself. *It's a hole in the wall. Nothing more.*

Lighting the way, Simon entered first. Despite the regulator in her mouth, Veronica held her breath as she passed through the opening.

More a tunnel than a cave, the rock walls refracted the light from Simon's underwater lantern, creating sharp shadows and making the dark waters feel more ominous.

The thought that something might grab her fins and pull her back out made her yank her knees to her chest before she could stop herself, scraping her shins along the tunnel's bottom.

She winced, gritting her jaw to keep from shouting and losing the precious air. She would not let this stupid phobia take over her.

But neither would she be unprepared. She pulled out the bowie knife that was strapped to her thigh. It was long and wicked, but would it be enough to ward off an ocean predator?

Knock it off!

Keeping her focus on Simon's fins and being careful not to cut herself on either the knife or the rough walls, she cleared her thoughts of anything but the Midas Stone. Ahead of her, the light spread outward. Simon must have cleared the mouth of the tunnel. She kicked her legs hard, anxious to be out of the passageway.

Simon was floating at the entrance, and she tried to push him out of the way so she could join him.

He waved her back and pointed, his light illuminating the water in front of them.

Something long and silvery swam in the water ahead of them. Circling. Its dorsal fin and black, lidless eyes told her all she needed to know.

Shark.

Veronica exhaled as instantaneous panic overwhelmed her. Her heart pounded in her ears, and her breathing was loud and hard.

Then Simon grabbed her hand and squeezed hard. She caught a glimpse of his eyes behind the mask. He was worried. Didn't know what she would do.

Welcome to my world. She swallowed and tried to slow her breathing. The shark swam past them. She squeezed Simon's hand as hard as she could but didn't blow her air again. She would beat this if it killed her.

It might.

Shut up.

She could not depend on Simon to get her past this. She

itched to pull out Lily, but shotguns were useless underwater. Besides, if she didn't face this fear, alone, it would haunt her forever.

It's a small shark, she told herself. *Not even five feet. It's more scared of me than I am of it.* She forced her muscles to unclench, and one by one, her fingers pried free.

Grasping the rough edge of the tunnel, she entered the cave. It wasn't very big—maybe twenty feet across—but what caught her attention was that the floor sloped upward until it was free of the water. *Dry land.*

Thank God, there was safety only twenty feet away.

Past a shark.

Simon touched her arm. She jumped. The shark caught the movement and widened its circle, swimming closer to them.

Both froze as it swam so close that its tail brushed against them on the sidestroke.

Veronica swallowed hard and took a deep, controlled breath, holding back panic with rigid control.

Simon touched her again, and this time she was ready. He pointed toward the wall and started creeping along the rock.

Veronica followed. Her shaking hands gripped the walls, pulling her along. They went five feet before the beast passed by again. Veronica held her breath.

Fearless, she told herself. *Be fearless.* Before she could think to stop herself, she reached out—*oh God, oh God, oh God*—and touched the tail, letting it glide over her palm as the shark slipped by.

She'd done it. Touched it. She wanted to throw up and shout success at the same time.

They started moving, again. Five more feet and the floor began its upward slope. The shark circled around, but this time stayed in the deeper water behind them.

Veronica's head cleared the water, and she let the regulator fall from her mouth. Simon had taken off his fins and was half-way out of the water but kept his light pointed toward the water.

Keeping her eye on the shark, Veronica took off her fins, the feel of rock comforting and solid beneath her aqua socks. Two more feet and the water stopped at her waist. She'd touched the shark. It was real. Not a monster. An animal. And animals weren't to be feared. Respected. But not feared.

Another glance told her the shark was on the opposite side of the cave, but it didn't matter. Panic broke over her, and she ran out of the water and onto bare rock.

Chapter 16

Leaning over, hands on her knees, Veronica pulled off her mask and took a few seconds to catch her breath.

"You okay?" Simon asked, his hand on the small of her back.

Still a little shaky, she straightened and sheathed her knife. "Yeah. I'm good." She wasn't over her phobia, but she knew she could beat it if forced and that was enough for now. "I take it that it's not shark repellent in the case?"

He held it up. "Not hardly, but I was wishing it were. When I saw the blue, I wasn't sure you'd be able to go through with it."

"And let you have all the fun?" she joked. "You wish."

His returning snicker echoed off the walls.

"Enough chitchat," she said. Let's get to work."

"Bossy," Simon retorted, but he ran the light along the cave to reveal a smooth, squared stone that was as high as Simon and set flush within the rock walls.

A door.

"I'll be damned," Veronica whispered.

This was *her* grave. Thalassas. The woman who saved the Stone and killed herself so it would remain a secret from men who would misuse it.

In Thalassa's hands, they would find it again.

Veronica ran a finger over the stone that made up the door. A thick covering of algae rubbed off on her finger. Beneath it, she caught a reflection of pale stone. "Marble?" she asked aloud.

"I didn't think it was tough enough to withstand the erosion of the sea. Not for that long, at least," Simon said. He wiped off more algae.

The door wasn't white. Wasn't marble. It was constructed from the same silver crystal that was set in the Eye, but so thick and marred by flaws it was impossible to see through.

"Impressive," Veronica said. The door was a find in itself, and under any other circumstance, she'd take the time to study it. But with the tide as their timekeeper, they had to move forward as quickly as possible. "Now what do we do with the Eye?"

"Let's find out," Simon replied, setting his light on the ground like a lantern.

Quickly, they cleared away the algae. Writing etched the edges of the stone, catching Veronica's attention. It wasn't difficult to read, and she followed its path around the perimeter. Something about the Maidens of Artemis rescuing the body. Guardians of the Stone. The One Most Favored. Thalassa.

"Veronica, look at this," Simon said, claiming her attention. He'd cleaned off the center of the door, uncovering a carved indentation. Veronica took the Eye from her dive bag and held it up. The indentation was the exact shape and size of the Eye of Artemis.

He gave her a go-ahead nod, his eyes bright, even in the partial illumination from the dive lantern.

Carefully, Veronica set the stone into the carved niche. It almost snapped into place. A perfect fit.

Nothing happened.

Both stepped back. "Now what?" Veronica said, hands on her hips and head cocked. "Shouldn't it do something?"

As if on cue, the crystal centerpiece of the Eye began to glow, scattering a silver light over the chamber.

The hair on Veronica's neck rose. The glow intensified, brightening to an almost unbearable level, the silver light washing out all shadows. Veronica's eyes watered, and she shielded them with her arm but refused to shut them. She had to see what she could. Whatever was happening, it wasn't what she would classify as normal. Not even close.

When she thought she couldn't take any more, the light pulsed twice, then faded.

She lowered her arm. "Is it over?"

On the tail of her question, the light increased again and she shielded her eyes again. Instead of silver, the light was a deep yellow-gold. And with the new light came sound. A great rumbling as if the very earth opened up.

The reverberations grew louder, almost deafening, and small pebbles fell from the ceiling above them. Veronica flattened herself against the rock wall, shielding her head with her arms. Simon did the same.

There was the sound of breaking glass. The cave went dark.

In tense silence, they waited for the phenomena to either stop or kill them.

The rumbling stopped. They were in total darkness. Total silence. With no idea of what they would see when they turned on their spare lanterns.

"You okay?" Simon clicked on the secondary light from his weight belt.

She felt fine other than the fact her pulse raced so fast she thought she might have a heart attack. "Yeah. You?" She took a deep breath and willed herself to calm down.

"I'm good, but what the hell was that about?"

Veronica unhooked her underwater flashlight from her belt. Turning it on, she blinked her eyes to adjust them. She pointed the light toward the door. "Look."

During the noise and light show, the giant silver crystal had slid backward on some kind of track. Veronica shone her light into the dark opening, revealing not the crypt they expected but a corridor that led downward, into the island's depth.

From what she could tell, there were steps carved into the rock, flanked by Doric columns every ten feet or so. The earliest and simplest of the Grecian columns, they were distinguished by their plain, twenty-sided shaft and were generally considered to be masculine in design due to their strong, straight lines and overall thickness.

It looked dark but harmless enough.

But she was betting it was anything but that.

"You thinking what I'm thinking?" Simon asked, his voice at her shoulder.

"That we better watch our step?" Veronica answered. "No one takes this much trouble to hide something and then leaves the main pathway free and clear."

"The question is how many traps and how lethal?"

He paused. "We should check the codex again."

Veronica rolled her eyes. "Don't you think that one of us would remember if there was mention of booby traps?"

She stepped over the threshold and into the corridor.

"Dammit, Veronica, what are you thinking!" Simon tried to yank her back out, but she evaded his grasp and stepped out of his reach.

"Wait," she commanded.

Both held their breath, waiting for a potential trap to spring, but there was only silence. The ground didn't open up and the ceiling didn't come crashing down. The rock surrounding Veronica remained solid. "So far, so good."

Simon stepped over the threshold. "That was about the dumbest thing I've ever seen you do."

"Someone had to go first." It was a bit reckless, but they also didn't have the time to watch every footstep. Who knew how long it would be before Michael and Deacon figured out their ruse? Once that happened, it would be best to have the Stone and be back in New York.

"I get that, but we're partners. We do this together. Not with you acting the cowboy and taking unnecessary chances," Simon said, the muscles bunching in his neck and shoulders the only physical indication of his tension.

"Okay," she acquiesced, knowing she'd say the same thing if the situation were reversed.

His jaw relaxed a fraction and he directed his light down the stairs.

The tunnel was wide enough for a single person to traverse, and he edged past her to examine the backside of the entrance stone. "There isn't an indentation for the Eye on this side. What do you think? Do we leave the Eye where it is or take it?"

Out of experience, Veronica hated to leave the door behind them open, but it was also doubtful that anyone would happen to *drop by* a cavern that was under water the majority of the day. Plus, if they removed the Eye, it was possible that the door would close, sealing them in. "Leave it."

He nodded his agreement. "I think so, too. Let's go."

"Carefully," she said.

Simon raised a dark eyebrow. "You're telling me?"

She raised her own in response, then gave him a gentle shove forward. Tanks still on their backs, each carrying their fins and goggles and with Simon's briefcase banging between his thigh and the wall, they walked single file down the carved steps with Simon leading.

Twenty feet down, the corridor turned ninety degrees. Twenty feet after that, it turned again, making their descent a slow squared spiral.

Veronica stopped to examine the columns that lined the corridor and wondered who carved it. Was it the priestess? Did they employ workers?

"Veronica," Simon called before he turned another corner.

This was not the situation to lose sight of each other, and she hurried forward as they continued downward.

And still no booby trap.

"This is too easy," Veronica said, her voice echoing down the space in front of them and bounding back.

"I was thinking the same thing," Simon replied. "If someone wanted to kill an intruder, I wish they'd get it over—"

He stopped in midstep.

Veronica stopped as well, a chill racing up her spine. "What's wrong?"

He didn't move. Didn't turn. Didn't flinch. Just stood there as still as a statue. "The step sank down. I think it's the trap we were talking about."

This was bad. Very, very bad. "Fuck me," she muttered.

"What?" Simon said.

"Nothing." She replied, already scanning the walls with her light, searching for a lever.

"Anything?" Simon asked.

She shook her head and realized he couldn't see her. "No." She edged closer to him, testing the stones before placing her weight on it. "Think you could come back toward me?"

He shook his head. "Not a good idea. We don't know which way the trap will spring or what form it'll take." He unbuckled the strap that held his tank on and slid the straps down his arms. "Take this."

"Why?"

"In case."

"In case what?" Her voice rose as she understood where the conversation was leading. He was going to sacrifice himself.

His right arm strained with the weight of the tank.

He continued. "I used to work for the government, you should know that."

"What?" Where did that come from?

"Government training. You asked me where I earned my 'Boy Scout' badges. The C.I.A. recruited me, but after a few years—"

"Shut up." She crossed her arms, suddenly very aware of what he was doing. He was tying up loose ends. Voicing his last regrets. Coming clean.

Whatever lame cliché one wanted to use, it came down to the fact that he expected to die at any moment.

She'd have none of it. "Cut the noble crap and let's focus on saving your lame ass."

"Lame ass?"

"Very." What did he think she'd do? Let him die?

His arm started to shake, straining with the weight of the tank. "I'm telling you my past. You wanted to know what I was holding back? This is it."

She wished she could reach out, but she didn't dare touch him. Her nerves were strained almost to their limit and if she felt him beneath her fingertips, she might break. "Tell me after we're done here. And you might want to put the tank back on before you drop it."

He surprised her and moved the tank to his back. "We'll talk about this later."

"Damn right," she agreed. She couldn't see his face, but

she would bet money that his right eyebrow was raised in that oh-so-familiar way.

She loved that quirk that told her he thought she was full of it or that she'd managed to surprise him.

She wanted to see it again.

She was not going to lose him. Not like this. "Lean toward the wall," she said.

"What are you doing?" His head turned but he didn't shift all the way around.

"Looking around."

He tried to protest, but she was already slipping past him with a wide-legged step, being careful not to knock him off the step that triggered the trap or add her own weight to it. If the switch to turn off the trap wasn't here, then it had to be farther down the corridor.

She passed him and shone her light down the corridor.

"Let it go." Simon's voice had an edge she'd never heard before. She turned her light on him, and in his eyes was fear, but not for himself. For her.

"I can't" she said, and moved forward. Her light found the blades five feet away and lodged in the ceiling. Side by side and sickle-shaped, they would slice Simon to ribbons.

Standing on her toes, she got as close as she could, but it was too high for her to reach. The light reflected off the blades.

"What's that?" Simon asked.

"Knives. Big ones." She squinted, trying to find a better perspective, "They go too far up into the ceiling, but I can't tell how far."

"Great, I'll be sliced into steak tartare," he said. "Any ground clearance once they swing?"

"I doubt it." She ran a hand over her damp hair and came back with handful of dry sand. "What the…?" She looked up, squinting when sand hit her eyes. There was a steady stream coming from the center of the blades.

A counter-balance.

Her stomach rolled, and she swallowed hard as she realized what it meant. When the sand ran out, so was Simon's time.

She should tell him. Should. But didn't. He might try something stupid. Something heroic.

"Veronica, go down to the Temple," Simon said, his voice concerned, but she sensed it was more for her and less for his own fate. "You might find something there to use as a wedge to keep the knives from dropping."

"That's not an option," she responded.

He shone his light on his face and managed a grim smile. "I promise, I won't go anywhere."

He'd risked freedom in Istanbul to wait for her, and now he asked her to abandon him? She shook her head.

"Veronica, go. This is the only way. As long as I don't move, it'll be fine," he assured her.

She blinked back unexpected tears. She didn't know how much sand had to fall before the blades were triggered, but her gut told her if she went to the Temple, he would be dead by the time she returned.

There had to be another way. All traps, no matter how lethal, were capable of being turned off.

She had to believe that.

The codex weighed heavily in her dive bag, and she rested her hand against it. If she had time…but she didn't. There was no time for a search. Only action.

"This is our expedition," Veronica answered, fighting to keep her voice steady. "I won't go without you." And she set off down the corridor, light weaving as she looked for something, anything, that might help them.

"Please don't let there be another trap," she prayed under her breath. "Please."

Behind her, Simon yelled at her to get to the Temple. She ignored him. Turning the corner, she passed another column and ran her light from top to bottom. It was carved with symbols, and one of them was an arrow on the column base—the same one that was on the map.

She didn't believe in coincidence. Dropping to her knees, she pressed it. Punched it. Nothing happened.

She scanned the other carvings. There was a circle in the base as well. The symbol for the Stone? She tried to manipulate it.

Still nothing.

Simon didn't have time for games. Where was the key? She took three steps down and stopped. She jumped to her feet and headed for the next column down the corridor but stopped before she traveled three feet. *Wait.* The arrow was on the *base* of the column? Doric columns didn't have bases. Ionic? Sure. Corinthian. You bet.

But not Doric.

She shed light on the other columns farther down the corridor. All were baseless unlike the one with the arrow.

Perhaps that was the key. It had to be!

She turned back, running the few feet. "Come on," she muttered. She pressed the arrow again with the same result. Nothing. Veronica growled in frustration and skimmed the base with her hands, hoping for a button. A lever. Anything that might stop the knives. "I know you're here. Where are you?" she muttered.

She started to press all the carvings on the column, but they didn't move. She shrieked in frustration.

"Veronica?" Simon called out. "Are you hurt?"

"Fine! I'm fine!" There had to be a trick. Something she was missing. The answer had something to do with the map since it had both symbols. But the Eye was still jammed in the door, and without the Eye, the map was inaccessible.

Fist clenched, she hit her thigh in frustration. "Damn it, think!" She'd spent hours looking at that map. Hours. She unclenched her fist.

She could do this.

Shutting her eyes, she slowed her breathing and tried to visualize it. The shape of the island. The pattern of the crystal fractures. The arrow and the circle, overlapping each other to show the location of the cave.

Overlapping.

A loud scraping echoed past her.

"Veronica, something's happening!" Simon's shouted.

Time's up. Wrapping her arms around the column, she pressed both symbols at once. "Please." They slid inward.

The scraping stopped, and for a moment, she thought her heart would do the same.

A moment later, Simon was at her side, dropping to his knees and pulling her into his arms. "Are you okay? I heard you scream."

She stared at him in stunned surprise. "Am I okay? I swear, of all the stupid—"

He silenced her with his mouth, his lips crushing hers. "You're welcome" was all she managed to get out as he kissed her harder.

After marking the wall with the silver greasepaint so they wouldn't miss the trigger step on the way back, they made their way as fast and safely as possible down the stairs to what they hoped was Thalassa's Tomb. Two turns. No tomb. No booby trap. The third turn. More nothing. On the fourth, she ran into Simon's back with a thud. "You could warn me...."

She saw that the corridor had ended, opening out into another cavern.

And what a cavern. Thirty feet across and another thirty in height, it glittered with granite and flashed of white limestone. Water dripped from the ceiling, echoing through the cavern.

Carved into the walls was a temple.

Veronica knew her mouth hung open and it didn't matter. There were no words big enough to describe the feeling. Even without the Stone, this was the find of a lifetime.

Walking down the last twenty steps, they made their way across the short, ten-foot courtyard and to the steps that led into the Temple. Veronica swung her light across their path. There were tide pools in the few crevices that dotted the area. No large animals from what she could see. Some anemones, limpets and barnacles, and watermarks on the wall, but that was enough to frighten her. "Simon, this cave floods during the tide."

"I noticed them too. I'd also bet money that when the tide comes in, the outer door will close, even with the Eye in it," he said, taking it one step further.

"Another trap," Veronica said. "They knew that someday, someone would find this place, and when they did…" She didn't finish the thought. Didn't need to when the reality was sharp as a knife. "We should hurry."

They came to a halt at the bottom of the stairs. The Temple wasn't as grand as the Temple to Artemis on Ephesus, but being intact and perfect, it didn't need to be.

The columns surrounding the Temple were Ionic style, as opposed to the corridor's Doric columns. The Ionic columns had longer flutes, giving them an almost feminine feel, which seemed appropriate for a Temple to Artemis.

The frieze above the entrance was carved with reliefs. If she was reading it correctly, the reliefs told a story. A young woman stood in a small boat with a bigger vessel bearing down on her, and she had a knife in her hands, pointed at her breast. *Thalassa.* Next, what could only be Artemis, lifting Thalassa's body and giving her to her maidens.

Finally, Thalassa being laid to rest, the maidens at her feet, mourning her.

"Incredible." Veronica whispered, awed by the tale.

"Yeah," Simon replied. "Ready?"

She slipped the knife from the sheath strapped to her thigh. "Yes."

He pulled out his as well.

In tandem, they walked up the steps. Like most temples, this one was rectangular, but longer than Veronica originally thought. A statue stood in the center of the room.

Sheathing their knives, they walked to it. What would normally be a statue of a Greek god or goddess was replaced with something far more important and once, Veronica was sure, far more real.

It was a woman carved in gold, breathtaking in detail. Veronica knew it was much more than a simple carving. This statue was once a living, breathing human being.

She came up to Veronica's shoulder and was as petite in structure as she was in height, with sculpted cheekbones, a delicate nose and small chin. Her hair was plaited into a thick braid that fell over her shoulder. Her clothes were simple, almost toga-like, except for what seemed to be a kirtle cinching the garment in at the waist.

One delicate hand clenched the knife that was thrust into her heart, but her eyes were closed, and a Mona Lisa smile gave her a serene appearance. This young woman welcomed death.

Thalassa.

Her other hand was outstretched as if offering a great gift.

In her open palm was a single stone. Formed from what might be granite, it was covered with thin veins of gold.

The Midas Stone.

Chapter 17

Veronica and Simon looked at each other. "You know there's got to be a trick to taking it," she said.

"You think?" Simon replied.

She gave him a halfhearted shrug. "Let's figure out how to take this Stone without getting killed. Maybe we should split up. We'll get more ground covered that way."

Simon raised his eyebrow. "Not a good idea."

"Why not?" Veronica argued. "We're on limited time. You said it yourself—this whole site will lock down once the tide turns."

"I could be wrong."

"There's a first," she snapped. "A man saying he's wrong."

Simon stared at her, dumbfounded. "Funny, but I still don't like it."

"How about if I promise not to touch anything that seems even vaguely threatening?" she suggested.

He waited, unconvinced.

She rested her hand on his forearm, knowing it was his concern for her that moved him. "Let's get this done and get out of here. We're wasting time."

His expression softened. "Okay. But be careful."

She grabbed him by the wetsuit. "You, too. Remember, I saved you last time." She gave him a quick kiss before he could retort, then set off to the right of the Temple. Scanning the columns as quickly and efficiently as possible, she looked for a clue to the booby trap she presumed kept the Stone safe.

But the columns had no markings or carvings.

"Damn it." There had be something. She searched the bases, praying for a sign, but nothing out of the ordinary caught her eye.

When she reached the back wall and turned to follow it, she saw Simon's light paralleling hers. His stopped. "Veronica." His voice echoed in the dark expanse. "I found it."

She broke into a jog.

He stood in front of another door. This one was made of gray granite speckled with mica and quartz. Flush with the wall, it was such a perfect fit that the edges were almost invisible.

In fact, both she and Simon might have missed it altogether except for the indentation—in the shape of a hand with the fingers spread wide—that was in the middle of the rectangular entryway.

Veronica held up her open right hand. It was smaller than hers, but not by much.

"Let's do it," she said, her breath coming fast.

Simon gave a curt nod.

She placed her hand in the indentation the way a tourist would match a handprint at Grauman's Chinese Theatre.

The door slid into the wall like a pocket door, revealing a room. She guessed the door weighed a thousand pounds, but it slid as if it weighed nothing. She shone her light around the edges of the entryway, but there was nothing to indicate how the door worked.

They illuminated the room with their flashlights.

It wasn't a big room. Perhaps ten feet in depth and width. The walls were bare. In the middle, serving as a table, was a short stone pillar. On it was a *lecythus*—a tall, slender-necked vase.

"Let me go in first," Simon said.

Veronica didn't move. "Why? 'Cause you're the guy?"

"Yeah." He set the metal case down. "There could be another trap, and I don't want you killed."

Veronica still didn't move. "Did it occur to you that I might feel the same way about you going in there? I almost lost you back there, and frankly, I don't want to go through that again."

His hard gaze softened.

She continued. "This doorway was made to fit a woman's frame. If you go, you might trigger a trap. Think about it. The women who built this were petite. I doubt they would have triggered the trap on the step. That was made to catch someone who was heavy. Like a man in armor."

His eyes skimmed her frame. "Then you're in as much danger, because you're not as small as the women who built this place."

Veronica stiffened. "I'm not that big, either, and I weigh a hell of a lot less than you."

He didn't relax, but he set his light down. "I don't like this."

She heard the acquiescence in his voice. "Neither do I. But we all have to do things we don't like. That's why I let you be on top sometimes."

His lips twitched. "I'll be right behind you."

Taking a deep breath, she edged through the narrow entry,

the granite scraping her shoulders even as she stepped into the darkened room.

The door slid shut before Simon could follow, trapping her in the room.

"Simon!" Veronica whirled around and pounded on the door, but the granite was so thick, there was little chance he could hear her.

"But if there was a way out of the first trap, there's a way out of this one." She surveyed the door. There was another indentation, and with the exception of fitting the left hand, it was similar to the one on the other side.

"Here goes." She put her hand in it.

The door didn't budge.

"I knew that was too easy," she muttered.

She ran a hand over the smooth stone, and contemplated using Lily for a brief moment, but the chance a ricochet would hit her was good in the small room.

She went to the pillar in the center of the room. It was five feet high and a foot across. She studied the *lecythus*. A *lecythus* was given as a funeral offering—that didn't bode well. Slowly, she picked it up.

No blades came at her, the floor didn't drop out from her feet or the ceiling cave in.

Her breath whooshed out in relief.

Carved from the same crystal as the Eye and the door, the vase was cool and damp against her skin. She held it up to the light. Etched into the crystal were words surrounding the base of the flask.

Strange. Generally, there were painted scenes and nothing more.

Whoever carved this had beautiful craftsmanship but lousy syntax. The words weren't in the usual order—or at least none that made sense to her. She couldn't be sure, but it was something about a priestess…or maybe believer…becoming one with the holy vessel to gain the blessing…or was that the curse? "Of the Stone," she finished aloud. It didn't make sense. Stones didn't give blessings. That was the job of immortals.

She noticed that it was also sealed shut with wax. She thought of Alice in Wonderland. "Drink me?" It didn't seem like a good idea.

She swung the light in a circle again, but a different solution didn't offer itself, and she knew she was being herded to a single, inevitable decision.

"Let's get this over with." Pulling out her knife, she wedged the tip under the hard wax and popped it free. The small vase was filled with a dark liquid. Water? She sniffed. It smelled sweet, with a hint of something familiar. She reassessed her decision. Not water. Wine.

In the original myth, it was Dionysus, the God of Wine, who gave King Midas the gift of gold. It seemed he played a part here as well.

Now the writing made some sense. A follower of Artemis drank the wine, or whatever it was, to become one with the holy vessel.

She shut her eyes and gave her version of a prayer. "Artemis, please watch over me. Over us. Let this work." She toasted the air, then took a tiny, cautious taste. The wine was sweet on her tongue, reminding her of apples and oak.

Her tongue didn't burn off. Nothing happened. She didn't feel any different, and the door didn't open.

"Fine. Be that way," she said to the silence.

She tipped the flask higher and took a generous swallow. It was thick in her mouth with an oily texture.

Grimacing, she swallowed.

The burning in her stomach was almost instantaneous. Veronica doubled over, with a cry. "Help me," she cried out to no one. Fire raced through her body, consuming her. Shaking violently, she managed to set the vase back down on the pillar before she gave herself over to the pain, clutching herself as the fire centered on her chest then flowed down her arms in a fiery trail.

She was sure she was having a heart attack.

The screaming sensation stopped at her hands and centered on her palms like red-hot coals. She clenched her hands together, rocking with pain.

Then there was nothing but blackness and screaming.

Veronica opened her eyes to total darkness. Confused, she blinked. Where was she? Her hand throbbed and she remembered. The flask.

How long had she been out? She pressed the stub of her watch and it illuminated. Not even five minutes.

She sat up with a groan. Her head felt as if someone had filed it with rocks and then given it a good shake.

She had to get out. Get to Simon. Let him know that she was fine—other than a horrible hangover from drinking thousand-year-old wine.

She rubbed her sore hands on her thighs then started feeling the floor, searching for her light. She must have dropped it when she passed out. She prayed it wasn't broken.

She found it a few feet away. She picked it up and it made an ominous rattling. When she clicked the on button, the lack of illumination didn't surprise her. "Fine," she said.

Knees wobbling, she crawled to the wall and used it to push herself upright. Taking a moment to breathe, she started feeling for the indentation. It hadn't worked before, but the burning in her hands gave her hope that it would no longer be an issue. Slowly, she made her way around the room, dragging her hand along the wall until she found the indentation. She placed a burning palm in the imprint, and the door slid open.

She staggered out and into Simon's arms, her knees finally giving out. He held her up.

"Simon, I'm sorry," she said, pressed against his chest. "I should have listened."

"Don't be" he said, "You were safer in there."

"What?" That was when she noticed they were not alone.

Deacon Gilchrist had found them. Also dressed in a wet-suit, he stood behind Simon with a Glock pointed at the back of Simon's head.

"Hello, Veronica." A familiar voice coincided with something hard being jabbed into her ribs from behind.

She froze. "Hello, Michael."

"I'll take that." He took the knife from the sheath on her thigh and Lily from the makeshift holster on her back. "You took long enough, but I am so glad you could join us."

Grabbing her by the braid, he pulled her away from Simon and yanked off her backpack in the same motion.

One hand holding her scalp, she jerked the length of hair from his grasp and turned to land a punch. He dodged her fist, and she stumbled past him, her legs still weak. "Too slow," he teased. His head-to-toe black neoprene offset his choirboy-blond hair and gave him a menacing appearance.

Deacon's deep laughter made her shiver and she spared him a glance. He was enjoying this. He gave Veronica a nod. "Nice job. Thanks for opening the door."

"Bite me," Veronica growled.

"Veronica, stay calm," Simon said angrily.

"Excuse me?" She replied, her anger growing. Deacon and Michael were holding them hostage and she was supposed to remain calm? "You think I should relax?"

"He has a gun."

"I know."

"Shut the fuck up," Deacon roared, thwacking Simon in the back of the head for emphasis.

Veronica clamped her jaw shut.

"Have a lover's spat on your own time," he said. "Now, you," he spoke to Veronica. "Tell me what happened in there, and don't lie. If you do, I'll know, and while Michael has issues with shooting people, you know I have no such inhibition." He cocked the gun. "And it won't be easy. Or quick. I can make your boyfriend hurt for a very long time."

"How did you find us?" Veronica asked. The more Deacon talked, the more likely they'd find an opportunity to overpower him and Michael.

"Deacon was never in Athens," Michael said. "He was watching you the entire time. When you set up a phony trail to Ephesus but went to Delos, we realized you'd cracked the code, so we set a phone trail of our own." He sighed with dramatic regret. "You got careless, Veronica. Very, very careless."

She bit her lip. He was right. They'd underestimated them.

"And thanks for solving that booby trap on the stairs," Deacon added. "Otherwise, we could have been killed."

Damn. It hadn't reset.

"Now, talk," Deacon said. "You're wasting my time."

Her gaze slid to Simon. His expression was unreadable.

"Put your hand in the impression," she explained. "The door opens. Easy as that."

"What happens once you're inside?"

"There's a similar impression on the other side. Put your hand in it and the door opens again."

Deacon shook his head. "What did I tell you about lying?"

Her skin broke out in goose bumps at the cold undercurrent to his voice. Or was it the damp air? "I'm not."

"Sure you are. If getting out was as easy as that, why was

Simon trying to blow the door?" Deacon took a few steps back. "Can't have him dying right off, can we?"

"No!"

Deacon squeezed the trigger. The sound of the shot reverberated throughout the room, and Simon fell to his knees, clutching his shoulder.

"Simon!" Jerking away from Michael, Veronica ran to him, dropping beside him. "Where are you hit?" What had she done?

"S'okay," Simon whispered, his voice tight.

Her gaze zeroed in on the blood oozing from between his fingers.

He increased the pressure. "Don't tell them jack."

Deacon jerked her to her feet. "As I was saying. Tell me *everything*."

Simon met her horrified gaze and shook his head, his lips pressed together. He was as white as marble.

Sorry, she mouthed. Nothing was worth seeing him bleed to death. Not the Stone.

Nothing.

She glared at Deacon. "When you go in, there is a *lecythus* in the middle of the room."

"What's a *lecythus?*"

"Funeral flask," Michael answered.

She crossed her arms, physically reining in the urge to punch Michael in the face. "Drink from it. The door opens. Simple as that."

"And?" Deacon prompted. "Or I shoot him again."

"Whatever is in the flask won't kill you," she answered, her voice dead flat. "But you will pass out for a minute or two. Afterward, you can open the door. I don't know why it works, but it does. That's it."

"Other than the parlor trick of reopening the door, what else does it do?" Deacon asked.

She shook her head. "I don't know."

Deacon cocked the gun again.

"I said I don't know," Veronica screamed, furious.

Deacon lowered the weapon. "I believe you."

Shoving past her, he placed his hand in the imprint and the door slid open.

"Do you think this is a good idea?" Michael asked.

"If it gets us the Stone, it's a great idea," he replied, stepping through.

The door slammed shut. Veronica went to Simon but Michael grabbed her away. "It's you and me now," he said, running a fingertip down the inside of her arm. "Wanna kill some time?"

"I'd rather kill something else," Veronica snarled.

"Yeah, I know what you mean." He glanced at Simon and laughed. It was cold. Humorless. Different from anything she'd ever heard from him before.

"Do it and I'll never help you," she said through gritted teeth.

Michael pressed his weapon into her side. "Let's take a walk."

"No," Simon said. "She stays."

"You're in no position to argue," Michael said.

"Don't worry," Veronica urged. "He won't hurt me." Or she hoped he wouldn't. Michael always claimed he loved her. She'd be fine, but the way he looked at Simon. She shuddered. She wasn't so sure Michael would give him the same consideration.

Michael drew her toward one of the pillars, and his face changed. Lost some of its hardness. "Deacon's going to kill you."

She didn't need Michael to tell her that but hearing it aloud was more unnerving than she'd thought it would be. "I know."

"I can save you if you let me."

"Is this to make up for Brazil?" The question slipped out before she thought to stop it.

The muscles in Michael's jaw tightened. "I never meant to abandon you. Never."

Veronica took a deep breath and ran a hand over her damp hair. Despite the tightness of his jaw, there was an air of desperation about him. A need to be believed.

There was no more ignoring the fact or denying it. She believed him, and despite her protest, she always had. She'd known Michael could never hurt her. Not intentionally. "I know," she whispered.

He lowered the gun until it hung limp in his hand. "You do?"

"Yes," she said with a regret so deep it pained her. What would he have done if she'd admitted that earlier? she wondered. If she'd loved him enough, forgiven him, could she have talked him out of working for murderers? She laid a palm against his cheek. "I believe you."

"Veronica." He wrapped his arms around her and pressed his lips softly to hers. She'd heard the hope in his voice. The elation. Felt his love for her in his touch.

God help her, she could not return it. She knew he never meant to harm her, but that didn't mean she forgave him.

He was a whore for the black market. Everything she loathed and everything she fought against. He'd lost her respect and trust when she found out about his other life, and without those two pieces, there was no love. If he'd left his life behind, she might have forgiven him, loved him. But he'd made his choice.

And it wasn't her.

Michael froze, as if he could read her every thought. He cupped her cheek in his hand. The gesture was as familiar as breathing. Veronica squeezed her eyes shut for a split second, remembering how eager she used to be for his touch.

His touch changed, the pressure increased until he pushed her away. Once again, his gun was aimed at her face. "You can't forgive me, can you?"

She shook her head, knowing it was useless to lie. He knew her too well.

His full mouth twisted. "Let's go. The others are waiting." He grabbed her arm, his fingers digging into her bicep as he yanked her along.

When they reached Simon, he shoved her down beside him, and she fell to the stone floor.

"You okay?" Simon asked. "Did he hurt you?"

"Hurt her?" Michael barked. "That bitch has a heart of stone. Short of killing her, I don't think she can be hurt."

Simon's eyes narrowed, and he looked like a bull ready to fight.

Veronica grabbed his hand. "Let it go."

Michael's eyes narrowed, and she knew that whatever part of him that once cared for her was gone. "I see you've made your decision." He picked up Lily, ripped off the plastic wrapping, and aimed it at Veronica. "Good thing you won't have to live with it."

The door behind them slid open, and Deacon stumbled out.

Chapter 18

Deacon held his hands out, palms facing them, his smile wide and almost beatific except for the Glock holstered at his thigh.

This isn't good, Veronica thought, and in the same instant, Simon grabbed Michael at the knees. The men hit the stone floor with a thud, and all hell broke loose.

Veronica rolled out of the way and stayed in a crouch as she waited for Deacon to start firing. But the only sounds that broke the silence of the great Temple were those of the fist-fight in progress.

She searched for Deacon. Far from caring about Michael, he was skirting the fistfight and walking toward the golden statue of Thalassa.

What was he up to?

Simon grunted in pain as Michael's fist connected with his wounded shoulder. There wasn't time to find out. She had to help Simon. Michael was on top of him and Simon barely held Michael's gun hand at bay with his good arm.

Lily was next to them, and she scrambled over to grab her, but the men rolled again and the shotgun was punted out of reach toward Deacon. "Damn it!" she shouted, trying to grab Michael instead and missing.

Grimacing, Simon twisted Michael's hand, and the Glock dropped to the stone floor then skittered away as the two men rolled on top of each other.

Veronica dove for the weapon before it was knocked out of reach and, this time, was rewarded with the feel of cool metal in her palm.

She cocked it. It wasn't Lily, but it would work. She edged closer to the fight, hoping for a clear shot. She didn't want to be the girl in the movie who stood around wringing her hands while her man got the crap kicked out of him.

She also didn't want to shoot the wrong person.

They almost ran into her, and she jumped aside.

"Get out of the way," Simon shouted, rolling over and on top of Michael. He smashed his fist into Michael's jaw again and again until he stopped moving.

With a groan, Simon rolled off him and Veronica helped him to his feet.

She barely spared Michael a glance. "You okay?" She went to touch Simon's shoulder and stopped herself.

He nodded. "Sure, I'm fine."

She knew he was lying. He hid it well, but his face was paler than before. He was going into shock.

"Michael is the least of your problems." Deacon's comment boomed through the Temple.

He stood next to Thalassa, his flashlight on the ground, pointing upward and illuminating the scene. "I can't believe it's mine." He reached for the Stone.

"No!" Veronica and Simon shouted in unison.

Deacon held the Stone and yelled in triumph as he held the Stone up like a primal hunter might hold a prize pelt toward the sky. Veronica saw Deacon's eyes were almost glowing. She and Simon both took a step back.

Deacon laughed again, and it prickled over her skin like an army of fire ants. Still laughing, he picked up the flashlight. The light winked out.

Veronica corrected her earlier assessment. Deacon didn't seem to glow. He *was* glowing. His hands, to be specific. They had an aura about them that was unmistakable. Like the sun's halo during an eclipse.

"I'll be damned," Simon whispered, and flipped on his flashlight. He pointed it toward Deacon.

Their adversary still stood beside Thalassa. In his right hand, his fist clenched the Midas Stone.

In his other hand was a solid gold flashlight. Deacon hooted. Crowed. Did a single twirl of triumph like a giddy drunk.

His smile almost split his face. "Thank you, Veronica. I would never have found this if it wasn't for you."

Veronica covered her mouth and swallowed to keep herself from retching. What had she done?

With her other hand, she raised Michael's gun. He couldn't be allowed to keep it. She'd started this and now she'd finish it. "Put it down, Deacon."

Deacon's smile faltered. "You wouldn't hurt me, would you, Pumpkin?"

"Don't make me shoot you, Deacon," she shouted, her hand shaking.

Deacon laughed and she knew he would never give up the Stone. Not while he was alive. Her hand shook harder.

"Give me the gun, Veronica. This is my expertise," Simon said, his hand gripping her wrist.

She couldn't seem to unclench her fingers, and Simon sounded a million miles away. She only saw Deacon, the man she was going to kill.

"Veronica, love. Let it go." Simon sounded closer now. His hand slid up hers, his palm on the back of her hand. "He's not worth it. Let's just get out of here."

He leaned in closer, his breath caressing her skin as if it was breathing life into her, and the world came back into focus. "Simon?"

"The tide is coming in," Simon whispered in her ear.

She heard the sound of trickling water. Tides were slow to make a difference on an expanse like a beach, but when entering a relatively small, contained area like the Temple, it wouldn't take long before they all drowned.

"Now, give me the gun," Simon said. His hand was warm against hers as he pressed the weapon downward. She let her arm relax.

"We're going, Deacon," Simon shouted.

"Keep the damned Stone," Veronica finished.

"You're not going anywhere." Deacon held up the Stone. "You want this. Admit it." Dropping to the ground, he placed his hands palms down on the floor of the Temple. "You can have it."

The glow emitting from his hands was as bright and blinding as the sun and filled the Temple with its light. It was both horrible and compelling in its magnificence.

Around Deacon, the floor turned to gold in a circular wave that rippled up the wall, across the ceiling, and then toward her and Simon, moving as fast as man could walk.

He meant to kill them by turning them to gold.

She raised her hand and fired, but the gun clicked on an empty chamber. She squeezed the trigger again. The clip was empty. "Crap!" She threw the gun to the floor.

"Run!" Simon shouted, pulling her backward and toward the antechamber. She pressed her hand into the indentation, and once again the door opened. "Go," he said, trying to push her through the opening.

She resisted. Something was happening to Deacon. To the wave of gold that was eating the floor. "Wait." She grabbed Simon's arm. "Look." Simon swung the flashlight around and illuminated the Temple.

The oncoming tide of gold was slowing.

Deacon screamed. A shrill, violent cry unlike anything Veronica had ever heard. Her attention shot back to him.

Something was wrong. The light from his hands grew dimmer with each passing second. Suddenly, his body jerked violently, as if he were trying to free himself from where he touched the floor but couldn't.

Even as he screamed, Deacon's face distorted, shriveled and seemed to collapse inward. The macabre scene was both horrifying and compelling and neither Veronica nor Simon could look away.

The glow from his hands flickered out, but Simon's light was like a spotlight on Deacon's smoking, shriveled corpse.

"What was that?" Simon whispered.

"I don't know," Veronica replied, horrified. "It's as if the energy were sucked from his body. His life force. Something." She realized she still had a death grip on Simon's arm and let go, shaking the blood back into her hand. "Do you think it's safe?

"Let's find out." He rolled the flashlight where stone met gold. The flashlight reached the edge of the gold and kept on rolling, unchanged. Simon collected their knives and handed her one, sheathing the other. "Give me a minute, then we need to go," Simon said.

"Do you think it's safe?" Veronica asked. "If we leave this

place intact, who knows what might happen. Who might find it."

Simon shook his head. "No one found it for a thousand years. It's safe. And even if they did, it's just a Temple. It can't harm anyone."

Veronica wasn't convinced. This place was more than *just* a Temple. It was now also Deacon's tomb. "If someone finds it, they're going to ask questions."

"Right now, this Temple is the least of my worries. What matters is that we're going to die if we don't leave. Now."

His jaw looked as inflexible as his command sounded, but Veronica refused to give in so easily. "I wish we could stay. Learn more," she said. Despite all that happened, leaving such a perfectly preserved Temple seemed like sacrilege. But she could see his point. If they drowned, this conversation was moot. "We'll talk more about this. I'm not letting it go."

"Fine, but let's do it up top," Simon said, his eyes leveling her. "Now let's get the hell out of here."

"What about Michael?" she asked. "Do you want to leave him?"

"Your call."

"I'll get him. Can you give me a minute?"

"Alone?" Simon's eyes darkened.

She nodded, and squeezed his forearm. "He can't hurt me. Not anymore."

Simon lay his hand over hers. "Hurry. I'll gather the weapons."

Veronica's footsteps were noiseless as she approached her former lover. She stood over him. She'd grown up with Michael, and while she loved the boy he once was, that boy was gone. She despised the man who lay at her feet. This man didn't deserve mercy, and he sure didn't deserve forgiveness. He'd tried to kill her with her own gun.

Still, she couldn't leave him to drown. If she did, she'd never forgive herself. That didn't mean she had to make it easy. She pushed him with her foot. "Wake up."

He groaned. She pushed him again. "Michael, you ass. Get up or you're going to drown."

His eyes flickered open, and he stared up at her with nothing but malice.

"That's enough," Simon said, suddenly by her side and taking her by the arm.

She pivoted on her foot, not bothering to give Michael a second glance. "Right."

Trailing the detonation wire behind them, they stopped at Thalassa's statue and Deacon's shriveled, lifeless body. "We should leave the Stone," Simon said.

Veronica didn't hear him. "Oh, Lily," she cried. The shotgun was turned to gold. She picked her up. She weighed a ton, but there was no way she was leaving her down here.

"Veronica," Simon said softly, taking Lily from her. "The Stone. Do we leave it or take it?"

She wiped her eyes. "Can't leave it. Michael."

Bending down, Simon hesitated, then picked the Stone up and closed his fist around it. There was no glow. Nothing. He opened his hand. "Just a rock. Whatever Deacon did, it must have killed it." He tossed it to Veronica.

She caught it in midair, and the instant it touched her hands, she knew it was anything but a simple rock. Her breath hissed in at the sudden steady, familiar pain that burned through her veins and came to center on her hands.

"Veronica?" Simon reached for her.

She leapt out of the way, horrified. "Don't touch me. Don't touch me."

"What's wrong?"

She heard the worry in his voice and took another step back. "The wine. It was in the wine." She'd all but forgotten it in the chaos.

"Wine?"

"From the antechamber." Her voice was sharper than she intended. Her hands glowed from the heat. Power flowed through her like electricity. It was heady, consuming, to *know* she could transmute material, anything, to pure gold.

This was what godhood feels like, she thought. And it was good.

It was also horrifying. Overwhelming and uncontrollable.

She took another step back, wanting to drop the Stone but scared to do more than stand there. How was she supposed to turn this damned thing off?

"Veronica!"

She and Simon turned at the screech. Now fully awake, Michael stumbled toward them. "Veronica!" He screamed her name despite his broken jaw.

Michael stretched his hand out in demand, shouting louder as he came at them.

Simon stepped in front of him, his larger body blocking Michael's progress like an unmovable wall.

But Michael was wiser now, and he went directly for Simon's shoulder, sending him to his knees with a single punch.

Then Michael turned and came toward Veronica, his hands clenched, mouth twisted, and madness in his eyes

Godhood felt more like hell as she realized what he was going to do. "No. Michael! Stay away!"

Before she could drop the Stone or run, he grabbed her hand and was dead before he could clench his fingers around her wrist—a perfect golden statue.

"Oh, my God." Veronica dropped the Midas Stone and

then joined it on the floor as fatigue roared through her. What was happening? Through bleary eyes, her focus was on Michael's face, now frozen for eternity into a madman's mask.

What had she done? What had she done?

The only sound was the water as it began to fill the cave. The only sensation? The coolness of the golden floor against her cheek.

Then there was warmth. Skin. Simon. He knelt next to her. Woozily, she let him help her to her feet. For a moment, she swayed and it took all her strength to remain upright.

She touched the gold statue that was once Michael. Her fingers traced the mouth she once kissed. Soothed the hair she once ran her fingers through. "He's dead. I killed him."

"No. His greed killed him," Simon corrected her. "We'll be dead, too, if we don't get out of here."

"The Stone?" she asked.

"Got it." He patted his dive bag.

For the last time, she touched the statue that was once Michael. Friend. Lover. Enemy. "You got everything you wished for," she said, her voice breaking. "Was it worth it? Was it?"

Then she and Simon ran, hesitating when they reached the entrance to the Temple. The water was to the top stair now and lapped onto the Temple floor.

She tried to walk, but her muscles refused to cooperate, and she sagged against Simon. "Go. I'll follow."

Simon's finger dug into her arm. "You move or by God, I will carry your ass out of here and then we're both dead, since, as I pointed out earlier, you're not a small woman."

Her jaw dropped and she stiffened as angry energy surged through her. "Are you saying I'm fat?"

He gave her a fast, hard kiss. "Not at all. I'm saying that you're beautiful and can we go now?" He took her hand.

He was playing her like a fiddle—pissing her off on purpose just to get her riled and ready to fight. She yanked her hand from his. "You lead."

As they sloshed through the waist-high water, every step felt as if her feet were weighted with bricks. They made their way to the stone stairs, the incoming tide turning them into a slippery waterfall.

By the time she reached the top of the ten steps that led to the small courtyard, Veronica was barely able to breathe, and she knew her sudden weakness had something to do with the Stone and how it used her to transform Michael into gold.

Simon stopped, letting her catch her breath.

She leaned against the wall. "I don't think I can make it," she explained. "However the Stone works, it used my energy to do it."

Simon pressed his lips tighter. "Fine. You stay, then I stay."

"You'll die," Veronica tried to shout, but it came out as a whine. "Go."

He pressed a hand to the wall on either side of her head, his eyes bored into her. "No."

"Bastard!" She just wanted to be left alone. She was tired, and not just in body, but to the depths of her soul. King Midas had said the Stone was a curse. She knew exactly how he felt. She'd thought the Stone was going to save her career. Bring her the fame, recognition and respect she craved. Instead, it brought death, bitterness and heartache. She wished she'd never seen the Midas Stone, and now it was her responsibility.

"I get that a lot." Simon pulled away and took her hand in his. "Now let's get out of here."

His touch was warm, and somehow gave her the strength to put one foot in front of another.

The tears came even as she cleared the first step.

* * *

Veronica was sure she was going to die. Her legs were as useless as putty. Her lungs burned.

Simon didn't sound much better. With each step, he winced, and she knew his shoulder bled freely.

They had to be close to the top. Had to be. The ground had stopped shaking, but rock still fell all around them. Behind her, there was a great crash, a shift of rock, and she slipped as the stairs fell away.

She screamed, caught her footing and propelled herself to the next step.

"Faster," Simon shouted about the noise.

She sent up another silent prayer. Please, let something go right. *Don't let this godawful hunk of rock be our tomb.*

They turned the corner, and Simon's light reflected off the silver crystal door.

They were at the top, and the door was still open. Finally, something had gone their way.

Thank you.

Quickly, they crossed the threshold. The water was up to her knees. The outer cave wasn't faring any better than the inner one.

A piece of granite as large as her head brushed her shoulder and crashed into the water next to her. The whole place was coming down. She tugged the Eye of Artemis free and the door slid shut as smoothly as if the cave wasn't falling in around them.

She and Simon waded deeper into the water.

A familiar fin split the surface. Veronica froze. She'd been pushed around, threatened, almost crushed, and she could not deal with this shark. Not now.

"It won't hurt you. Go." Simon shouted over the noise.

She dug in her feet. She'd give the beast a minute, and maybe it would go away. As it was, she was so drained that every breath was a struggle.

"If you stay, you'll die," Simon said, and he shoved her into the water.

Grabbing the wall, Veronica's first impulse was to swim back, but intelligence overrode instinct, and she swam for the opening.

Simon pulled himself along the opposite wall.

She watched the fin pass by her and pressed her back into the rock, sure it would attack. But it slipped by and headed toward Simon.

Blood in the water.

"Simon. Look out!"

As quickly as the shark came in to attack, Simon's ten-inch knife was in his hand. The shark dove and Simon went under as well. There was a thrashing, and for a moment, she thought Simon was dead and a white-hot fury erupted in her. A raging anger that gave her strength.

She kicked and swam toward the commotion. She and Simon had come too far to die because a million-year-old product of evolution didn't have the brains to get the hell out of a collapsing cave.

If Simon was dead, she'd kill the shark, she vowed. Make it pay.

Simon bobbed to the surface, and Veronica pulled harder with her arms. A very much alive shark swam past her, brushing her side as it went to the opposite side of the cave.

She reached Simon. "Are you okay? Did it bite you?"

"I'm good. It tried, but it's damned small." He flashed his light over the water, searching for the blue.

"Too bad it doesn't know it," Veronica said. "I'm betting it's really pissed off, too." Still on her adrenaline high, she pushed Simon ahead of her. For once, he didn't argue.

"Yeah?" Simon said. "I'm not exactly thrilled with the situation."

Veronica watched for the fin as they swam for the opening, but the blue wasn't showing itself. Simon dove into the hole.

Veronica took a deep breath and followed, feet first, pushing her self backward with the knife in her hand. There was no way she was letting the shark sneak up on her.

She squinted into the receding darkness.

The shark swam into the hole with the speed of a snake, and for a beat, all Veronica saw were rows of teeth and cold, black eyes. Her nightmare had come for her.

Then she screamed, bubbles rising from her mouth as she lashed out with her knife, striking the blue on the nose.

It thrashed, trying to get at her, and she lashed out repeatedly even as Simon pulled her forward by her feet.

When she opened her eyes, she was in the Mediterranean and the sky was still dark overhead. Simon bobbed beside her.

"Where's the shark?" she said, frantic to know. Waiting for it to complete the nightmare and grab her by the feet.

"Don't know," Simon replied. "I think it swam off. You scared the crap out of it."

"Ditto." Fear made her hands tremble, and it took three tries before she sheathed her knife. "Let's get to the boat before it decides it wants a rematch."

Veronica reached the boat first and helped Simon up the ladder.

Adrenaline and willpower had kept the pain of Simon's wound at bay, but now that they were safe, he collapsed on the deck. She couldn't blame him. She felt the same way.

She fell beside him, rolled over to her back and stared at the night sky. It was beautiful.

For five minutes, she didn't want to think about death or sharks or Michael. She wanted to close her eyes and forget she ever heard about the Midas Stone.

* * *

When Veronica opened her eyes, the sky was just starting to show the first signs of light.

Shirtless, Simon sat on the deck next to her. His shoulder was bandaged with what appeared to be his ripped up T-shirt, and he wore clean shorts. His feet were bare.

She was still in her wetsuit. She sat up, yawning. "How long was I asleep?"

"About two hours."

"Why didn't you head back? We need to get you to a hospital."

He leaned against the railing. "And tell them what? They'd have to report a gunshot wound, then we'd have the authorities after us. Again."

She nodded toward his shoulder. "Will that be okay without professional attention?"

"I'll be fine," Simon assured her. "The bullet went clean through."

Eww.

"I'll heal," Simon said confidently.

She smiled in relief, more grateful than she could say that Simon would be okay.

Automatically, she reached behind her to remove Lily from her back holster but stopped when her hand met air. "Lily?" she asked, her voice breaking, her heart not wanting to believe what her mind already confirmed.

"Under the towel," Simon said, compassion in his eyes.

Slowly, Veronica pushed aside the oversize yellow terry towel that was on the desk next to her.

Gleaming in the morning light was her shotgun. The one piece of equipment she knew she could count on. Her good-luck talisman. The symbol of who she was.

Now, solid gold, and never to be shot again. Veronica ran

her hand up the barrel, and her eyes teared. "Oh, Lily," she said, wiping her eyes, hating that she was crying in front of Simon. *It's just a shotgun,* she told herself. She could buy another.

But the self-assurances didn't help, and she couldn't stop crying. "Crap." She looked over at Simon with weepy eyes. "You probably think I'm dumb. It's just a gun."

Lily...and Michael. Gone forever.

He moved over on the bench. "Come here," he said tenderly.

Still crying, she went to him and let him comfort her, let him stroke her hair and murmur that it would all be okay as she sobbed on his shoulder.

When her tears subsided to hiccups, she sat up and ran a hand over her hair, knowing she was a soggy, red-faced mess. "Sorry," she said, embarrassed.

"Don't be," Simon said. "It's been a long day."

"Thanks," Veronica sniffed.

She and Simon sat in silence, watching the sun rise over the water. Finally, Simon picked up his dive bag. It was weighted down with the Midas Stone. He made no move to hand it to her. "You realize that once word gets out about what we have, we'll be famous. We won't have a peaceful moment for a very long time."

She squeezed her eyes shut and saw Michael's face.

Simon was right. Peace would be a long time coming.

"I have no idea how it works," Alyssa said, handing Veronica her written report. "I ran every test I could think of and came up with nothing. As far as I can tell, it's a rock. The material is close to obsidian, but I'm not even sure that's right."

Veronica handed the report to Simon. She had hoped Alyssa could figure out the science behind the Stone, but it was almost as enjoyable seeing her sister stumped.

Alyssa was *never* stumped.

"Watch this," Alyssa said to Simon. Taking an apple from her desk drawer, Alyssa rolled it across the desk. "Veronica, can you transmute that, please?"

Veronica sighed and picked up the Stone in her left hand, flinching as it seemed to burn into her skin. The pain never got any better. In fact, she swore it grew worse with each successive use of the Stone.

One thing that remained consistent was the rate in which the Stone sucked energy from her body. She and Alyssa had soon figured out that it was all based on the size of the object she was trying to change to gold. With something as small as a piece of fruit, it wasn't too much of a problem. But changing Michael to gold, even inadvertently, had almost killed her. And God help her if she tried something bigger.

She remembered what the Stone did to Deacon, and now she knew why. Once her adversary tapped into that kind of energy and attempted to transmute the Temple from stone to gold, he was unable to pull away—much like sticking his hand in an electrical outlet.

She shuddered, remembering how he had collapsed in on himself.

"Veronica? Is there a problem?" Alyssa asked.

"No." Focusing the energy that was almost tangible now, she reined it in and touched the apple. It turned to gold as if it had never been anything else. She set the Midas Stone back in its box and rubbed her hand.

It still burned.

"See that?" Alyssa said, pointing to the golden apple. "Somehow, the energy is focused through her hands, allowing the Stone to tap into it and transmute the material. We've done a few experiments, and she can control it to some extent. Keep it from turning the desk under the apple from turning to gold, but as to how it taps *her* energy?"

Alyssa picked up the Stone with a manicured hand, surveyed it then set it back. "I have no idea. Not without that catalyst."

Simon set the report down on the table. His arm still in a sling, he leafed through it one-handed. "Are you saying it's magic?"

Veronica snickered, knowing how Alyssa would react to such a suggestion.

Alyssa glared at her and frowned at Simon. "Of course not. I'm saying that it's beyond our ability to determine how it works."

"Then it is a gift from the gods," Simon said, egging her on.

"Are you sure you're a scientist?" Alyssa's frown deepened. "I'm saying that whoever created it knew something we don't and that knowledge died a long time ago. Or they discovered it by accident and were never able to duplicate it." She crossed her arms as if satisfied by the conclusion. "That's the more likely case. Otherwise, we'd have more of these things floating around."

"That's not much help," Simon said. "Maybe if we research more on the mythology…"

Veronica tuned them both out. Did it matter if they figured out how the damned thing worked? She'd been struggling with the Stone's existence and her own part in Michael's death since they came home. Asking herself if it was worth the sacrifice.

Once she published her findings, she'd have what she wanted. Her colleagues would be forced to acknowledge that she wasn't a crackpot. Joseph and Chris would also get the same overwhelming recognition. She'd be famous. Her reputation as an archaeologist would be assured.

She'd have everything she ever wished for. Sacrificed for.

Which made destroying the Stone that much harder.

"Simon?" she said.

"Yes?" The animated excitement died from his face as he saw her expression. "What's wrong?"

"About the Stone." She took a deep breath. He wasn't going to like her decision, but she hoped he'd agree to it. If not, she'd do what she had to, anyway. She took another breath, unable to believe she was going to say the next sentence. "We have to destroy the Stone. Get rid of it. We can't even publish our findings. The Stone's very existence could send the world into an economic tailspin, and then there's the whole issue of the government cracking its secret." She knew she was babbling but couldn't seem to stop herself. "It could be used as a weapon. And if the government doesn't discover the secret, it might want to use me to help. I can't—"

"I know," Simon interrupted her.

"You know?" She repeated the comment, confused.

He raised a familiar eyebrow and her heart skipped as she remembered how she almost lost him on the stairs.

"I had the same thoughts," Simon said. "When I talked about never having peace, I meant you. Not me. If you publish, you'll never be free, and I guarantee you that you'll never go out in the field again." His expression softened, and he took her hand in his, his thumb stroking the calluses that proclaimed her profession. "I'm only sorry that we can't use it to prove your theory."

"Thanks." Relief flowed through her, and she smiled in both her body and soul for what she thought was the first time since their return. "I'm sorry, too, but I'm not the first scientist who's been called a crackpot, and I won't be the last." She shrugged. "It's part of the game."

"True," he agreed, looking contrite.

"I'll just have to keep searching. There's something else out there. Other sites. Other artifacts." Her smile broadened as she thought about the possibilities. "Ones that don't threaten all mankind."

He grinned in return.

She wrapped her arms around him, being careful of his shoulder. "Thank you," she whispered. Simon was a good man. Strong. Loyal. And with his priorities in order.

So not like Michael.

His arm tightened around her, making her feel safe. She was okay with that. They were a team. They were lovers. She could trust him to keep her safe, and he could trust her to do the same.

Unfamiliar tears welled in Veronica's eyes.

"How do you two plan to get rid of it?" Alyssa interrupted, her voice soft.

Kissing Veronica's neck, Simon released her. "I have an idea about that."

"I figured you might." Veronica rubbed away the tears with her knuckles. What was it about Simon that made her cry?

"I know a great camping spot up in Vermont," Simon said. "We could take a long weekend. Sleep under the stars. Remember what it feels like not to get shot at, almost drowned, beaten or attacked by killer sharks."

Veronica grinned. "I like the idea, but what about the Midas Stone?"

"You ever skip rocks?"

Her grin broadened. "Not in a long time, but I have the perfect one to practice with."

Chapter 19

"Let me see that again," Veronica said, trying to snatch the check from Simon.

Simon closed the door to the Sotheby's auction office and held the check over his head, trying to make her jump for it.

She crossed her arms instead. "If you're going to be that way, you can just forget it."

With a laugh, he handed it to her.

The final sale—the sale of the golden apple—was complete. It was the first piece of fruit she's transmuted in her sister's lab, but afterward, she'd had Alyssa go to the grocery store and fill a basket with everything from bananas to mangoes. Then she'd spent the afternoon transmuting the produce, despite the fact that the process would leave her drained.

It had been worth it. Now she was able to pursue archaeology sans investors, and if people wondered where the golden fruit came from, then Sotheby's would send them away.

She kissed the ink on the check, glad that the famous auction house had taken them on despite the stipulation that she and Simon were to remain anonymous.

The additional three percent commission probably hadn't hurt.

As for the codex and the Eye, she'd done the honorable things and had Rebecca mail them both, making sure they could not be tracked back to her. She smiled at the irony of making both parties sign for the return of the artifacts.

The Vatican police were sure to be surprised. As for Fakir...she wasn't sure what would shock him more—the return of the Eye or the investigation that was sure to follow since she had anonymously alerted the Turkish Antiquities Authority about his illegal archaeological possessions.

"Happy?" Simon asked.

"Yeah." She was. Mostly. Money couldn't buy some things, like her reputation or the return of Chris's life.

But the money helped. She had asked Simon if he would split the proceeds of the various sales with Joseph and Chris's widow, and he'd agreed without even a hint of hesitation.

She knew he would.

Thoughtfully, she rubbed the paper between her fingers. The check represented power and money—they were Michael's downfall. She'd make sure they weren't hers. She'd lived the lesson, watched those desires destroy someone she cared for.

It was a lesson heeded.

"You're too quiet. Feeling all right?" Simon asked.

"Just thinking," she said.

"About Michael?"

Was she that obvious? "Does it bother you?"

Simon smiled tenderly at her, shaking his head. "You loved him for a long time. If you didn't mourn him, I'd wonder what was wrong with you."

"Thanks." Veronica slid her hand into Simon's, interlocking her fingers with his. He was a good man. She wasn't sure what would happen now that he was healed and the Stone was gone.

Once the check was deposited and split four ways, he could go anywhere he wanted.

But she hoped he'd stay.

"Veronica?"

"Yes?"

"Have you given any more thought on going back to the Temple?" He stroked her hair with his free hand, letting the dark strands slip through his fingers.

She leaned into his touch. Excavating the Temple was tempting, and the archaeologist in her wanted to return. She met Simon's eyes and saw the same desire in his dark, steady gaze. The Temple was the find of a lifetime. Hell, two lifetimes. And they both lived for the thrill of discovery.

But her emotional wounds were still to raw to even contemplate returning.

She drew Simon's hand to her lips and kissed his knuckles.

"Not ready to decide?" he asked.

"No," she murmured. Because the Temple was more than a potential excavation to her.

It was Michael's grave and the death of her girlhood dreams. She'd thought her dreams of love and Michael had died when he betrayed her in Brazil. And when he'd pointed Lily at her in the Temple, she was sure that any micron of feeling for him was long gone.

She couldn't have been more wrong. Her dreams only truly died with Michael's passing and the hope he took with him.

Veronica pressed their joined hands to her chest. "Ask me again next year?"

"Deal," he said with a smile. "I have infinite patience."

She returned the grin, her heart lifting at his effortless acceptance of her request. "It's easy to have patience when you know we have a copy of the codex and even though we don't have the Eye, I'm guessing you can get your hands on enough explosives to blow open the door."

"Who? Me?"

His right brow arched upwards in what she considered a very unconvincing attempt to appear above question.

With a resigned sigh, she stood on her toes and kissed his mouth. "Thanks for understanding."

"My pleasure," Simon replied, moving to trap her between his torso and the wall. "Besides, I have something else in mind. I heard a rumor that a villager outside Cairo found evidence that the griffin was a real animal."

She brought their joined hands up between them. "Really? The eagle-lion creature?"

"Mmm-hmm." He kissed her fingertips.

Her skin started to tingle, and her inner archaeologist snapped to attention. "What kind of evidence?"

"A feather or skeleton. Something like that," he said, working his way over to the fleshy part of her palm where he began nibbling. Was he serious about the griffin? She couldn't tell.

"Doing anything Saturday night?" he whispered.

And she realized she didn't care. Going anyplace with Simon was bound to be an adventure. Smiling slyly, she wrapped her arms around his neck. "Going to Egypt. Wanna come?"

* * * * *

If you enjoyed what you just read,
then we've got an offer you can't resist!

Take 2 bestselling
love stories FREE!
Plus get a FREE surprise gift!

Clip this page and mail it to Silhouette Reader Service®

IN U.S.A.
3010 Walden Ave.
P.O. Box 1867
Buffalo, N.Y. 14240-1867

IN CANADA
P.O. Box 609
Fort Erie, Ontario
L2A 5X3

YES! Please send me 2 free Silhouette Bombshell™ novels and my free surprise gift. After receiving them, if I don't wish to receive any more, I can return the shipping statement marked cancel. If I don't cancel, I will receive 4 brand-new novels every month, before they're available in stores! In the U.S.A., bill me at the bargain price of $4.69 plus 25¢ shipping & handling per book and applicable sales tax, if any*. In Canada, bill me at the bargain price of $5.24 plus 25¢ shipping & handling per book and applicable taxes**. That's the complete price and a savings of 10% off the cover prices—what a great deal! I understand that accepting the 2 free books and gift places me under no obligation ever to buy any books. I can always return a shipment and cancel at any time. Even if I never buy another book from Silhouette, the 2 free books and gift are mine to keep forever.

200 HDN D34H
300 HDN D34J

Name	(PLEASE PRINT)	
Address	Apt.#	
City	State/Prov.	Zip/Postal Code

Not valid to current Silhouette Bombshell™ subscribers.

Want to try another series?
Call 1-800-873-8635 or visit www.morefreebooks.com.

* Terms and prices subject to change without notice. Sales tax applicable in N.Y.
** Canadian residents will be charged applicable provincial taxes and GST.
All orders subject to approval. Offer limited to one per household.
® and ™ are registered trademarks owned and used by the trademark owner and
or its licensee.

BOMB04   ©2004 Harlequin Enterprises Limited

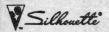